*after*burn / *after*shock

Never mix business with pleasure. Never bring politics into the bedroom. In a way, I did both when I took Jackson Rutledge as a lover. I can't say I wasn't warned.

Two years later, he was back. Walking into a deal I'd worked hard to close. Under the tutelage of Lei Yeung, one of the sharpest businesswomen in New York, I had picked up a thing or two since Jax walked away. I wasn't the girl he once knew, but he hadn't changed. Unlike the last time we'd drifted into each other's lives, I knew exactly what I was dealing with…and how addictive his touch could be.

The inner circle of glamour, sex and privilege was Jax's playground—but this time, I knew the rules of the game. In the cutthroat business world, one adage rules all: keep your enemies close and your ex-lovers closer.…

Now a major motion picture!

PRAISE FOR SYLVIA DAY

OTHER BOOKS BY SYLVIA DAY

CONTEMPORARY ROMANCE

The Crossfire® Saga

Bared to You

Reflected in You

Entwined with You

Captivated by You

One with You

PARANORMAL ROMANCE

The Renegade Angels Series

A Dark Kiss of Rapture

A Touch of Crimson

A Caress of Wings

A Hunger So Wild

The Dream Guardians Series

Pleasures of the Night

Heat of the Night

HISTORICAL ROMANCE

The Georgian Series

Ask for It

Passion for the Game

A Passion for Him

Don't Tempt Me

SYLVIA DAY

*after***burn** / *after***shock**

ISBN-13: 978-1-62650-983-2

Cover Design by Croco Designs

ACKNOWLEDGMENTS

My gratitude to
Kimberly Whalen, Ann Leslie Tuttle, and Dianne Moggy
—the fun, fearless women taking this journey with me.

And to my dear readers, who inspire me every day. Thank you!

1

IT WAS A breezy fall morning when I entered the mirrored glass skyscraper in midtown Manhattan, leaving the cacophony of blaring horns and pedestrian chatter behind to step into cool quiet. My heels clicked across the dark marble of the massive lobby with a tempo that echoed my racing heart. With damp palms, I slid my ID across the security desk. My nervousness only increased after I accepted my visitors badge and headed to the elevator.

Have you ever wanted something so bad, you couldn't imagine not having it?

There were two things in my life I'd felt that way about: the man I'd stupidly fallen in love with and the administrative assistant position I was about to interview for.

The man had turned out to be really bad for me; the job could change my life in an amazing way. I couldn't even think about walking away from the interview without nailing it. I just had this feeling, deep inside me, that working as Lei Yeung's assistant was what I needed to spread my wings and fly.

Still, despite my inner pep talk, my breath caught when I stepped out onto the tenth floor and saw the smoked-glass entrance to Savor, Inc. The company's name was emblazoned in a metallic feminine font across the double doors, challenging me to dream big and relish every moment.

Waiting to enter, I studied the number of well-dressed young women sitting around the reception area. Unlike me, they weren't wearing last season's styles secondhand. I doubted any of them had held three jobs to help pay for college, either. I was at a disadvantage in nearly every way, but I'd known that and I wasn't intimidated…much.

I was buzzed through the security doors and took in the café-au-lait walls covered with photos of celebrity chefs and trendy restaurants. There was a faint aroma of sugar cookies in the air, a comforting scent from my childhood. Even that didn't relax me.

Taking a deep breath, I checked in with the receptionist, a pretty African-American girl with an easy smile, then I stepped away to find a bare place against the wall to stand. Was my scheduled appointment time—for which I was nearly half an hour early—a joke? I soon realized that everyone was set for a brisk five-minute audience, and they were marched in and out precisely on time.

My skin flushed with a light mist of nervous perspiration.

When my name was called, I pushed away from the wall so quickly that I wobbled on my heels, my clumsiness mirroring my shaky confidence. I followed a young, attractive guy down the hall to a corner office with an open, unmanned reception area and another set of double doors that led into Lei Yeung's seat of power.

He showed me in with a smile. "Good luck."

"Thanks."

As I passed through those doors, I was struck first by the cool modern vibe of the decor, then by the woman who sat behind a walnut desk that dwarfed her. She might've been lost in the vast space, with its stunning views of the Manhattan skyline, if not for the striking crimson of her reading glasses, which perfectly matched the stain on her full lips.

I took a moment to really get a good look at her, admiring how the strip of silver hair at her right temple had been artfully arranged into her elaborate updo. She was slender, with a graceful neck and long arms. And when she looked up from my application to consider me, I felt exposed and vulnerable.

She slid her glasses off and sat back. "Have a seat, Gianna."

I moved across the cream-colored carpet and took one of the two chrome-and-leather chairs in front of her desk.

"Good morning," I said, belatedly hearing a trace of my Brooklyn accent, which I'd practiced hard to suppress. She didn't seem to pick up on it.

"Tell me about yourself."

I cleared my throat. "Well, this spring I graduated magna cum laude from the University of Nevada at Las Vegas—"

"I just read that on your résumé." She softened her words with a slight smile. "Tell me something I don't already know about you. Why the restaurant industry? Sixty percent of new establishments fail within the first five years. I'm sure you know that."

"Not ours. My family has run a restaurant in Little Italy for three generations," I said proudly.

"So why not work there?"

"We don't have you." I swallowed. That was way too personal. Lei Yeung didn't seem rattled by the gaffe, but I was. "I mean, we don't have your magic," I added quickly.

"We…?"

"Yes." I paused to collect myself. "I have three brothers. They can't all take over Rossi's when our dad retires and they don't want to. The oldest will and the other two…well, they want their own Rossi's."

"And your contribution is a degree in restaurant management and a lot of heart."

"I want to learn how to help them realize their dreams. I want to help other people achieve theirs, too."

She nodded and reached for her glasses. "Thank you, Gianna. I appreciate you coming in today."

Just like that, I was dismissed. And I knew I wasn't going to get the job. I hadn't said whatever she'd needed to hear to make me the clear-cut winner.

I stood, my mind racing with ways I could turn the interview around. "I really want this job, Ms. Yeung. I work hard. I'm never sick. I'm proactive and forward-thinking. It won't take me long to anticipate what you need before you need it. I'll make you glad you hired me."

Lei looked at me. "I believe you. You juggled multiple jobs while maintaining your honors GPA. You're smart, determined and not afraid to hustle. I'm sure you'd be great. I just don't think I'd be the right boss for you."

"I don't understand." My stomach twisted as my dream job slipped away. Disappointment pierced through me.

"You don't have to," she said gently. "Trust me. There are a hundred restaurateurs in New York who can give you what you're looking for."

I lifted my chin. I used to be proud of my looks, my family, my roots. I hated that I was constantly second-guessing all of that now.

Impulsively, I decided to reveal why I wanted to work with her so badly. "Ms. Yeung, please listen. You and I have a lot in common. Ian Pembry underestimated you, isn't that right?"

Her eyes blazed with sudden fire at the unexpected mention of her former partner who'd betrayed her. She didn't answer.

I had nothing to lose at this point. "There was a man in my life who underestimated me once. You proved people wrong. I just want to do the same."

She tilted her head to the side. "I hope you do."

Realizing I'd come to the end of the road, I thanked her for her time and left with as much dignity as I could manage.

As far as Mondays went, that was one of the worst of my life.

"I'm telling you, she's an idiot," Angelo said for the second time. "You're lucky you didn't get that job today."

I was the baby of the family, with three big brothers. He was the youngest. His righteous anger on my behalf made me smile despite myself.

"He's right," Nico said. The oldest of the Rossi boys—and biggest prankster—bumped Angelo out of the way to set my meal in front of me with a flourish.

I'd chosen to sit at the bar, since Rossi's was packed as usual, the dinner crowd boisterous and familiar. We had a lot of regulars and often a celebrity or two, incognito, who came here to eat in peace. The comfortable mix was a solid sign of Rossi's great reputation for warm service and excellent food.

Angelo bumped Nico back with a scowl. "I'm always right."

"Ha!" Vincent scoffed through the kitchen window, sliding two steaming plates onto the service shelf and ripping the corresponding tickets off their clips. "Only when you're repeating what I said."

The ribbing coaxed a reluctant laugh out of me. I felt a hand at my waist the moment before I smelled my mother's favorite Elizabeth Arden perfume.

Her lips pressed against my cheek. "It's good to see you smile. Everything happens—"

"—for a reason," I finished. "I know. It still sucks."

I was the only one in my family who'd gone to college. It'd been a group effort; even my brothers had pitched in. I couldn't help feeling like I'd let them all down. Sure there were hundreds of restaurateurs in New York, but Lei Yeung didn't just turn unknown chefs into name brands, she was a force of nature.

She spoke frequently about women in business and had been featured on a number of midmorning talk shows. She had immigrant parents and had worked her way through school, making a success of herself even after being betrayed by her mentor and partner. Working for her would have been a powerful statement for me.

At least, that's what I'd told myself.

"Eat your fettuccine before it gets cold," my mother said, gliding away to greet new patrons coming in.

I forked up a bite of pasta dripping with creamy Alfredo sauce as I watched her. A lot of customers did. Mona Rossi was closer to sixty than fifty, but you'd never know it from looking at her. She was beautiful and flamboyantly sexy. Her violet-red hair was teased just high enough to give it volume and frame a face that was classical in its symmetry, with full lips and dark sloe eyes. She was statuesque, with generous curves and a taste for gold jewelry.

Men and women alike loved her. My mom was comfortable in her skin, confident and seemingly carefree. Very few people realized how much trouble my brothers had given her growing up. She had them well trained now.

Taking a deep breath, I absorbed the comfort around me—the beloved sounds of people laughing, the mouthwatering smell of carefully prepared food, the clatter of silverware meeting china and glasses clinking in happy toasts. I wanted *more* out of my life, which sometimes made me forget how much I already had.

Nico came back, eyeing me. "Red or white?" he asked, setting his hand over mine and giving a soft squeeze.

He was a customer favorite at the bar, especially with the women. He was darkly handsome, with unruly hair and a wicked smile. A consummate flirt, he had his own fan club, ladies who hung out at the bar for both his great drinks and sexy banter.

"How about champagne?" Lei Yeung slid onto the bar stool next to me, recently vacated by a young couple whose reserved table had opened up.

I blinked.

She smiled at me, looking much younger than she had during our interview, dressed casually in jeans and a pink silk shell. Her hair was down and her face scrubbed free of makeup. "Lots of rave reviews about this place online."

"Best Italian food ever," I said, feeling my heartbeat quicken with renewed excitement.

"A lot of them say a great place got even greater over the past couple of years. Am I right in assuming that's due to you putting into practice things you've learned?"

Nico set two flutes in front of us, then filled them halfway with bubbling champagne. "You're right," he said, butting in.

Lei caught the stem of her glass and stroked it with her fingers. Her gaze caught mine. Nico, who was good at knowing when to disappear, moved down the bar.

"To get back to what you said…" she began. I started to cringe, then straightened up. Lei Yeung hadn't made a special trip just to berate me. "Ian underestimated me, but he didn't take advantage of me. Blaming him would give him too much credit. I left the door open and he walked through it."

I nodded. The exact circumstances of their split were private, but I'd inferred a lot from the reports in industry magazines and filled in the rest from gossip columns and blogs. Together they'd had a culinary empire comprised of a stable of celebrity chefs, several restaurant chains, a line of cookbooks and affordable cookware that sold in the millions. Then Pembry had announced the launch of a new chain of eateries bankrolled by A-list actors and actresses—but Lei hadn't been part of that.

"He taught me a lot," she went on. "And I've come to realize he got as much out of that as I did." She paused, thoughtful. "I'm getting too used to myself and the way I've always done things. I need fresh eyes. I want to feed off someone else's hunger."

"You want a protégée."

"Exactly." Her mouth curved. "I didn't realize that until you pointed it out. I knew I was looking for something, but I couldn't say what it was."

I was totally thrilled but kept my tone professional. I swiveled toward her. "I'm in, if you want me."

"Forget about normal hours," she warned. "This isn't a nine-to-five gig. I'll need you on weekends, and I might call in the middle of the night…. I work all the time."

"I won't complain."

"I will." Angelo came up behind us. All the Rossi sons had figured out who I was talking to and, as usual, none of them were shy. "I need to see her every once in a while."

I elbowed him. We shared a sprawling, half-finished loft apartment in Brooklyn— all three of my brothers, me and Angelo's wife, Denise. Most of the time we bitched about seeing one another too often.

Lei thrust out her hand and introduced herself to Nico and Angelo, then to my mom, who had wandered back over to see what the fuss was about. My dad and Vincent gave shoutouts through the service window. A menu was set in front of Lei, along with a basket of fresh bread and olive oil imported from a small farm in Tuscany.

"How's the *panna cotta?*" Lei asked me.

"You'll never have better," I replied. "Have you already had dinner?"

"Not yet. Lesson number one—life's too short. Don't put off the good stuff."

I bit on my lower lip to hold back a grin. "Does that mean I got the job?"

She held up her flute with a brisk nod. "Cheers."

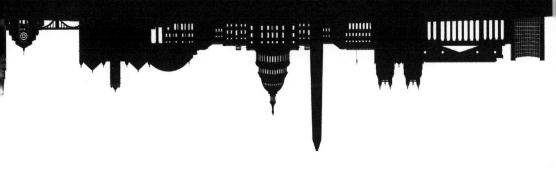

2

One year later…

"GOD, THE RUSH," Lei said, her feet tapping beneath the dining table. "It never gets old."

I grinned, having caught the bug from her over the months we'd been working together. We'd experienced a lot of highs, but today—a cloudless late-September afternoon—was special. After months of finessing and wooing, we were going to close a deal that would snag two of Ian Pembry's brightest stars. Payback for what he'd done to Lei long ago and a major coup for us.

Lei had dressed for the occasion and so had I. Her Diane von Fürstenberg wrap dress was vintage and her signature red. Paired with black boots, she looked fierce and sexy. I debuted a dark gold shell snagged from Donna Karan's fall collection and the cigarette pants the designer had paired with them. The ensemble was chic and reflected a new me, a Gianna who'd evolved a lot over the previous year.

Impatient to finalize everything, I looked toward the entrance of the hotel bar and felt a surge of adrenaline when the Williams twins appeared as if on cue. Brother and sister made a striking pair, with auburn hair and jade-green eyes. They were a great team in the kitchen, having made a name for themselves with down-home Southern cooking updated with gourmet ingredients. The package they presented sold deluxe books and cute little tins of seasonings, but the truth wasn't so pretty. Behind the scenes, they hated each other.

And that had been Pembry's fatal mistake with his dynamic duo. He told them to suck it up and make it work, because they were making millions off their sibling success story. Lei had offered them what they really wanted—the chance to split up and shine on their own, while still capitalizing on their supposedly playful rivalry. Her plan was to build a chain of restaurants with dueling kitchens in the world-famous Mondego casinos and resorts.

"Chad. Stacy," Lei greeted, rising to her feet along with me. "You're both looking fabulous."

Chad came over and pressed a kiss to my cheek before he even said hello to Lei. He'd been flirting with me for a while and it had become part of our negotiations with him.

I'll admit I'd been tempted to do more than flirt on occasion, but thoughts of his sister retaliating held me back. Chad wasn't a saint by any means, nursing a fierce ambitious streak. But Stacy was a real piece of work and she hated me more than her brother. Despite all my friendly overtures, she'd taken an instant dislike to me and that had seriously hindered the whole process.

Personally, I suspected she was sleeping with Ian Pembry—or had been once—and was carrying a torch for him. I thought that was why she didn't like Lei, either, but maybe she was just one of those females who hated other women.

"I hope your rooms are comfortable," I said, knowing damn well they were. The Four Seasons didn't have its five-star reputation for nothing.

Stacy shrugged, her glossy hair sliding over her shoulder. She had an angelic face, pale with a smattering of freckles that were adorable. It was disconcerting how someone so sweet and innocent-looking, with a syrupy Southern accent, could be such a raging bitch. "They're all right."

Chad rolled his eyes and held out my chair for me. "They're great. I slept like a rock."

"I didn't," his sister griped, sliding gracefully into her chair. "Ian kept calling. He knows something's up."

She slid a side glance at Lei, as if gauging the impact of her words.

"Of course he does," Lei agreed easily. "He's a smart man. Which is why I'm surprised he didn't do more to keep you both happy. He knows better."

Stacy pouted. Chad winked at me. Usually I didn't find winking cute, but it worked for him. Part of his good-oleboy charm that was tempered by how sexy he was. There was something about him that hinted he might spank you with a spatula as expertly as he cooked with one.

"Ian did a lot for us," Stacy contended. "I feel disloyal."

"You shouldn't. You haven't signed anything yet," I said, having learned reverse psychology worked best with her oppositional nature. "If you feel that your identity as the Williams twins has more potential than being Stacy Williams, you should absolutely go with your gut. It's got you this far, after all."

Out of the corner of my eye, I watched Lei's lips twitch with a repressed smile. It gave me a thrill that she was pleased, since she'd taught me pretty much everything I knew about herding egos where we wanted them to go.

"Don't be an ass, Stace," Chad muttered. "You know this casino deal is a prime opportunity for us."

"Yes, but it may not be the *only* opportunity," she argued. "Ian says we need to give him a chance to deliver."

"You told him?" her brother snapped, scowling. "For fuck's sake, the decision isn't just yours to make! This is my goddamn career, too!"

I shot a worried glance at Lei, but she just gave a nearly imperceptible shake of her head. I couldn't believe how cool and unruffled she looked, considering this deal would be the one to finally even the score between her and her mentor-turned-nemesis.

The Hollywood eateries Ian had pulled out from under her went bust when the celebrity investors got over the novelty of it and went looking for other tax shelters that didn't involve personal appearances. And two of his heavy-hitter chefs had gone back to their home countries, leaving a lot riding on the young shoulders of the Williams twins.

"The Mondego deal is exclusive to Savor, of course," Lei said. "What's Ian offering you?"

What the hell had gone wrong? I glanced between the two siblings, and then at my boss. I had the contracts in my lucky satchel under the table. We were in the home stretch and suddenly our prime bet was backing away.

Later on, I'd recognize the ripple of awareness that shimmered across my skin for what it was. At the time, I thought it was foreboding, my instincts warning me that the deal had tanked long before we'd sat down at the table.

Then, I saw him.

Everything in me stilled, as if the predator couldn't see me if I didn't move. He came into the bar with a sultry stride that made my hands curl into fists beneath the tablecloth. That walk of his was easy and smooth, confident. And yet it somehow signaled to the female brain that he was packing heat between those long, strong legs and knew how to use it.

God, did he.

Dressed in a gray V-neck sweater and dress slacks of a darker hue, he looked like a successful man with the day off, but I knew better. Jackson Rutledge never took a day off. He worked hard, played hard, fucked hard.

I reached for my water glass with a shaking hand, praying he wouldn't recognize me as the girl who'd once fallen hopelessly in love with him. I didn't look the same. I *wasn't* the same.

Jax was different, too. Leaner. Harder. His face made more stunning by the new sharpness in the angles of his jawline and cheekbones. I took a deep, quivering breath at the sight of him, reacting to his presence as if I'd been physically struck.

I didn't even realize Ian Pembry was walking beside him until they stopped at our table.

"What are the chances Jackson Rutledge is related to Senator Rutledge?" Lei asked with silky evenness as we slid into the backseat of her town car. "Or any of the Rutledges for that matter?"

Her driver pulled away from the curb and I fumbled with my tablet just to have an excuse to keep my gaze averted. I was afraid to reveal too much, that her perceptive eyes would see how shaken I was.

"One hundred percent," I said, my eyes on my tablet screen and the gorgeous face I'd thought—*hoped*—I would never see again. "Jackson and the senator are brothers."

"What the hell is Ian doing with a Rutledge?"

I'd been asking myself the same thing as the deal I'd worked so hard on fell apart in front of me—we'd come with contracts and pen in hand and left empty-handed. Unfortunately, I'd lost track of the conversation the moment Jax had allowed Stacy to press an exuberant kiss to his cheek. The roaring of blood in my ears had drowned out everything.

Lei's crimson-tipped fingers tapped a silent staccato on the padded door handle. Manhattan spread out all around us, the streets crawling with cars and the sidewalks with people. Steam billowed sinuously from the subways buried below, while shadows claimed us from above, the sun kept at bay by towering skyscrapers that choked out the light.

"I don't know," I answered, slightly intimidated by the energy she radiated, that of a tigress on the hunt. Did Jackson have any idea what he'd stirred by getting in Lei's way?

"Jackson's the only one of the Rutledge males not serving in political office somewhere in the country," I continued. "He manages Rutledge Capital, a venture capital firm."

"Is he married? Any children?"

I hated that I knew the answer to that question without looking it up. "Neither. He plays the field. A lot. Prefers pedigreed blondes in public, but won't turn down a roll in the hay with something…*flashier* in a pinch."

I couldn't help remembering how Jax's cousin-in-law, Allison Kelsey, had once described me. *You're flashy, Gianna. Guys like to fuck flash. Makes 'em feel like they're banging a porn star. But that's what turns them off, too. Enjoy him while it lasts.*

Allison's melodious voice and cruel words echoed in my mind, reminding me why I straightened my naturally wavy dark hair and had stopped maintaining the French-manicured acrylic nails that had made me feel sexy. I couldn't do anything about the genetics that gave me an overly generous ass and big boobs, but I'd toned the rest of myself down, striving to be classy instead of *flashy*.

Lei looked at me sharply. "You got that from a five-minute search?"

"No." I sighed. "I got that from five weeks in his bed."

"Ah." Her dark eyes took on an avid gleam. "So he's the one. Well, this just got interesting."

* * *

During the remainder of the ride back to the office, I braced for Lei to tell me the conflict of interest was a problem. I scrambled to find a way to downplay it.

"It wasn't serious," I told her as we rode the elevator up. *At least not for him…* "More like an extended one-night stand. I don't think he even recognized me just now."

And hell if that hadn't stung. He hadn't even looked at me.

"You're not a woman a man forgets, Gianna." She looked thoughtful. "I think we can work around this, but are you up for it? If this is going to get personal for you, we need to talk about that now. I don't want to make you uncomfortable. I also don't want to put my business at risk."

My first instinct was to lie. I wished Jax had meant as little to me as I had to him. But I respected Lei and my job too much to be untruthful. "I'm not indifferent to him."

She nodded. "I can see that. Glad you're honest about it. Let's keep you on this for now. You'll throw Rutledge off balance and we'll need that. And you're my in with

Chad Williams. He likes doing business with you."

I breathed a sigh of relief. She was wrong about Jax, but I wasn't going to blow my shot by pointing that out. "Thank you."

We exited onto our floor and were buzzed through the glass doors. The receptionist, LaConnie, raised her brows at me, obviously picking up on our agitated vibe. We should have returned triumphant, not frustrated.

"Any idea why Rutledge would have a sudden interest in the restaurant industry?" Lei asked, returning to her earlier question as we headed to her office.

"If I had to make a guess, I'd say one of the Rutledges owed Pembry a favor." That was the way the Rutledge family operated. They worked together like a tightly knit team, and even though Jax wasn't a politician, he still played the game.

Lei went directly to her desk and took a seat. "We'll need to figure out what chip he's cashing in."

I caught the undercurrent of annoyance in her voice and understood it. Ian Pembry had been undermining Lei in countless ways for years, but Lei had bided her time—it had been a study in patience that she admitted had made her a better businesswoman. She was determined to prove she'd learned his last lesson in betrayal well and I was determined to help her.

"Okay." I knew a little of what she felt. It still made me angry that I'd jumped into bed with Jax. I'd known who he was, knew his reputation, yet I'd thought I was sophisticated enough to take him on.

Worse, I'd deluded myself into thinking he cared. He lived in D.C.; I was in Vegas. For five weeks he'd flown out to see me every weekend and the occasional weekday. I'd told myself a guy as beautiful and sexy as Jax wouldn't go through all that trouble and expense just to get laid.

I hadn't considered how rich he was. Rich enough to find it entertaining to jet cross-country for a piece of tail and cautious enough to find it convenient that his inappropriate mistress was far away from both the public eye and his family.

My desk phone started ringing, and I hurried out of Lei's office to answer it. My station was set up just outside her doors, making me the last barrier visitors faced before they had an audience with her.

"Gianna." LaConnie's voice came clipped and quick through the receiver. "Jackson Rutledge is in the lobby, asking to see Lei."

I hated the way my heart gave a little kick over hearing his name. "He's here?"

"That's what I said," she teased.

"Have him sent up. I'll be around in a minute to show him to the conference room." I placed the receiver carefully back into its cradle and then walked back into Lei's office. "Rutledge is about to arrive at reception."

Her brows rose. "Is Ian with him?"

"LaConnie didn't say so."

"Interesting." She glanced at the diamond-encrusted watch on her wrist. "It's nearly five o'clock. You can stay for the meeting with Rutledge or head out, your choice."

I knew I should probably stay. I was already feeling like I'd lost ground by freaking out at the Four Seasons. I'd been too shell-shocked by Jax's unexpected appearance to grasp how the situation with the Williams twins had changed. Sadly, I wasn't in any better shape now.

"Instead of sticking around, maybe I should use this time to reach out to Chad," I suggested. "Get a feel for where he's at with this. I know we wanted to take the Williams twins together, but even if we get just one, it'll hurt Pembry in a significant way."

"Good plan." She smiled. "It'll do Rutledge some good to get better acquainted with me, don't you think? If Ian's led him to believe I'm an easy mark, it would be smart to prove otherwise now."

I almost smiled at the thought of Jax and Lei butting heads. He was far too used to females falling all over him, for both his devastating good looks and his family name, which was as close to royalty as America got.

"I'll do some digging after I talk to Chad—" I backed out of the room "—and see if I can find the connection between Pembry and the Rutledges."

"Good." She steepled her fingers together and rested her chin on the tips, studying me. "Forgive me for asking, Gianna—but did you love Jackson?"

"I thought we loved each other."

Lei sighed. "I wish that was one lesson women didn't have to learn the hard way."

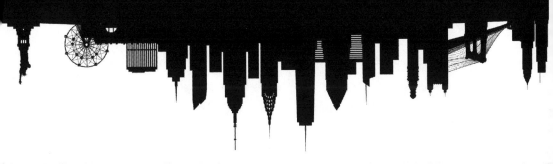

3

I GRABBED MY purse out of my desk drawer before I headed up to reception, clutching it like a talisman that would hurry me away from Jax before he realized who I was. The walk up to the front seemed to take a very long time.

It was a tough pill to swallow, realizing he still affected me so strongly. He'd only been part of my life for a short time. I'd had two other lovers since him and thought I had moved on.

He was studying a display of our bestseller cookbooks when I rounded the corner and my breath caught. His tall, powerful frame was now shown off to full advantage in an expertly tailored suit, a sign of respect for Lei I couldn't help but appreciate. I'd never seen him dressed so formally in person. We'd met at a bar, of all places. I'd gone out with some classmates, and he was attending a bachelor party.

I should've known it wouldn't turn out well.

But God, he was magnificent. His dark hair was close-cropped on the sides and back, slightly longer on the top. His eyes were a brown so dark they were nearly black. Thickly lashed, they were relentless in their intensity. Had I really thought they were soft and warm? I'd been blinded by that lush, sensual mouth and wicked dimple. There was nothing soft about Jackson Rutledge. He was a hard and jaded man, cut from a ruthless cloth.

He raked me from head to toe with a slow, intense look that made my fingers flex as I approached him.

It was well-known that he was a connoisseur of women. I told myself I could be anyone and get that look from him, but I knew better. My body remembered him. Remembered his touch, his scent, the way his skin felt against mine…

From the way he was looking at me, the same recollections were heating his blood, too.

"Hello, Mr. Rutledge," I greeted him formally, because he still hadn't acknowledged that he knew who I was. I spoke each word carefully, in a controlled voice not quite my own. I usually didn't have to think about sounding too Brooklyn anymore, but he made me forget myself.

He made me want to forget everything.

"Ms. Yeung will be out in just a moment," I continued, deliberately stopping a few feet away from him. "I'll show you to the conference room. Can I get you some water? Coffee? Tea?"

His chest expanded with a deep breath. "Nothing, thank you."

"This way, then." I passed him, managing a strained smile for LaConnie as I walked by her. I could smell him, that subtle hint of bergamot and spice. I could feel his gaze on my back, my ass, my legs. It made me hyperconscious of my walk, which made me feel awkward.

He didn't say a word, and I was afraid to, my throat too dry to make speech comfortable. I felt a terrible yearning— the almost desperate need to touch him the way I'd once had a right to. It was hard to believe I'd had him in my bed. Had him inside me. How had I ever had the courage to take on such a man?

I was relieved when we reached the conference room, the door handle feeling blessedly cool as I pushed it down.

His breath gusted softly over my ear. "How long are you going to pretend you don't know me, Gia?"

My eyes slid closed as he purred the name only he had ever used.

Pushing the door open, I stepped inside, holding on to the handle so there was no mistaking that I wouldn't be staying.

He walked right up to me, standing face-to-face. He was a little more than a head taller—even though I wore heels. His hands were in his pockets, his head bowed over me. He was in my personal space. Too intimate. Far too familiar.

"Please step back," I said quietly.

He moved, but not in the way I wanted. His right hand slid out of his pocket, and then down my arm, from elbow to wrist. I felt his touch through the silk of my navy blouse and was grateful that the long sleeves hid the goose bumps.

"You've changed so much," he murmured.

"Of course. Enough that you didn't recognize me earlier."

"Jesus. You think I didn't know it was you?" He turned away, but that didn't lessen his impact. The back view was just as splendid as the front. "You could never hide from me, Gia. I'd recognize you blindfolded."

Shock and confusion held my tongue for a moment. We'd gone from distant and impersonal to searingly intimate in a heartbeat. "What are you doing here, Jax?"

He walked to the windows and looked out at New York. In the near distance, Central Park was a splash of green already touched with autumn-red and orange, a vibrant burst of color in a concrete jungle. "I'm going to offer Lei Yeung whatever it takes to make her go play in someone else's sandbox."

"It won't work. This is personal."

"Business should never be personal."

I stepped back toward the threshold, eager to escape. The conference room was spacious and airy, with floor-to-ceiling windows on one side and clear glass on the other. The walls at either end were a soothing pale blue, with an expensively stocked bar to the right and a huge display screen to the left. Still, Jax dominated his surroundings, making me feel caged.

"Nothing's personal, right?" I said, remembering how he'd just failed to show up one day. And every day after that.

"Things were between us," he said, his deep voice husky. "Once."

"No, they weren't." *Not for you…*

He turned abruptly, causing me to take another cautious step back even though we stood a room apart. "There are no hard feelings, then. Good. There's no reason not to pick up where we left off. My meeting with Yeung won't take long. When I'm done we can head to my hotel and get reacquainted."

"Fuck you," I snapped.

His mouth curved, revealing that delicious dimple. Oh, how that changed him, concealing how dangerous he was with a touch of boyish charm. I hated that playful little indentation as much as I adored it.

"There you are," he said, with an unmistakable note of triumph. "You almost had me fooled into thinking the Gia I knew was gone."

"Don't toy with me, Jax. It's beneath you."

"I want you beneath me."

I'd known he would say that, if I opened the door, but I'd had to hear it. I had to hear him spell it out. He was direct when it came to sex, sensual and natural as an animal. I loved it, because I'd been that way with him, too.

Greedy. Insatiable. Nothing else had ever made me feel as good.

"I'm seeing someone," I lied.

Visually, he didn't bat an eye, but somehow, I got the impression that struck a nerve. "That Williams guy?" he asked too casually.

"Hello, Mr. Rutledge," Lei said, sweeping in on her killer Jimmy Choo slingbacks. "I'm going to assume this is a pleasant surprise."

"It can be." He turned his attention to her so completely, I felt dismissed.

"I'll leave you two to it," I said, walking out. Lei's gaze caught mine and I understood the silent message. We'd be talking soon.

I didn't look at Jax again, but I still got the same message from him.

I called Chad Williams as soon as I passed through the turnstiles in the lobby. "Hey," I said when I heard his smooth Southern drawl. "It's Gianna."

"I was hoping you'd call."

"Do you have dinner plans?"

"Ah—I can break them."

I smiled, feeling a little guilty about preempting whoever was going to be ditched, but it felt good to have a little ego-stroking. My confidence had taken a beating from seeing Jax again.

I couldn't forget how he'd been with me long ago. Frisky, teasing, affectionate. If I closed my eyes, I could still feel him come up behind me, sliding my hair out of the way to press his beautiful mouth against my throat. I could still hear the way he'd groan my name when he was inside me, as if the pleasure were too great to stand.

"Gianna? You still there?"

"Yeah, sorry." I started pulling out the pins that restrained my straightened hair into a sleek chignon. "I know a charming Italian place. Cozy. Casual. Excellent food."

"You've got yourself a date."

"I'll call the car service. I can pick you up in about fifteen minutes. Will that work?"

"I'll be waiting."

True to his word, Chad was standing on the sidewalk when the car pulled up. He wore loose-fitting black jeans, boots and a dark green Henley that went great with his eyes. As far as dates went, he was prime.

He started toward the cab, then jumped back with a curse as a bike messenger sped by.

"Christ almighty," he muttered as he settled into the seat beside me. He looked me over as we merged back into rush-hour traffic. "I like your hair down. It suits you."

"Thank you." It'd taken me a while to get used to wearing it up. It was so thick and heavy, the weight of it gave me headaches...like the one I had at that moment.

"So," I began, "I have to confess—"

"Hope it's sinful."

"Uh, no. I'm taking you to my parents' place."

His brows rose. "You're taking me to meet your folks?"

"Yep. They own a restaurant. We won't have trouble getting a table without a reservation—usually impossible on a Thursday night—and they won't rush us off, either."

"You planning on keeping me around awhile?" he teased.

"I'd like to. I think we could work really well together."

Chad nodded, sobering. "Stacy knows what you're offering is exactly what we need, but...she's sleeping with Ian and it's screwing everything up."

"I figured." Ian Pembry was a suave and distinguished fifty-year-old man with silvery gray hair and striking blue eyes. He wasn't handsome in the usual sense, but he had charisma and a bank balance that made a lot of women overlook his flaws. Stacy had her work cut out for her; since Lei, he'd never stayed with any lover long. "What's he offering you to stay with him?"

And where does Jax fit in? Had seeing me knocked him for a loop at all?

"Ian says he can put something together like you've presented and he can do it better, because Lei doesn't have what it takes. That's why she's poaching his talent."

"You know that's crap."

"I do, yeah." He smiled. "You wouldn't be working for her if she was second-rate."

"And the Mondego resort chain is five-star all the way," I reminded him. "They wouldn't work with someone second-rate, either. This is the opportunity of a lifetime, Chad. Don't let Stacy take it away from you."

"Goddamn it." His head fell back against the seat rest. "I don't think we can make it separately. That's why the idea of the dueling kitchens was going to work."

"It *will* work. But you can do it on your own, too."

He looked at me, his gaze searching. "Give it to me straight, Gianna. You'll say anything to close this deal, won't you?"

I thought about Jax and what he'd said about business not being personal. For me it was always personal. I cared.

"I've got my reasons," I admitted, Jax now being one of them. I'd worked too hard to have him stroll in, toss his money around and ruin everything. "But I wouldn't screw you over. It doesn't get Lei or me anywhere if you're not successful. I promise you, I won't disappear as soon as the ink is dry."

"And now I'll know how to track you down through your folks," he said, relaxing.

"Over thirty years in the same location."

"I guess that's as good a guarantee as anyone can get."

My family pulled out all the stops when we got to Rossi's, deducing who Chad was from my previous descriptions. We were seated at a corner table and everyone came by to introduce themselves, giving Chad a heaping dose of Rossi hospitality.

I had Chad take the bench seat facing the rest of the restaurant, while I took the single chair across from him. I wanted him to feel the energy, to see the faces of customers enjoying a great meal. I wanted him to remember why he wanted what Savor was offering him.

Over a toast, he said, "You're right. This place is great."

"I'm never going to lie to you."

He laughed, and I enjoyed the sound. It was a bit wild, a lot free. Very much like the man himself. I was attracted to him on a comfortable level. Nothing like the explosion of body and mind I'd felt from the very first second I'd laid eyes on Jax, but then no one elicited that reaction but Jackson Rutledge.

"Smart bringing me here," he said, running his fingertip around the lip of his wineglass. I suspected he'd prefer beer, but he didn't ask for it. "Making me see you've got the business in your blood, too. It's not just a job."

"My family just opened our second Rossi's in Upper Saddle River."

"Where's that?"

"New Jersey. Posh as hell. My brother Nico is spearheading it. Just passed the three-month mark."

"So why not hook your family up with the Mondego?"

"It's not what they want. They want this—" I gestured around the restaurant with a sweep of my hand. "Community. Franchising was never their dream."

He studied me. "You make it sound like your dreams are different."

I sat back. "I suppose they are. I want to help them get what they want, but I want something different."

"Like what?"

"I haven't found it yet." *Although I thought I had. Once upon a time…* "I figure I'll know it when I see it."

"Maybe I could help you pass the time while you're waiting," he suggested boldly.

I smiled. "It's an idea, isn't it?"

Maybe he was what I needed. It'd been too long since my last boyfriend. I'd been working hard, leaving little time for socializing. I didn't fool myself into thinking I would magically have immunity to Jax if I got laid, but it wouldn't hurt. It would certainly take the edge off life in the interim, and Jax wouldn't be staying in New York long. His life and work was split between D.C. and northern Virginia, and soon enough, another Rutledge would need him for something. He was the family fixer.

I leaned forward, opening myself to the possibilities.

Chad's mouth curved in a very male smile, the slightly triumphant one of a man who knew he was going to score. He reached for my hand, his gaze drifting over my shoulder in a lazy way. Then he stilled, his brows lowering in a scowl. "Fuck."

I knew who he was looking at before I turned around.

4

AN ALL TOO FAMILIAR CHARGE swept over my skin. I decided not to turn and give Jax the satisfaction of seeing my face, which probably showed my surprise, frustration and irritation.

He had cast-iron balls to come into Rossi's after the way he'd broken my heart. My family would remember him— remember that last night we'd all spent together. We'd been in New York on a quick weekend trip to introduce him to the family I talked so much about. We'd stayed long after the restaurant closed, eating and drinking and laughing with my brothers and my parents. They'd fallen in love with him just as I had. That was the night I'd come to believe we were in it for the long haul.

I hadn't seen him again until he'd walked into the bar at the Four Seasons.

Chad looked at me. "You invited Stacy, too?"

"No." Confused, I finally looked over my shoulder. Seeing Jackson helping Stacy out of her jean jacket made my teeth grind. Chad hadn't known where we were going, but Jax had guessed.

And sure enough, he made a beeline toward us with Stacy. My mom got in their way, her smile wide as ever but proverbial feathers ruffled in full mother-hen mode.

I looked at Chad. "We could sneak out the back."

He laughed, but his eyes were hard.

Angelo came over. "Is he meeting you?" he asked, jerking his head toward Jax.

"No…" I looked at Chad. "They don't have to sit with us."

"Good." He sat back, glaring. "Talk about keeping the wrong company. Stace can go ahead with Ian's deal, if she wants. I'm sticking with you and the Mondego."

"All right." Angelo looked at me. "I'll make sure they're seated somewhere else."

I took a gulp of my wine as my brother walked away.

Chad studied me for a moment. "He has your back."

"That's the Rossi way."

"Stace and I used to be like that. Before Ian showed up."

"Really?" I tried to ignore the sensation of Jax's gaze. I could *feel* him looking our way. "What happened?"

He shrugged. "Hell if I know. It all went to her head. I don't even know if she thinks about the food anymore. She's too busy trying to be rich and famous."

My mom came by with more wine, setting her hand on my shoulder as she refilled our glasses. I felt the gentle press of her beautifully manicured nails and heard the silent question: *Are you okay?*

I set my hand over hers and squeezed, answering. I wasn't okay, but what I could say? I wouldn't give Jax the satisfaction of refusing him service and neither would my family. He'd get excellent food, our best server and complimentary wine of his choice.

They'd pull out all the stops. Kill him with kindness. Show him that we weren't petty and small. But oh, what it would cost us. All of us. My safe place felt invaded, his potent energy permeating the space and my senses. Every nerve tingled with awareness.

Lori, one of the waitstaff, came over to take our order. Chad and I decided to split the pasta for two. All through the appetizer and salad courses, I was expecting Jax to come over. I was terribly aware of him, unable to give Chad the attention I'd been able to before. He was subdued, too, his gaze staying firmly on his food or on my face, both of us studiously avoiding looking at other patrons.

In my mind, I was certain Jax was having a wonderful time just to spite me. Why was he taking Stacy out when she was Ian's latest fling? Or was she freely available to both of them? After all, she'd showed no hesitation and a lot of pleasure in kissing Jax's cheek when he first showed up.

Just before the main course was served, Chad excused himself to go to the bathroom, and I checked my smartphone. I'd missed a call from Lei. When Chad came back with a beer in hand, I smiled and said, "I'll be right back."

I headed toward the bathrooms, but ducked into the back office instead, closing out the noise when I shut the door behind me. I speed-dialed Lei and set the phone to my ear.

"Gianna," she answered. "I have to applaud you for your choice in men."

"Can I pick 'em or what?" I walked over to the far wall where a family portrait hung. I'd been around twelve years old in the picture with braces on my teeth and wild hair. Nico, Vincent and Angelo had been varying degrees of gangly. My dad was immortalized in his prime, as was my mother, who'd aged little since. "How'd it go?"

"As expected. You guessed right, by the way. Jackson said he's stepped in as a favor for someone."

"I haven't had a chance to dig for more details, I'm sorry— I've been with Chad since I left—but it's probably a Rutledge. When Jackson's not gambling with millions, he's cleaning up after family members à la Olivia Pope." *And dating beautiful women…* "As for Chad, he's on board, but I think we'd be wise to get a new contract drawn up ASAP before something happens to change his mind. Jax isn't going home gracefully. He crashed the dinner hour at Rossi's, bringing Stacy along for the show."

Lei laughed. "I'm sorry, but I like him."

My mouth quirked ruefully. "Happens."

"Ian called."

"Oh? How'd that go?"

"He asked if I'd see him tonight."

"Ah. Maybe that's why Jax has Stacy. Babysitting duty." Irritatingly, that filled me with relief.

"Could be. I said no in any case. I feel like our men are circling the wagons, which means we need to keep doing what we're doing. Honestly, I haven't had this much fun in years."

Our men. I snorted and turned in time to see the door opening…and Jax appearing. "I have to go, Lei, but I'm here if you need me."

"We'll hit it again fresh in the morning. Good night, Gianna."

"You, too." I set my phone aside.

We sized each other up for a long minute. He was wearing the gray sweater and slacks from earlier in the day, the casualness more familiar—and beloved. A lock of his dark hair fell over his brow, softening the severity of his beauty. He had his back against the door, his hands in his pockets, his legs crossed at the ankles. But only an idiot would fail to sense the predatory alertness in him. His hooded gaze was watchful and knowing, seeing way too much.

"I miss the curls in your hair," he said finally.

I backed up to my father's desk, resting my butt against it. I crossed my arms. "That's a seriously delayed response." *A couple years too late…*

"You were closing in on the kill when I got here. Are you thinking about fucking Chad Williams because you want to, or because you want him to sign on the dotted line?"

Some other woman might have held her tongue because the question didn't deserve an answer. I didn't say anything because I was too hurt. I'd never seen Jax deliberately mean or cruel—he'd just disappeared from my life.

"Gia…"

"Don't call me that."

"What would you prefer?"

My foot tapped restlessly. "I'd rather not see or hear from you."

"Why not?"

"I would think that'd be obvious."

His wonderfully sensitive mouth tightened. "Not to me. We know each other. We get along well. Very, very well."

"I'm not fucking you again!" I snapped, feeling the walls close in on us. He'd always had that effect on me. When he was with me, I didn't register anything else.

"Why not?"

"Stop asking me that!"

Jax straightened, and the office got even smaller. My breathing quickened, my gaze darting to the door at his back.

"It's a valid question." He engaged the lock without taking his eyes off me. "Tell me why you're so angry."

A surge of panic got the better of me. "You fell off the face of the earth!"

"Did I?" He took a step toward me. "Are you saying you didn't know how to find me?"

I frowned, confused. "What are you talking about?"

"It had to end, and it did." He came closer. "Quietly. No messy scenes. No ugly memories. We—"

"Neat and tidy." I sucked in a sharp breath, more wounded than I could say. I lashed out in self-defense. "So why rehash and screw it up?"

"Can't we be friends?"

"No."

Jax stepped into my space. "Can't we do business together?"

"Nope." I unfolded my arms, feeling the need to take the defensive. "You made this personal from the get-go."

He smiled, flashing that damned dimple. "You're sexy as hell when you're mad at me. I should've pissed you off more often."

"Back off, Jax."

"I did. It didn't take."

"Actually, it did. Go back to your world and forget me again."

"My world." The smile faded along with the light in his eyes. "Right."

He'd stopped his advance, so I skirted him quickly, aware that I had been gone too long and Chad was waiting.

Jax caught my arm, his hand flexing around it. He spoke in my ear. "Don't fuck him."

I shivered. We stood shoulder-to-shoulder, facing in opposite directions, which mirrored our entire relationship. I smelled him, felt his warmth, was reminded of other occasions when he'd whispered in my ear.

Jax knew how to seduce and he never shirked the effort. Even when I'd been a sure thing, he'd get me hot long before he took me to bed. Giving me long, searing looks, touching me often, murmuring naughty promises that made me blush.

"Are *you* celibate, Jax?" I retorted.

"I will be, if you are."

A harsh laugh burst out of me. "Yeah, right."

He held my gaze. "Try me."

"I'm not interested in playing games."

The doorknob rattled, making me jump. "Gianna? Are you in there?"

Vincent. "Yes," I called out. "Hang on."

"Don't fuck him," Jax repeated, his eyes dark and hard. "I mean it, Gia."

I shook free and fumbled the lock open, pulling the door wide.

My brother paused with the office key in his hand, then glared over my shoulder at Jax. "You got a death wish, Rutledge?"

Rolling my eyes, I pushed Vincent back. "Leave it alone."

"Sniff around somewhere else," Vincent went on, blocking the doorway as soon as I moved out of the way.

I briefly considered intervening, then decided against it. They were big boys. They could figure it out by themselves.

When I got back to the dining room, I found a large to-go bag sitting on the table in front of Chad, who stood when he saw me.

"What do you think about taking this back to the hotel and eating in peace?" he asked.

I looked around the dining room, easily spotting Stacy's bright hair gleaming in the muted glow of the wrought-iron chandeliers. She was staring daggers at Chad and me.

"I've got a better idea," I said, grabbing my belongings. "I know someplace we can go where no one will find us."

I took him to my sister-in-law Denise's beauty salon in Brooklyn. She closed up shop, found some paper plates and we feasted on lukewarm-but-still-delicious *ragù bolognese* in the stylists' lounge in back, away from the smells of dye and hair spray.

"You've got a New York accent," Chad noted after we'd been swapping crazy customer stories for a while. "I never noticed before."

I shrugged. "Yeah. As heard on TV in ten thousand cop shows."

Chad laughed.

"It's because she's on her own turf," Denise explained.

I didn't add anything. No biggie that he'd noticed. The accent always came out when I was hanging with family or friends, when my defenses were relaxed and I felt more like the me I used to be.

"It's cute," he teased, exaggerating his own. "Y'all know I've got one, too."

"She's gotten good at hiding it," Denise said, her platinum hair with hot pink tips arranged into artful braids. She had piercings in her nose and brow, and a sleeve of tattoos on her left arm. She was also five months pregnant and just beginning to show. I was so excited about that. I was dying to be an aunt.

My smartphone started ringing in my purse, and I reached over to the counter to dig it out. Maybe Lei needed me after all. She hadn't been kidding about the hours when she'd hired me. I'd had 2:00 a.m. calls and weekend calls, but I loved them all because those happened when she was really pumped about something.

Looking at the screen, I didn't recognize the New York number and was about to let it go to voice mail when I decided to indulge Chad with my accent a little more.

"Gianna Rossi's office," I answered naturally. "How can I help you?"

Silence greeted me, then… "*Gia.*"

I held my breath, rocked by the way Jax said my name. The way he used to when we were lovers and he'd call just to hear my voice.

"Say something," he said gruffly.

Fortified by the sight of my stricken face in the unforgiving mirror, I replied with chilly calm. "How did you get this number?"

"Give me a break," he snapped. "Talk like you used to. The *real* you."

"You're the one who called me."

He bit out something under his breath. "Have lunch with me tomorrow."

"No." I slid out of the chair and walked toward the front of the beauty shop.

"Yes, Gia. We need to talk."

"I don't have anything to say to you."

"Then listen."

I rubbed the tip of my stiletto over a crack in a floor tile. Denise had just started turning a profit and there were improvements she wanted to make to the shop. Still, the location was newly hip again and she'd been smart to go with gorgeous vintage pinups on the walls and great retro décor that distracted the eye from minor flaws.

God, I was a mess over Jax. My scattered brain was bouncing random thoughts all over the place.

I focused on the man driving me crazy. "If I have lunch with you, will you go away and leave me alone?"

"I won't promise that."

"Then I won't go," I countered. "You've got no right to invade my life like this. None of this is your business. You shouldn't be butting in—"

"Damn it. I didn't know you were in love with me, Gia."

My eyes closed against the pain of hearing those words from his lips. "If that's true, you didn't know me at all."

I hung up.

5

"I FOUND SOMETHING tying Pembry with the Rutledges," I told Lei first thing Friday morning, following her into her office as she arrived for the day. "An article in *FSR* magazine."

She glanced aside at me. "How long have you been here?"

"Half an hour, maybe." But I'd been up late doing my homework, unable to sleep. I needed to know why Jax was meddling in my life and how to get him back out of it again. I didn't want an apology from him or an explanation.

I didn't want to be friends. I didn't want any reason to hope, because it'd become painfully obvious to me that I was still in love with him. And now, he was becoming aware of it, too.

I'd learned my lesson the first time, and he'd confirmed it—our relationship had to end at some point. No do-overs.

I slid the article from *Full-Service Restaurant* across her desk. "A tiny mention of Pembry supporting and contributing to Rutledge campaigns in a bigger piece on restaurateurs and politics."

"Hmm." Her astute gaze lifted to meet mine. "I lived with Ian for five years. He never once voted in any election. And he's too much of a tight-ass to spend the kind of money it takes to get the Rutledges' personal attention."

Lei leaned back, twisting her chair side to side. "That said," she went on, "I can't see a venture capitalist taking an interest in Ian's business over mine without some personal motivation. It doesn't make fiscal sense."

Lifting my hands, I admitted, "I don't get it, either."

"Would Jackson tell you what sparked his interest in Ian if you asked him?"

"Maybe." I took a seat in front of her desk. "But he's not the deciding factor here. Stacy prefers Ian. Chad prefers us. We've got a grip on this."

"Aren't you curious?"

"Not enough to go out of my way to talk to him. He's starting to realize I took our fling more seriously than I should have and that's…awkward."

Lei's gaze was warm with sympathy. "I guess the best solution is to get this wrapped up. I'm talking with the team at Mondego today about moving forward with just Chad. They're not as excited—no surprise there—but I think I have an appealing alternative."

I leaned forward, and she smiled at my eagerness.

"These two." She swiveled her monitor around to face me, revealing two very different women. One darkly exotic, the other a fresh-faced blonde. "I've been keeping my eye on them for a few months now. Isabelle, the brunette, specializes in regional Italian, while Inez, the blonde, has a flair for regional French."

A soft laugh bubbled up. "Dueling kitchens international."

"More work to get the menu right, but when you can't deliver two, up the ante to three."

"Awesome."

Lei rubbed her hands together. "With any luck, we'll still be cracking open bottles of bubbly."

I heard my desk phone ringing through the open door and stood.

She pushed her phone over to me. "You can get that here."

Picking up the receiver, I hit the button for my line and answered.

"Miss Rossi, Ian Pembry. Good morning."

I raised my brows and mouthed *Ian* to Lei. Her mouth curved.

"Good morning, Mr. Pembry. I was just thinking about you."

"I was waiting for you to call, then I got impatient." The warm amusement in his voice hit me the way I suspected it hit most women. There was no doubt about it; he had a great bedroom voice.

"Would you be available for lunch sometime?" I asked, shooting a look at Lei to make sure she'd be okay with it. She nodded.

"I'm flattered you'd choose me over Jackson," he said, putting my back up. "But I was hoping for dinner instead. I have an engagement tonight and I need a date."

Reaching over, I hit the speaker button. "What about Stacy?"

"She's wonderful, of course, but I'd prefer to take you. You'll want to come along, Lei," he posited, addressing her directly, "and look out for your girl, which is fine. The more the merrier. It's a formal event. Be at the Midtown heliport by six."

Lei grinned, clearly enjoying the exchange although she didn't reply.

"You're assuming I don't have plans on a Friday night," I said.

"Don't be offended, Miss Rossi." He sounded amused. "It's a compliment on your dedication. Lei wouldn't have hired you if you didn't put the job first. See you tonight."

The line clicked off, and I set the receiver back in the cradle. "Well…what do you think?"

"I think we need to go shopping."

When I returned to my desk, I found a package waiting.

I ripped into the brown paper wrapping and discovered a foiled box of chocolates inside. The surge of desire that pierced me at the sight of that particular brand— Neuhaus—and the memories it evoked quickened my breathing. My skin heated.

I'd had the Belgian truffles only once before, when I'd sucked them off the tips of Jax's fingers. He'd melted them with the heat of his touch…then painted words over my body that he'd licked off with wicked lashes of his tongue.

Sexy Gia. Sweet. And my favorite—*mine.*

My thighs clenched, and I crossed my ankles, my core tightening in greedy demand. My body didn't care that he'd dumped me without a word. It wanted Jax. Desperately.

The note attached was simple and unsigned.

I'd know you blindfolded.

I couldn't tell you where Lei took us to buy gowns. It was a small, unmarked storefront that had a permanent Closed sign on the door. Appointments only. The moment Lei's town car pulled up out front, we were ushered inside a showroom of quiet luxury and served champagne with ripe strawberries. There were no price tags in evidence anywhere.

The next hour passed in a blur of silks and taffetas. I was dazzled.

There had been times working with Lei that I had been exposed to a world far beyond anything I knew. I always struggled to hide my wide-eyed awe on such occasions, striving to take my cues from Lei, who seemed so natural and at ease. I had to remind myself that her background wasn't so different from mine. She'd acquired polish over the years and so could I.

I was eyeing a black gown with lace cap sleeves when Lei set her hand on my shoulder.

"That's too old for you," she said.

I glanced at her. "I think it looks understated and elegant."

"It does, for a woman my age. You're twenty-five. Enjoy it."

"I have to be careful," I explained. My boss was slender as a reed, graceful and lithe. I was too curvy. "My boobs are too big. And so is my butt."

"You're sexy," she asserted bluntly. "You play it down at work, which I understand and appreciate, but don't waste it. It's a terrible myth that a successful woman can't be sexy without it ruining her credibility. Don't buy into it."

I caught my lower lip between my teeth. Looking around the showroom, I was intimidated by the reek of wealth it exuded. I was out of my league. The walls were draped in billowing ivory silk, for Christ's sake, instead of wallpaper. And the finger sandwiches they had just brought out were sitting on a platter I was positive was pure, heavy silver. "Can you help me? I'm afraid I'll make the wrong choice."

"That's what I'm here for, Gianna." She gestured at one of the three women helping us. "Let's see what you've got for young, beautiful and voluptuous."

The whistles I got when I stepped out of my bedroom a few hours later both excited me and made me nervous. Denise had come home early to do my hair, bringing Pam, one of her stylists, with her to do my makeup. Angelo was sprawled across the couch watching stuff he'd recorded on the DVR, passing the time until his eight o'clock shift at Rossi's.

"Wow," my brother said, sliding up into a sitting position. "Who are you and what have you done with my sister?"

"Shut up," Denise and I retorted in unison.

"She looks like a movie star," Pam said, returning from the kitchen, where she'd been cleaning her cosmetic brushes. "One of the real goddesses, I'd say. A Raquel Welch or Sophia Loren."

"Who?" Denise frowned.

But I got it. I'd always thought of my mom the same way.

The gown we'd chosen in the end was still black, but *much* sexier. A jeweled brooch held the one shoulder strap together, with inky satin ruched across the bust, cinched at the waist with a thin diamond belt, then slit down the right leg from midthigh to hem. It occurred to me that it was a good thing Vincent was already at Rossi's. He might've freaked a little at how much of my legs were showing. Nico, who was living in Jersey now, would've loved it.

Denise plopped down on the sofa with two beers in hand, passing one over to her husband and setting the other on the coffee table for Pam. She'd been sticking religiously to water and fruit juice since she had found out about the baby.

Gold hoops glittered from between the crimped mass of her hair. "Is Chad going, too?" she asked.

"I have no idea."

"Is Jax?" Angelo added tightly.

I shrugged, but my pulse leaped. I had tried not to think about Jax when I'd been getting ready, but I couldn't help hoping he could see me dolled up. I looked hot.

"You know better," he warned. "Yeah," I agreed, "I do."

My smartphone rang, and I knew Lei's driver had arrived. "Gotta run!"

I hurried across the refinished hardwood of our joint loft to grab my heels, clutch and wrap from the bench by the door, waving at Pam before I exited through the open sliding front door. I skipped the temperamental old freight elevator and took the three flights of stairs to reach the street. Lei's driver was used to the delay.

Nico, Vincent and Angelo had bought the loft with the expectation of fixing it up and selling it for a profit. I'd moved in after college and eventually bought Nico's share when he moved to New Jersey. Then Vincent and I had split the cost of Angelo's share when he'd moved out with Denise, giving the two of us 50 percent stake each. We'd been considering selling out when Denise found out she was pregnant, and she and Angelo moved back in to save money.

I liked coming home to a full house and missed Nico. I wasn't sure what I'd have done with myself living alone. I think having someone around all the time had helped me focus on work and date less than I normally would have. I'd been comfortable with that, but maybe I had just been hiding from the fact I was nursing a broken heart. Maybe I should've faced that sooner. Certainly it was time to face it now.

Breathless from the rush, I slid into the open backseat of the town car and we headed to Lei's. Her part of New York was a lot different from mine. She lived in Manhattan, a bridge distance away that could've been another world. We crossed the East River with the sun still hanging in the sky, the light's reflection on the water broken by an industrious towboat.

It amazed me that I'd once believed Jax could fit in here. I had come to associate him so completely with D.C. that I could no longer imagine him anywhere else.

Except my bed. I had no trouble imagining him there....

I was considering how best to finagle information out of Ian Pembry when the car pulled to a stop in front of Lei's apartment building.

I'd seen her dress earlier, but it had a whole new impact with the hair and makeup to match. Emerald-green and Grecian in design, it glided over her willowy body as she exited her apartment building with a smile for her doorman. The rich hue of her gown showed off her flawless pale skin and emphasized the red of her lips, while a beautiful jeweled clip accented the silver strands at her right temple.

She settled on the seat beside me and I immediately caught her tension.

"You okay?" I asked.

"Sure."

We were quiet as we took the short ride to the heliport, both of us lost in our own thoughts. Turning a corner, my gaze caught on a dog park and the boisterous furry bodies running wild and free inside it. Their playful exuberance and undisguised pleasure made me smile, despite the somber turn my reflections had taken all day.

I hated to admit it, but I was hurt that Ian knew about Jax inviting me to lunch. When Jax had called, I'd thought the request had come from the heart. I had believed it was personal, that he truly wanted to connect with me, even if it was only to apologize. I guess I'd always expected too much from Jax. When it came to him, my instincts were seriously faulty.

By the time we were strapped into a helicopter and lifting into the air, my attention had turned outward to Lei. She stared out the window as the ground dropped farther away, laying the city out for us in a spectacular blanket of setting-sun-drenched concrete and sparkling glass. I followed suit, absorbing the panorama. The entire day had been reflective of my experience working with Lei. My family had a microscopic view of the world and they liked it. I'd always wanted something bigger, a view with a much wider lens.

"Do you know where we're going?" I asked.

She shook her head. "Ian's making a point with this outing. I expect we'll be wowed."

Around eight o'clock I found myself exiting a limousine in front of a sprawling mansion in D.C. I'd been growing more anxious by the mile, starting when we boarded a private jet at the airport and increasing exponentially when the flight attendant advised us of our destination.

"He's outdone himself," Lei muttered as Pembry descended the sprawling home's wide front steps to greet us.

The restaurateur looked impressively dapper in a classic tuxedo, his silvery-gray hair slicked back. He greeted me first by kissing the back of my hand, then turned his blue eyes onto Lei.

"You're toying with one of my people," she said coldly, watching impassively as he lifted her hand to his mouth. "You never used to be cruel."

"I used to have a heart," he drawled, "and then someone broke it."

My gaze darted between the two, trying to read the vibrating tension between them. I got the sense I was being played and that everyone understood the rules but me.

Fine. If I kept my mouth shut and my ears open, I could catch up.

Ian turned and offered me his arm. "Shall we?"

He led me up the front steps with Lei trailing behind. A glance back at her proved she did so regally, her head held high on that long neck I envied. Light spilled out of the open double doors and limousines discharged their passengers in steady waves behind us. It was an amazing party and I hadn't even crossed the threshold.

"I trust the flights were pleasant," he said.

I glanced at him and found him watching me too carefully. "Yes, thank you."

"Have you been to D.C. before?"

"My first time."

"Ah." He smiled, and I could see a hint of his charm. "Maybe you'll consider spending the weekend. I have a town house in Georgetown. You're welcome to use it."

"That's kind of you."

Laughing, he unlinked our arms and set his hand at the small of my back, urging me through the doors before him. "I hope you'll say more than a few words at a time as the evening progresses, Miss Rossi. I'd like to get to know you, especially since both Jackson and Lei have taken such an interest in you."

My steps slowed when I saw what looked to be a receiving line. "What is this event?"

"A private fund-raiser," he murmured near my ear.

I suddenly understood what Lei had meant by cruelty. "For a Rutledge?"

Amusement colored his voice. "Who else?"

Passing through the receiving line went quickly, with brisk handshakes from the men and slightly warmer handclasps by the women. All of them were perfectly groomed, without a hair out of place, and all had big practiced smiles with blindingly white teeth.

I was glad to get through and accept a glass of champagne from the tray of a smiling waiter. I was even happier to see Chad, who looked as uncomfortable as I felt. His face brightened when he saw us, familiar faces in an unfamiliar crowd, and he headed our way.

"I took the liberty of pairing Chad with you, Lei," Ian said, his gaze sliding over her.

I searched the room for Jax. I didn't see him, but then there were so many people milling around the ballroom we'd been shown to. A ballroom, for God's sake, in someone's *house.*

Who lived like this?

I swallowed a large gulp of the cool wine in my glass. Jax lived like this. The sleek businessman I'd seen at Savor fit in here, but not the lover I'd known.

You only thought you knew him....

Chad came up to me, sliding one finger beneath the collar of his dress shirt. "Can you believe this? I just met the governor of Louisiana. And he knew who I am!"

Ian's smile was smug. But I still didn't get it.

"How do politics and the food-service industry mix?" I asked him.

"Strange bedfellows, I admit." He took my empty glass and swapped it for a fresh one as a waiter walked by. "But everyone eats."

"Not everyone votes," Lei said, catching her own glass.

"You were always much more conscientious about that than I," Ian agreed. "What about you, Gianna? I can call you Gianna, can't I? Do you exercise your right to vote?"

"Isn't politics one of those topics it's wiser not to discuss?" I eyed a passing tray of hors d'oeuvres and realized my nerves were too shot to even consider food.

"Why don't we dance instead?" he suggested.

Figuring it might be a rare chance to speak to him alone, I agreed. Chad took my glass of champagne and downed it.

"I'll warn you that I'm not a great dancer," I told Ian as he led me over to the area reserved for dancing. I'd taken a few classes to build my confidence, but I never had a chance to dance formally outside of the studio and little time to practice anything beyond the basic steps. I had definitely never danced to a live orchestra before.

"Just follow my lead," he murmured, pulling me close.

We blended into the few couples on the floor.

I was so focused on not stepping on his feet that I didn't say anything for the first minute or so.

"Tell me how you know Jackson," he said.

"I don't know him." And that was the truth, in every way that mattered.

Ian's brows rose, his blue eyes searching my face. "Yesterday wasn't the first time you'd met."

"Since I'm sure you knew that before you brought him into the mix, I'm more interested in how you two know each other."

"I know his father, Parker Rutledge. He introduced us." He looked past me. "Speak of the devil."

My spine stiffened. I turned my head, my steps faltering as I watched a man who looked eerily like Jax dancing with a very pretty younger woman.

The urge to leave the event was insanely strong. I had no business at a political fund-raiser, no place in a world that had nothing at all to do with my own. I couldn't figure out how a pair of twin chefs had led me to this point in time and didn't really care to puzzle it out at the moment anyway. A sinking feeling that the night would go from bad to worse was getting stronger.

"What was the reason you brought us here, Ian?"

He countered with a question of his own. "How ambitious are you, Gianna?"

"I'm loyal to Lei."

He smiled. "I was, too. Unfortunately, you won't find her to be as faithful in return. You know as well as I do that it's not in Chad's or Stacy's interest to break up. They need each other."

"They can make it on their own. They're both talented in their own right." My feelings of irritation grew. "Why couldn't we have discussed this in New York?"

"I'm fighting for my livelihood. You have to expect that I'll pull out all the stops."

"Lei's in your league. I'm not."

"You feel out of place here," he said softly, soothingly. "I know these people. I would love to help you make connections and find your way."

I stared up at him. "Why are you offering me that? Because of Jackson? If you think I want to insinuate myself into his life, you couldn't be more wrong about me."

The song ended and I pulled back, ready to find Lei and see if she wanted to leave, too.

Pembry wisely got the hint and guided me off the dance floor. I was almost home free when a tall figure stepped into my path. I looked up and caught my breath, thinking for a split second that Jax had shown up after all.

Then I realized it was his dad.

"Ian," Parker said, thrusting out his hand in greeting. His voice carried power in it, just as his posture did. The Rutledge patriarch controlled a family with serious political clout. His reach and influence were staggering if you thought about it, which I couldn't help doing when he turned those dark eyes to me. "I don't think I've met your lovely companion before."

I was startled to hear his slight accent, one I couldn't place.

Ian did the honors. "Parker, this is Gianna Rossi. Gianna, Parker Rutledge."

"Hello," I said.

"Miss Rossi, a pleasure. This is my wife, Regina."

I looked at the blonde beside him, the one he'd been dancing with, and thought she couldn't be much older than me. She certainly wasn't old enough to be Jax's mother. Even a great plastic surgeon couldn't preserve someone that well. "Hello, Mrs. Rutledge."

Her smile didn't reach her eyes. "Regina, please."

"Dance with me, Regina," Ian said, holding a hand out to her with a flourish.

She looked at Parker, who gave a nod. She looked back at Ian. "I want you to tell me about that new chef you brought with you tonight. What type of food does he cook?"

"Modern Southern."

"Really?" They moved off. "I'm having a dinner party in a few weeks. Do you think...?"

"You'd never know it from looking at her," Parker said, setting his hand at my waist before I could decline. "But she loves to eat."

"I have a hard time understanding people who don't."

Parker swept me into the dance with a flourish and I held on, forcing myself to breathe.

"Regina also loves a great party," he continued. "But then she's young and beautiful. Like you."

"Thank you."

"Your interest is hospitality, isn't it? I believe that's what Ian told me. You must enjoy a great party, too. What do you think of this one?"

"It's..." I scrambled for an answer. "I'm still taking it in."

He laughed and the sound wasn't anything like Jax's warm chuckles. Parker had a booming laugh, one that drew attention. It was oddly infectious. I felt my mouth curve reluctantly.

"Gianna," he said, again with that hint of a regional accent. "An unusual name, isn't it? Jackson knew a Gianna in Las Vegas a few years ago."

As I'd expected, the evening was quickly moving from uncomfortable to disastrous. I had assumed I'd been a secret. Instead, it seemed Jax had been telling everyone about me. That didn't give me the warm fuzzies.

"It's a family name," I answered tightly, feeling terribly awkward.

"It must have been a pleasant surprise, seeing him again."

I studied him. Would Jax look like his father when he reached the same age? I hoped not. I hoped he'd have more laugh lines around the eyes and less tension around his beautiful mouth.

"I'm more surprised that Ian felt the need to involve him in our business."

"I involved Jackson," he murmured, looking over my head with narrowed eyes. "Ian did me a wonderful favor when he introduced me to Regina, so I help him whenever I can." He looked at me again. "I wasn't aware of you, though. I'll assume Ian was."

Unease slid down my spine. I felt like a clown fish swimming with sharks, in way over my head.

"*Excuse me.*"

God. The sound of Jax's voice reverberated through me.

"I'm cutting in."

Parker stopped and I turned my head, my heart pounding when I came face-to-face with Jax.

"I didn't think you'd show," Parker said to his son.

Jax glanced at me, then back at his father. "You didn't give me a choice."

For a second, I considered slipping away while the two men were occupied with staring hard at each other. Then Jax's arm slipped around my waist from behind, pulling me into him and away from his father.

Parker glanced at me. "I'll bow out and see you at dinner, Gianna. Enjoy yourself."

Jax rounded me, cutting off my view of his dad's retreating back. "You look amazing," he said softly, pulling me closer.

My shoulders ached with tension. "I'm glad you approve."

He took the first step and I followed.

"Breathe, Gia," he admonished. "I've got you."

"I don't want to be here."

"That makes two of us." He caressed my back with a soothing brush of his hand. "I hate these things."

"But you fit right in."

His eyes were shadowed with an emotion I couldn't name. "I was born into it. I don't live in it."

The heat of his body began to soak into mine. Every breath I took was filled with his scent; every movement he made sent echoes of memories sliding through me.

"That's better," he coaxed. "Relax into me, baby."

"Don't."

"You're in my world now, Gia. My rules."

I shook my head. "I was tricked into coming here."

He pulled me closer, his lips at my temple. "I'm sorry."

"You just had to get that out, didn't you? I don't see why. Clearly I wasn't the dirty little secret I thought I was."

"Not dirty." His voice lowered. "Except when you wanted me that way. A little rough, a lot hard. Jesus. You used to turn me inside out."

I stepped on his foot on purpose.

His low laugh rippled through me.

"You've been drinking," I accused, smelling the faint trace of liquor on his breath.

"Driven to it." He pulled back, his jaw set. "I didn't know it'd be so damn hard to see you again."

"I'll make it easier. Help me and Lei get out of here."

"Not yet." His soft mouth brushed over my brow. "I spent a night with your family. You owe me a night with mine."

"Then do I get to disappear, never to be seen again?"

I really wanted to. Cinderella at the ball had turned into the unsuitable girl once more.

His chest brushed against my breasts as he urged me closer. "That's the plan."

* * *

Jax kept me dancing through two more songs, bluntly refusing to relinquish me to Ian or two other gentlemen who attempted to cut in. I got the message as loudly as I'm sure everyone else did: I arrived with Ian, but I was now with Jax.

At that point, I decided to play my Cinderella role to the hilt. I kicked the voice in my head that had been depressing me for the past two days into a corner and flexed my toes in my proverbial glass slippers.

"I want champagne," I announced abruptly.

Jax eyed me. "Is that right?"

"Yep."

His eyes took on a wicked gleam I recognized. "Come on."

Grabbing my hand, he led me off the dance floor and through the crowd. It surged around him, trying to pin us in, but he was adept at brusque acknowledgments and quick rejoinders. I caught sight of a familiar face, beautiful Allison Kelsey—the woman whose fiancé's bachelor party had brought Jax and I together—then the view changed to a brightly lit hallway. From there, Jax led me through a swinging door into a massive industrial-sized kitchen buzzing with activity.

I looked around, noting the multiple cooking stations and the black-and-white service uniforms I'd only ever seen in movies. Jax snagged a bottle of champagne out of the hands of a waiter, slipped his ring finger around the stem of a flute in a practiced movement, then pulled me out a side door into another hallway.

"Where are we going?" I asked, still wary of being alone with him. I wanted him. I'd never stopped.

"You'll see."

The sounds of the party grew louder, and I ignored the pang of disappointment I felt at the possibility of rejoining it. Seriously, I had to make up my mind.

Jax led me through open French doors onto a terrace overlooking a magical garden. At least it looked that way to me, with its torch-lit gravel pathways and handsome old trees sparkling with white lights.

"Whose house is this?" I queried.

"It's a Rutledge estate."

The way he said it conveyed more ownership than the words themselves. "Right."

"Pretend we crashed this party," he said, leading me down cobblestone steps to a crescent-shaped marble bench.

I sat, watching as he poured champagne for me and passed me the glass. "Seems like we've been pretending all along, doesn't it?"

Jax swigged straight out of the bottle and wiped his mouth with the back of his hand, careless and a bit defiant. "Maybe. I still know you better than you think I do."

"I don't feel like I know you at all."

"So get to know me," he challenged. "What are you afraid of?"

I sipped my champagne. "Spinning my wheels and dead ends."

"Can't you just enjoy the ride?"

Oh, I'd love it. A surge of heated yearning pierced me.

He set the bottle on the bench beside me. "I'm going to kiss you."

My breath caught. "No, you're not."

"Try and stop me."

I surged to my feet. "Jackson—"

"Shut up, Gia." He cupped my face in both hands and took my mouth.

For a moment I didn't move, frozen by the feel of his lips on mine, so soft yet firm. Achingly familiar. Tender. His tongue licked along the seam. I opened up to him with a low moan and he slid inside.

I dropped my flute. Distantly, I heard it shatter, but didn't care. My arms were draped across his broad shoulders; my fingers were in his silky hair. I was drinking him in, tasting champagne and Jax, lifting onto my toes to deepen the connection.

As always, he gave me what I demanded of him.

Holding me still, he ate at my mouth, stroking with the velvet lash of his tongue, nibbling with lips and teeth, sliding his lips back and forth across mine. Savoring me. Turning a simple kiss into an erotic melding that had me trembling with pleasure.

God, I'd missed him. Missed the way he made me feel.

He growled, the rough sound vibrating against me. His hands slid downward, rubbing along my back, holding me in place as he rolled his hips and brushed the thick length of his erection against my cleft. Desire shot through me, flushing my skin. He smelled delicious, the subtle fragrance of his soap mixing with the virile scent that was his alone. I wanted to wallow in him the way I used to, pressing my naked body to his until even air couldn't come between us.

"Gia," he murmured gruffly, his lips sliding along my cheek. "Christ, I want you."

I closed my eyes, my hands fisting in the thick strands of his hair. I was on fire for him, my skin feeling too tight and sensitive. "You had me."

"I made the right decision walking away." His breath gusted over my temple. "That doesn't mean I don't regret it."

A tiny voice of caution was screaming. "You'll hurt me."

"I'll worship you." One of his hands captured my nape. The other gripped my hip, urging me into the slide of his hardness against my clit. "You remember how it was. Hours with my hands and mouth on you, my cock inside you—"

"For how long?" My core was clenching, tightening in demand for an orgasm.

"Weeks." He groaned. "Months. Jesus, I'm so hard it hurts."

I struggled out of his hold. "I need more than sex."

He let me go, but his gaze was fierce and hot. "I'll give you everything I've got."

"For a few weeks?" I trembled from the effort of staying away from him when he was all I craved. "A few months?"

"Gia." Jax scrubbed his hands over his face. "Damn it. Take what I can give you."

"It's not enough!"

"It has to be. Christ… Don't ask me to turn you into one of them!"

I jerked back, startled by his vehemence. "What are you talking about?"

He turned his back to the house and picked up the bottle of champagne, drinking deeply.

Confused, I studied him and saw only mulish determination. I looked past him into the ballroom, seeing the glittering couples inside. Lei appeared at that moment, walking onto the terrace with Chad on her arm.

In that moment I understood how badly I wanted to unravel the mystery of Jax, bad enough that I didn't care how much it was going to cost me.

"Mind if we join you?" Lei asked as she and Chad approached.

Her eyes caught mine. I sank onto the bench, my body still throbbing with unappeased hunger.

Glancing at Jax, I found his eyes on me. A challenge was there in those dark depths. I held my hand out for the champagne, gripping the bottle by the neck when he handed it to me.

I lifted it in toast and drank to that dare.

6

DON'T DISAPPEAR. See me again….

Jax's last words, whispered in my ear as we said goodbye, haunted me on the flight back to New York.

If I tangled with him I'd get hurt, because I would hope. I wanted more. But what choice did I have? I had to know what had gone so wrong before and what was still holding him back now. I'd always assumed it was me—who I was, where I came from—not meshing with who he was and what he wanted long-term.

I glanced at Lei, who was seated across from me on the plane, as she opened her clutch and withdrew a folded piece of paper. She slid it over and I smoothed it out on the table in front of us. I read the first paragraph, shot a look down to see the signature at the bottom, then lifted my head.

"Oh, my God… You got Chad to sign?"

"It's a tentative agreement," she qualified, "based on getting Isabelle and Inez on board—and you overseeing the first restaurant—but it's got him on the hook."

"Wow." I refolded the document carefully, taking in the fact that I'd just been handed a major responsibility. "I can't believe you had this with you. Did you know he'd be there?"

"I suspected, knowing Ian."

I handed the agreement back to her.

"Rutledge took care of you tonight," Lei noted. "Ian tried to throw you to the wolves, but Jackson kept you too close for that."

And he'd wanted me even closer.

I shrugged off her unspoken query, not wanting to get into something so deeply personal. "By the way, Parker Rutledge explained the connection. Ian introduced Parker to the latest Mrs. Rutledge."

"Did he?" Lei's elegantly arched brows rose. "Then it's likely Ian knows Regina Rutledge intimately."

"Are you kidding?"

"'Fraid not."

"Okay, then."

She leaned her head back against the seat. "Let's enjoy the weekend. Turn off your phone, forget about work. Just recharge. We'll hit it fresh on Monday."

That sounded perfect to me. "I'm more than game, but I'll leave my phone on in case you need me."

Lei smiled. "I won't need you, I promise. I've got a date this weekend."

"All weekend?"

"I'm overdue."

I laughed. In the year I'd been with Lei, I hadn't known her to date. She was due for a good time, all right. So was I. "Rock it."

She shot me a look. "I plan to."

When I got home, it was just past two in the morning and everyone was asleep. I padded to my room on bare feet, eager to strip and scrub down to my bare skin.

I was reaching for the concealed zipper on the side of my dress when I caught sight of my reflection in the mirrored closet doors. I paused, really taking a good hard look at myself.

Was Jax attracted to the polished businesswoman I'd become in a way he hadn't been to the girl I was before? Was I okay with that?

"God." I sat on the edge of my bed, wishing someone were awake that I could talk to. If Nico had been around, he'd be up. He was a night owl.

Impulsively, I reached for the phone on my nightstand and speed-dialed him. It rang three times before he answered.

"Hey," he said. "This better be good."

I winced at his irritated and slightly breathless tone, suspecting I'd interrupted him when he had someone staying over. "Nico, hi. Sorry. I'll call back tomorrow."

"Gianna." He exhaled roughly and I heard rustling. "What's up?"

"Nothing. We'll chat tomorrow. Bye."

"Don't hang up on me!" he snapped. "You wanted me, you got me. Spill it."

I hung up, figuring the sooner I let him go, the sooner he'd get back to whatever he'd been doing.

A half second later, the phone started ringing. I answered quickly, hoping it didn't wake up the rest of the house. "Nico, come on. It's not a big deal. I'm sorry I bugged you so late."

"Gianna, if you don't start talking, I'm heading up there to kick your ass. Is this about Jackson?"

I sighed. I should have known he would've heard the news from someone. "I've got a free weekend. I thought maybe I could come visit. Give you a hard time. Harass you a little. Or a lot."

"Now?"

Actually, I'd been thinking about it, but… "No, tomorrow."

"Bullshit. You don't call after two in the morning to say you want to stop by tomorrow."

"You're busy."

"By the time you get here, I won't be." His voice softened. "You got a safe ride down?"

"Nico—"

"I'll call a service, have a car pick you up."

I closed my eyes, grateful for him and more certain than ever that hanging with him would do me a world of good. It'd been a few weeks since I'd seen him. Too long. "I need to shower and change."

"Thirty minutes. I'll see you when you get here." He hung up.

Setting the handset back into its cradle, I hurried to get ready.

It was creeping past four in the morning when I arrived at Nico's apartment complex. He'd called a few minutes before to check where I was and was standing on the sidewalk waiting for me when I pulled up. Dressed in sweats with a shadow of stubble on his jaw, he looked a bit dangerous in that badboy way so many women gravitated toward.

God knew Jax's alpha-male qualities could put me into heat.

"Hey," he said, taking my duffel bag from the driver and handing over cash. He slung his arm around my shoulder and led me toward his place. "It's good to see you."

"No, it's not." I bumped my hip into his and made us both stumble. "Sorry to crash your night."

"I got mine." He grinned. "She got hers, too, so it's all good."

"Gross. TMI." He was such a player. Always had been. "Is she anyone special?"

"Not in a serious way. Got no time for a relationship now. My hands are full with Rossi's Two."

He released me to unlock the lobby door, then led me through to the interior courtyard. I'd been to his apartment complex before to help him move in, but it felt different at night. Too quiet and unfamiliar. I wondered if he got lonely without the rest of us. It made me sad to think of it.

"I wish you had someone to take care of you," I said.

"You first," he retorted, deftly bringing it back to me. He was good at that.

We climbed exterior steps to his apartment. Once inside, I saw that he hadn't done much more to it since he'd moved in. It was a typical bachelor pad—sparse on decoration and laid out for comfort rather than aesthetics.

A large flat-screen TV dominated the living room, which had a black leather couch and love seat, coffee table and one end table with an open soda can on it. Light spilled into the otherwise darkened room from the open-plan kitchen and ajar bedroom door, trying valiantly to compensate for the lack of table and floor lamps.

"So, Jax is back," he said, watching me as I dropped onto the couch. "Vincent owes me a hundred bucks."

"Are you kidding?" I would've thrown a sofa pillow at him if he'd had any. "You bet on Jax?"

"Bet on you." He sat on the love seat, setting my duffel on the floor at his feet. "He was gonzo over you, which meant he was either going to put a ring on you or run scared. I figured he'd run, then come back around once the fear wore off. He's a guy, but he's a smart one. Question is, is he too late? I'm guessing no or you wouldn't be here."

"Maybe I just wanted to see you," I argued. "God knows why."

"Maybe," he said in a tone that told me he'd believe it when hell froze over and pigs flew. "You still love him?"

My head fell back against the sofa, and I closed my tired eyes. "Yeah. Damn it."

"And him? Where's he coming from?"

"He's confused."

"Should I smack him around some? Knock some sense into him?"

I laughed softly. "God, I miss you."

We slept past noon, went out to eat, then sat on the couch and played video games until my thumbs ached from using the controller. I left my smartphone in my purse, powered off and squashed any impulse to check it. I'd left a note for Angelo and Vincent about where I'd be. With Lei off the grid for the weekend, there was no one else who needed to reach me before Monday.

When it came time for Nico to head into Rossi's, I got up off the couch with him.

"Need an extra set of Rossi hands?" I asked.

He grinned. "Sure. I have an extra T-shirt around here somewhere."

By seven, I found myself helping out at Rossi's and remembering how much I loved the hands-on part of the business. I couldn't do it long-term, like my brothers, but I was reminded that helping out every now and then was good for my soul. Dressed in jeans and a black Rossi's T-shirt with my hair pulled back in a ponytail, I could almost believe I was back in high school. I didn't know any of the customers coming in, but they quickly picked up on my relationship with Nico, due in large part to the playful ribbing we indulged in.

Crossing my arms on the bar, I leaned over and teased, "Where's my Bellini order? Pick it up, Rossi. You're laggin'. I'm waitin'."

"Ya hear that?" he asked the pretty redhead sitting in front of him. "She's rushing greatness."

I felt a charge that raised the hairs on my nape an instant before I felt a hand on my hip. I turned my head…

And saw Jax.

Blinking, I stared, drinking in the sight of him in jeans and a Rossi's T-shirt from way back, before we updated the logo. It twisted me up a little to see that he'd kept the gift. And worn it some, judging by how broken in it was.

"Jax. What are you doing here?"

"What do you think?" He smiled.

Damn it. His dimple threw me for a loop.

I turned to face him, leaning back on the bar with my elbows and hitching my shoe onto the brass foot rail. It was a deliberately provocative pose and got me the response I'd been hoping for.

His dark eyes swept me from head to toe and back again, coming to rest on my mouth. "Have dinner with me."

"Okay."

His brows rose at my quick reply.

"Order up," Nico said behind me.

I turned back to him just in time to see him acknowledge Jax with a jerk of his chin and a handshake.

"Jackson," my brother greeted him. "I was just talking to Gianna about kicking your ass."

Jax grinned. "Good to see you, too, man."

Nico wagged a finger at him and moved back down the bar.

As I transferred the three Bellinis onto my tray, I felt Jax's hands come to rest lightly on my hips, an unmistakably proprietary move. His lips touched my nape, brushing softly. "I missed you," he murmured.

My hand shook slightly as I set the last tall, slender glass down. "Don't fuck with me, Jax. It's not cool."

"You missed me, too."

"Yeah, I did. Back up." I lifted the tray and headed toward the table awaiting the order. "Come on," I told him over my shoulder.

I dropped the drinks off, smiling at the party of three women who were clearly out on a girls' night. They eyed Jax, who leaned against the end of a booth with his arms crossed, his gaze on me as I leaned forward to serve.

"You training him?" the brunette asked, grinning at Jax.

"Tried to," I quipped. "Failed miserably."

"I'm asking her to try again," he said, winking at the table. A really rotten thing to do since it got the women all riled up…and me, too.

"Give it a shot, girl," the blonde encouraged. "Trying is half the fun!"

They were laughing as I walked away, exchanging words with Jax, who lingered as I hit the bar to drop off the empty tray.

"You okay?" Nico asked, intercepting me.

"Yep." I straightened my shoulders and abruptly decided on a course of action. Jax and I could dance around each other for days if I let us. I didn't have the patience for it. "I'm heading out for a bit."

He nodded and reached over to squeeze my hand. "Give him hell."

"Thanks." I pivoted and nearly ran into Jax, who'd come up behind me. "You staying somewhere?"

The faint amusement on his face faded into something darker. Hotter. "I've got a room, yes."

"Let me grab my purse."

He caught my elbow before I walked away. "Gia."

I looked at him, let him study me.

His thumb brushed over my skin. "There's no rush."

"In three days, you've popped up where I am across three different states. *Now* you're going to cock-block yourself? Really?"

A slow smile curved his mouth. "You've got a point. I'll go get the car."

A sleek BMW waited just beyond the front doors of Rossi's when I stepped outside. The car was a rental, but it suited Jax. He was standing by to open the door for me, his lips brushing over my cheek before I took the passenger seat.

It was addicting the way he touched me, as if he couldn't help himself.

Jax slid behind the wheel. The engine purred to life, and we set off.

Sitting back, I watched him drive, turned on by his confident handling of the powerful car. His grip on the wheel was light, his arm extended in a way that showed off the beauty of his chiseled arms. He was an inherently sexy man and I was crazy in love with him, able to adore every commonplace thing he did.

Which wasn't fair, I realized. I'd never recognized his flaws, although he surely had some. I had never acknowledged that there might be struggles in his life, circumstances and people who might pull him in different directions and away from me. I'd never scratched below the surface.

Reaching over, I set my hand on his thigh, feeling my palm tingle as the hard muscle bunched in reaction to my touch. He switched driving hands so that he could hold me in place, his skin warm and dry.

He glanced at me. "Are you nervous?"

"No." Wary, yes, but not anxious about it. "I want you."

He nodded and drove faster.

We didn't say anything further on the drive to his hotel or once we arrived. He parked and we entered a center courtyard via a key-card entrance at the side of the building. We took an elevator up, standing on opposite sides of the car, our gazes locked as the seconds ticked by.

The tension was so thick I found it hard to breathe, my lips parted as I pulled air into my lungs in a near pant. I could feel the need radiating off him, sensed the hunger tightening his muscles and sharpening his focus on every response of my body to his.

He was hard already, his cock straining against the button-fly of his jeans.

And I was wet and ready, aching between my legs, my breasts full and heavy. My nipples were furled so tightly they throbbed and stretched shamelessly toward him.

His gaze was there on my chest, caressing me, his tongue sliding along his lower lip in a blatant promise of what he'd be doing to me as soon as we were alone.

The elevator dinged to announce our arrival on his floor and he surged toward me, grabbing my hand in his and dragging me after him. A long hallway later, he was shoving open a door to a suite and then he was on me, grabbing me so tightly my feet left the floor. I dropped my purse and hung on.

Jax's mouth found mine as the door clicked shut, one arm around my waist and the other hand shoved into my hair, dislodging the elastic restraining my ponytail. The finesse he'd shown the night before was gone, only animal hunger left in its wake. His lips slanted over mine, his tongue plunging rhythmically into my mouth, luring me to climb his big body.

My legs wrapped around his lean waist, my arms caging his shoulders, my hips rocking to rub my cleft against the rigid outline of his erection. I moaned as the pressure drove me mad, the layers of denim between us too thick to relieve me.

"Jax," I gasped into his mouth.

"Hang on," he growled, pinning me to the door.

My legs straightened, my hands going to the front of my jeans. I popped the button open and yanked down the zipper, struggling against Jax, who was shoving up my shirt.

His hands found my breasts and squeezed through the thin satin of my bra. I gasped, shocked by the intimacy.

"Christ, you're gorgeous," he breathed, his thumbs circling the hardened points of my nipples.

My head fell back against the door, my lungs struggling for air.

His dark head lowered, his tongue licking me through my bra, his lips wrapping around me. He sucked hard, and I writhed, my hands clawing at the door behind me.

"Hurry, Jax. Damn it!"

His dimple flashed, then he was kissing me again, his body hard against mine, his hands between us as he wrenched his button-fly open. I barely had the sense to dig his wallet out of his pocket before he shoved his jeans down and out of the way. Fumbling, I found a condom and tossed the wallet on the tiled entryway.

I was ripping open the foil with my teeth when he started pulling at my pants, tugging them roughly. I stumbled, laughing, falling into him, letting him sweep me up again and lower me to the floor.

Kicking off my shoes, I wrestled with him, our arms and legs tangling as we fought our clothing and our own desperate urgency. Jax yanked off his shirt, pulled the jeans off one of my legs and ground out, "That's good enough."

He ripped my panties to get at me, hissed through his teeth when I sheathed him in latex. Then he pushed my thighs wide to sink between them.

His first thrust inside me had my back bowing off the floor.

"*Gia.*"

With his neck arched, shoulders straining, sweat glistening on his chest, Jax was impossibly beautiful. He throbbed inside me, so thick and hard, so deep. My heels dug into the carpet, my hips churning as I struggled to accommodate him.

"Baby, wait," he gasped, gripping my waist to hold me still. "I'm too close…."

"Jax…please!"

He looked down at me fiercely, his eyes glittering in the semidarkness of a room lit only by light spilling through the windows.

"Is this what you want?" He pulled back, sliding out of me. Then thrust.

"Oh, God," I moaned, quivering. "Don't stop."

One hand at a time, he linked his fingers with mine and pulled my arms over my head. Rolling his hips, he stroked deep on the inside, rubbing me perfectly on the outside. For all his impatience to get at me, once he was there, he took his time.

His lips touched my ear and he whispered, "Give it to me, baby. Let me feel you."

Rocking upward, I wrapped my legs around him and took it, climaxing with a low pained moan, shivering with pleasure as my sex clenched in desperate ripples around him.

"That's it," he coaxed hoarsely, beginning to move. "Ah, Jesus, you feel amazing."

I held on, his measured drives keeping me hot and wanting. My core tightened, reaching again.

"You're so hard," I whispered, loving the feel of him, the smooth slick glide.

"It's you." He kissed me, his hands tightening on mine as his hips lunged again and again, taking me with long, deep plunges. "Gia, baby…you're making me come."

His pace quickened, then he tensed, his head thrown back as the orgasm hit him. I watched, awed, as shudders racked his powerful frame. He groaned my name, his eyes squeezed shut, his neck straining as he came with such intensity it brought me off again.

Turning my head, I sank my teeth into his forearm, muffling my cries as the hunger sharpened painfully, then receded into a hot, sweet ache.

"Gia." He clutched me firmly, nuzzling his sweat-slickened face against mine.

Wrapped in him, filled with him, I released my bite and pressed my lips to the mark. Wishing it was possible to so easily brand him as mine.

7

JAX ROLLED TO his back beside me and groaned. "I can't feel my legs."

I laughed, knowing just how he felt. I was tingling all over, as if my entire body was reawakening after a long hibernation.

Which was sadly true.

He turned his head toward me. I looked at him.

"Hey," he said, reaching for my hand and lifting it to his mouth for a kiss.

"Hi." I studied him, seeing that soft warmth in his eyes I'd missed so much.

"I'm sorry we didn't make it to the bedroom."

"S'okay." I smiled. "I'm not complaining."

"I'll get you there as soon as I can walk."

"Getting old, Rutledge?" I teased, knowing that at twenty-nine, he was in his prime.

He looked at the raised ceiling with its pretty moldings. "Out of practice."

"Yeah, right." I threw my arm over my face, hiding my reaction. I couldn't think about him with other women. It made me crazy. "I read the papers, you know."

"Escorting a woman somewhere and fucking her are two different things." He leaned over me. Catching my wrist, he pulled my arm above my head and exposed my face. "But it feels good to know you've been keeping tabs."

"I wasn't."

Jax flashed his dimple at me. "Okay."

He rose up to his knees and sank back on his heels, removing the condom. His movements were easy and unaffected, but the sight of his half-hard cock glistening with semen made my mouth water.

I pushed up onto my elbows and licked my lips. "Come here."

He responded instantly, his cock stiffening and lengthening. "Jesus, Gia."

I moved toward him.

"Shower," he said hoarsely, pushing unsteadily to his feet, then holding out his hand to me. "I'll taste like rubber without one."

"I don't care."

"I do." He pulled me up. "Once I slide into your mouth, I'm staying there awhile."

I looked at him, taking him in, finding him so damned sexy standing there—tall and bare chested, his jeans open and shoved down, his cock exposed and curving upward toward his navel. I'd never seen anything so blatantly masculine and erotic.

This was the Jax I knew. And loved so much.

"Look at you," he murmured, his thumb brushing over my swollen lower lip. "You're so fucking sexy. So soft and beautiful."

"Right." My mouth curved as I checked myself out. My jeans and torn panties clung to one leg and my shirt was shoved up over my breasts. No doubt my hair was a mess. "Spoken like a man who just had an orgasm and wants another."

"Don't." He caught my chin, tilting my head up. "You can't ask me to give you everything I've got, then take it lightly. It's not fair."

"No," I agreed. "It isn't, is it?"

From the tightening of his jaw, I knew he got the message—*he'd* taken *me* lightly… then left me behind.

Crouching, he held my jeans down so I could pull my leg free. Then he caught my hand and led me around the wrought-iron-and-glass coffee table.

We crossed the taupe carpet to enter a bedroom boasting a king-size bed with a dark wood headboard matching the desk and armoire also in the room. There was a seating area by a window that stretched up to the high ceiling, and the entry into the bathroom was a beautifully simple archway.

I tried not to show how astonished I was when Jax flipped the light on, but was glad he didn't look at me because I was pretty sure I failed. The room was huge, with a shower that could accommodate three people and a separate sunken tub with jets. A television was embedded in the wall and the dual-sink vanity resembled the heavy wooden furniture in the bedroom.

I had to ask. "Did you book this room thinking you'd get me to come here?"

"I hoped." Jax let me go to turn on the shower. I whistled, impressed by the giant showerhead embedded in the ceiling, which sprayed water straight down like a waterfall.

He faced me with a smile that dazzled me. "Can I finish unwrapping you?"

A sharp ache spread through me. *Gia, baby, you're my present to myself after a long, hard day.* One of the many things he'd said to me back in Vegas that had made me love him.

I wondered suddenly if that was just who Jax was and the way he talked to whatever woman was with him at the time. Maybe he hadn't a clue about how sweet nothings like that could turn a girl inside out. Or maybe he did. The thought depressed me.

"Hey." He caught my chin, tilting my head back. "Don't check out on me now. I'm here. I'm in this."

"For how long? The weekend?" I backed away, some niggling sense of self-preservation warning me to get out while I was ahead. "I can't do this, Jax."

His jaw tightened. "Gia…"

I turned and hurried through the bedroom to get my clothes.

"What the fuck?" he snapped, grabbing my arm as I crossed over the threshold into the living room. "You wanted this."

"It was a mistake." A huge mistake. I was too invested in my feelings for him to find closure this way.

"The hell it was." He tugged me around to face him, grabbing me by the forearms so that I couldn't get away. "Why did you ask for this? You wanted to come here. You wanted me to make love to you."

"I wanted to *fuck* you," I growled, hating how he recoiled from my words. "I wanted to get past the tension so maybe you'd start giving me the truth. I don't want any more of your smooth-player bullshit. It's not real. *You're* not real."

"What the fuck are you talking about? This is as real as it gets, and you know it."

I yanked free and stalked farther into the living room, feeling foolish in only socks and my Rossi's T-shirt. "I don't have time for this."

"Time for what? Me?" Jax's long stride easily overtook mine. He reached my jeans first and stepped on the cuff, pinning them to the floor. His arms crossed his chest, displaying the raw power of his ripped body to perfection. He didn't care at all that his pants were still undone, although he'd hitched his boxer briefs up at some point along the way.

"I don't have the time or patience to pretend like we're building something here when we're not." I fixed my ponytail, trying to focus on putting myself back together—

at least on the outside.

His scowl depended. "Who's pretending?"

I threw up my hands. "Why do you talk to me like you do? All that crap about unwrapping and missing me and… and all of it! Why can't you just be real about what we have, what we've *always* had—nothing but great sex?"

"We're not just *fucking*," he growled, leaning forward. "You don't fall in love over nothing but sex."

"Do I have to be in love with you? Does it make it better for you if I am?" To my horror, I felt my eyes sting with tears. "You've already gotten into my pants. I don't understand why you have to act like this is a romance. Don't make something that should be simple so complicated for me!"

"Baby, we've never had simple." He exhaled harshly and reached up to rub the back of his neck. "What do you want from me, Gia?"

"I think we need to focus on what you want from me, since what I want is irrelevant."

He scowled. "That's not true."

My hands went to my hips. "I want a commitment, a chance, some effort made to see how far this thing between us could go. You've already shot that down. So what's left is what you want."

"I want you."

"You want to fuck me," I corrected. "Why can't you just be matter-of-fact about it?"

"Gia." He shook his head and sighed. "I'm an asshole to everyone else in my life. You're the one thing I've cherished. Don't make me stop."

"See? Like that! Why do you have to say stuff like that? Why can't you just say you like me or something—"

"Because I don't just *like* you. You get under my skin. I think about you damn near all the time and I get *hard*. I see you and I forget who I am. You don't know what you do to me." Jax's voice lowered dangerously. "You make me want to *rut*, Gia. I want to pull you beneath me, work my cock into you and ride until you've wrung me dry. You make me *need*—"

"Shut up!" God, I was quivering, my hunger stirring in response to the heated waves of desire sizzling off him.

"You know how it feels. You're feeling it, too. Let me give it to you."

"No!" The refusal cut deep, like restraining part of myself with barbed wire.

"Give me tonight." He reached for my hand and squeezed too tightly. "One night."

I laughed softly even as my sight blurred. "One night to screw me out of your system? That's a cliché, Jax. It never works. Great sex doesn't stop being great just because you gorge on it."

"So we'll have a night of great sex. We both want it. Need it."

"I don't need this." I tried to reclaim my hand, but he wouldn't let go.

"The hell you don't."

Nothing but the truth would work with Jax. He read me too easily, was too adept at homing in on a challenger's weakness and exploiting it.

"I can't do this," I said again, holding his gaze. "I'm not like the women you're used to sleeping with. I can't do it for fun or to scratch an itch. Not with you. I fell for you the last time. I can't do it again."

"You're still in love with me," he retorted bluntly. "Give me a chance to make that something you stop regretting."

I turned away from him, my gaze sweeping over a living room that was bigger than my bedroom back home. "I want you to take me back to Rossi's."

"That's a problem." He came up behind me, his arms wrapping around me. With his lips to my throat, he whispered, "I want to take you to bed. If you don't want me to talk, I won't say a word."

I closed my eyes, absorbing the feel of him behind me. The warmth of his body, the scent of his skin now musky with sweat and sex, the soft caress of his breath.

"You left the shower on," I said, latching on to something inane and far less personal.

"I'd turn it off if I wasn't afraid you'd bail while I wasn't looking."

"You can't keep me prisoner here."

"I don't want to. I want you willing. I want the Gia who demanded I bring her here and give her whatever she wanted."

I glanced over my shoulder at him, finding his eyes glittering at me from the shadows that caressed his beautiful face. I felt the pull inside me, that inexorable tugging between us. I didn't know how to turn it off or ignore it. Some sick cosmic joke had made me hardwired to crave him with every fiber of my being.

Did I have what it took to convince him to stay? I had what it took to get him to want more; that was a start.

"Tonight's not enough," I said quietly.

"Thank God. I just threw that out there to buy some time to convince you otherwise."

"You can't just walk away without a goodbye like last time." I turned in his arms.

"I want you to look me in the eye and say you're through when you decide you've had enough."

His lips thinned, but he nodded.

"I want monogamy."

"Damn straight. I'm not sharing you."

"I'm talking about *you* being monogamous," I said drily.

"That's a given." He cupped my face. "What else?"

"My hours are erratic. My job comes first."

"I fit into your life before—I can do it again."

I gripped his wrists. I could go on with the list of my wants, but what I needed at that moment was distance and some perspective. I needed some time to back up, catch my breath and my bearings, then I might be able to figure out the next best move to make. "I want you to turn off the damn shower and take me to dinner. I'm hungry."

He laughed, but it sounded strained. "You always did get hungry after sex. Can we actually take the shower first?"

"No." I leaned forward. "I want you to smell me on your skin for the next couple hours."

Jax groaned. "You want to punish me."

"Yep," I agreed. "That, too."

Nico shot me a knowing look when Jax and I returned to Rossi's. I stuck my tongue out at him.

We grabbed a table and ordered shiraz. I went with lasagna, Jax went with *pollo alla cacciatora*. While we waited for our food, I studied him, admiring the way the small candle on the table between us gilded him. He looked softer, more relaxed, his face impossibly more handsome.

He had the look of a well-fucked man, one who was sated and yet anticipating further pleasures ahead. I loved that I put that look on him, but I hated it, too. Because I wasn't in danger just from the things he said; it was everything about him that made me vulnerable. The effect he had on me was in large part due to the effect I had on him.

I made him happy. Content. And it was difficult not to feel as if that made me special, even though I knew better.

"So Regina is your stepmom, right?" I asked, giving my mind something else to think about.

"Yeah." He looked into his wineglass.

"How did that happen?" *Would he mention Ian and open that door…?*

"My mom died ten years ago."

"Oh." Seeing how he closed up alerted me—I'd touched on a painful subject. "I'm sorry to hear that, Jax."

"Not as sorry as I was," he muttered before gulping down his near-full glass in three swallows. He refilled, then looked at me. "Your mom looks great."

I nodded. "She's happy. Her kids are doing all right, business is good and she's about to be a grandmother."

"How's Angelo dealing with impending fatherhood?"

"Good. It threw off his plans to open another Rossi's, but that's probably for the best. Denise—his wife—has a new business of her own, so I think it would've been a strain for them if they'd tried juggling two startups and a new marriage."

"Do you like her?" he asked, his fingertips stroking up and down the stem of his glass.

"A lot. She's great." I looked at the party next to us, a family of four enthusiastically discussing how good their food was. "I thought I saw Allison at the fund-raiser last night. How are she and Ted doing?"

Honestly, I couldn't care less about Jax's cousin and his bitchy wife, but talking about Jax's mom made me realize that he knew more about me than I did about him. Aside from his family members who made news because they were in office, I only knew Allison.

"They're solid." He took another drink. "She's what he needs to run for mayor in the next election."

"It's good that she's there for him."

He snorted. "They barely talk to each other. But she knows how to work the press and she's very active in his campaign planning. He made a good choice with her. She fits him the way Regina fits my dad."

"I thought the political marriage/business partnership was a Hollywood stereotype."

"No." Jax reached over and lightly brushed the back of my hand. "You've got to be pragmatic about relationships. Marrying for love never works out well. My mom and dad were a love match and they made each other miserable. Now, Regina and Dad… They'll do just fine. She knows how to play the game."

"He seems like he genuinely cares for her."

"After what he went through with my mom, she's got to seem like a gift." He took another drink, then leaned back as our food was served.

His change in mood was another warning. Talking about his mother didn't seem to sit well with him. I'd have to be careful about approaching the topic. "Ian introduced them, right?"

"Which turned out to be really lucky for him, didn't it?" he said with an edge in his voice.

"Because he called in the favor and got you? You can't save him, Jax."

"I wasn't asked to." He shrugged, his gaze hard. "I'm just supposed to keep Lei Yeung at bay. I can do that."

Nico walked over with a steaming plate of pasta in hand. "Mind if I join you two?"

Jax pushed out the chair opposite him with his foot. "The more Rossis the merrier."

Sadly, the more Rutledges the scarier. And that had shaped Jax into the man he was.

I played with that in my thoughts as Jax and Nico settled into the easy banter of men, reminding me of how effortlessly Jax fit into my life...and how uncomfortable I was with his.

8

AFTER DINNER, JAX and I headed out to his rental. I paused before I slid into the passenger seat. "If I go back to the hotel with you, I'll need you to take me back to Nico's when he gets off work."

Jax rested his arm on the open car door. "You won't stay the night with me? I'd like you to."

I did want to. And once, back in the day, I had dropped everything in my life for his visits and ended up resenting him for that. I may not have learned to stay away from him, but I'd still picked up a thing or two about having a healthier relationship. "I came here to spend time with my brother."

His chest lifted and fell on a deep breath. "Fair enough. Can I schedule time for you to spend with me?"

We stood so close to each other, pressed into the space between the car and the door, but there was a gulf between us. I'd created it, but I still wished it didn't have to be there. "When are you thinking?"

"Any night this week and next weekend for sure."

I nodded, then got in the car. He shut the door and rounded the trunk, giving me time to think about how the rest of the night could go. More sex. More Jax. I craved both, but it would've been nice not have so many doubts and reservations. I missed how carefree we used to be. But then, I guess it was only that way for me. He'd been counting down the minutes all the while.

He got in and closed the door, but didn't start the engine right away.

"Listen," he began, "you should know this is hard for me, too."

"But you understand what's going on," I argued softly. "I'm clueless."

Jax twisted in his seat and reached for me, catching me by the nape and pulling me in. I closed my eyes, anticipating the moment when his parted lips would touch mine. His tongue caressed the curve of my mouth, a slow sweep that had me leaning closer for more.

"So sweet," he murmured. "I'm going to spread you across my bed and lick you from head to toe."

"You're good at that," I said breathlessly, a shiver of eagerness moving through me.

He pulled back, as if to start the car, then surged forward again, catching my lips in a heated, wet, ravenous kiss. His mouth ate at mine, his tongue stroking deep and fast. I was just as greedy for him, my hand sliding into his hair, holding him by the roots while I frantically tasted him. He cupped my breast in his hand, plumping it, his thumb and forefinger surrounding my aching nipple and tugging rhythmically. I moaned, turned on and needy.

"God," he groaned, releasing me and falling back heavily against the seat. "I want you. Right here. Now."

I was more than tempted by the thought. If we had been anywhere but right outside Rossi's, I might have climbed over the gearshift and gone for it.

"Drive fast," I told him.

He laughed hoarsely and turned his head against the headrest to look at me. "Fine. But when we get to bed, I'm taking it real slow."

"Jax!" Clawing at the sheets, my body arching away from the torture of his mouth, even as I craved more. I'd forgotten what he could do to me, how he could strip away my skin to get into the very heart of me, how his complete command of my body made me willing to do or say anything for the pleasure he could give.

He held me pinned at the thighs, his mouth on my throbbing sex, his tongue licking leisurely. The velvety strokes over my clit had me gasping, the need for an orgasm so fierce I was drenched in sweat, my legs vibrating from the strain.

"Please," I begged hoarsely, squeezing my heavy breasts, the tips swollen and tender from the long minutes he'd spent drawing on them with slow, measured pulls of his mouth.

His silky hair brushed over my skin. He lifted his head. "Please what, baby?"

"Ah, God… Make me come."

"Just a little more."

"Please!" I pushed my hand between my legs, desperate to bring myself off.

He nipped at my fingers and I cried out, panting.

His head lowered, his tongue tracing the swollen folds. He circled my clit, then rimmed the trembling opening below.

I grabbed his head, holding him to me, struggling to lift my hips to his mouth. Jax was too strong, restraining me easily, his breath hot against my sensitive flesh. He suckled gently, moving slowly along the length of my cleft, giving me just enough pressure to drive me insane.

"Let me turn around," I gasped. "Let me suck you."

His chuckle was filled with such wicked amusement it sent goose bumps racing across my skin.

And then he thrust his tongue inside me.

"Jax!"

He cupped my butt and lifted me, angling me into his working mouth. His tongue fucked me swiftly, the shallow plunges into my trembling sex driving me hard toward orgasm. His growl vibrated against my clit, his pleasure feeding my own.

I clutched at his hair, moaning, digging my heels into the mattress to rock against his lips.

"Don't stop," I sobbed, so close, my entire body tingling.

Jax surged onto his knees, elevating me. My legs spread wide, giving him limitless access. He devoured me, so hungry and greedy. I couldn't breathe for the pleasure. The frenzied licking against sensitive tissues overloaded my senses. I watched him, as he'd meant for me to. The sight of his dark head between my thighs, the rapid-fire flickering of his tongue, the beauty of his biceps hardened from supporting my weight… unbearably erotic.

He was gorgeous. Everything I'd ever wanted. And the fierce need that etched his face warned that his demands would take me to the edge before he was through with me.

Another low moan broke from my dry throat. "Oh, Jax… I'm going to come."

"Wait," he ordered. "I want you milking my dick when you lose it."

I gave a clenched-teeth scream of frustration as he lowered me to the bed and reared, snatching up a condom and ripping it open. He was sheathed and coming over me a heartbeat later, but it was too long. I had no patience. I caught him in the cage of my arms and legs, pulling him to me, lifting to him.

He allowed me to drag him down, his palms flat on the bed by my shoulders, his biceps thick and hard. He reached between us with one hand, fisting his penis and stroking the wide crest through my slickness. I gasped and his eyes darkened, his cheeks flushing as he notched into the grasping opening to my sex.

"Jax," I growled in warning.

He thrust hard, sinking deep in one lunge, wrenching a cry from me as I fell hard into orgasm. Neck arched and eyes squeezed shut, I lay taut as the pleasure pulsed through me, my core tightening on the powerfully thick cock inside me.

"Fuck, yeah," he groaned, grabbing fistfuls of the sheets and pumping that long, rigid column of flesh into my quaking body. The climax grew, spurred by the rhythmic blows of his pelvis into my clit…the feel of his erection plunging relentlessly.

I writhed, helpless, lost to him, struggling to hang on to the part of my soul that wanted to surrender.

"That's it, baby." Jax's lips were at my ear, his breath hot and quick. "Dig those claws into me."

My nails were grasping at his sweat-slicked back, feeling the muscles flex as his body worked to service mine. His buttocks tensed and released beneath my calves, his thighs bunching and powering the drives of his hips.

His teeth sank into my earlobe and he groaned, his rockhard abs contracting against my stomach, his sweat and mine sealing us together.

"Those noises you make," he gasped. "God…they make me so hard."

And he was. Like stone.

"So g-good." I swallowed past a dry throat. "Jax…it's so good."

"You were made for me," he said fiercely. "No one else, Gia. You're *mine.*"

He drove the point home with every plunge, fucking me so thoroughly I couldn't think beyond the need to come again.

My body was no longer my own.

Jax was the only one who could do this to me…make me mindless…an animal. I wasn't *me* when I was in bed with him; I was *his.* Willing and ready to do whatever he wanted, to take whatever he chose to give me, knowing he would make me come again and again…

I whimpered, feeling his grip tighten, his muscles gathering as his own pleasure grew.

He nuzzled his damp face against me. "So tight and hot… *Gia.*"

I realized then that he was clinging to me as desperately as I was to him, that urgency laced every breath, every touch. He was screwing me as if he'd die if he stopped, as if it were possible to fuck me hard enough to delve even deeper beneath my skin.

My eyes stung with tears when the orgasm hit, stealing my breath and causing spots to blur my vision. A low noise poured out of me, unrecognizable as mine.

"Ah, sweetheart." He kissed me, absorbing the sound, slowing until he was just circling his hips, stirring his raging erection inside me. "I love that sound you make when you come. It tells me how good you feel, how much you love my cock… my mouth…my hands."

How much I loved him.

I was sprawled beneath him, wide open and possessed, while he felt like a dream. Something I'd conjured.

"Feel me," he breathed, pushing up to look down at me. His eyes were so dark, his face flushed, the skin stretched tight with lust over the sculpted angles of his face. "Inside you—" he rolled his hips, then caught my hand, lifting it to his slick chest "—and you inside me."

"Jax—"

He took my mouth, kissing me deeply, his tongue rubbing along mine. His hips circled slowly, making me feel every throbbing inch of him. The leisurely, deliberate stroking over tender nerves kept me hot and edgy. He remembered me well, knew just how to keep me revved and needy.

"I missed you, Gia," he whispered into the kiss. "Did you ache for me, too?"

When I didn't reply, he brushed the wet tendrils of my hair away from my face and searched for the answer.

My sex rippled along his length. His eyes closed and his lips parted, his body tightening. "Not yet. I'm not coming yet."

"Please…" I was begging and I didn't care. I just wanted him to come. I wanted it more than my next breath.

"I'm not rushing this." He reached behind him to grab my wrist, bringing my right arm up and over my head. His other hand pushed beneath my buttock, lifting me into a smooth, easy thrust. "Umm…perfect. It's always been perfect."

I wanted to tease him, to play the game as coolly as he was, but I couldn't.

"Stop thinking and feel, baby," he murmured, nibbling on the corner of my mouth. "Let me make you feel good. That's all I want. To make you feel good."

Turning my head, I caught his lips and let him.

Nico eyed me as I slid onto a bar stool at Rossi's after closing and I knew he saw my makeupless state, which betrayed the shower I'd taken just a half hour before. He had been cleaning up the bar, but he stopped and pulled out a beer, popping off the top before sliding the bottle over to me.

"Forgot how much I like Jax," he said conversationally.

I nodded. I liked Jax, too. Thing was, I didn't know which Jax was the real one.

"You two going to work it out?"

"No, it's temporary. But this time, I know the rules."

"Maybe I don't like him so much." Nico popped open a second beer and took a long pull. "He's in love with you, you know."

"He's in lust," I countered drily, picking at the label on the bottle. "And that's okay, I can live with that. It's the other stuff—the way he talks to me sometimes, as if there's more, and the head trip I'm on about why he left and came back— that's hard for me to deal with."

"My offer to knock some sense into him still stands."

I smiled. "Might be easier and more effective to knock sense into me."

"Can do that, too." He tapped his bottle against mine. "But you've got plenty of sense. You know what you're doing. You just wish you weren't doing it. He obviously doesn't have a clue or else he wouldn't risk letting you get away. He'll never find better."

"Ah, God, don't get sappy on me now. I can't take it." I wasn't entirely kidding. I felt weepy and emotional. Sex with Jax did that to me.

Nico grinned. "Fine. Get off your ass and help me clean up so we can get the hell out of here."

With a sigh, I slid off the bar stool. "Shit. I should've stuck with sappy instead."

An insistent pounding on Nico's door woke me Sunday morning. I rolled off the couch with a curse, stumbling over with the intention of bitching out whoever it was.

When I blinked wearily through the peephole, however, I saw beloved faces.

Pulling off the security chain and turning the dead bolt, I opened the door to my brothers and Denise. "What the hell?" I groused.

"Yeah. What the fuck?" Nico wandered in from the bedroom wearing sweatpants that barely clung to his hips. Brother or not, I could still appreciate what a good-looking man he was. "You know what time it is?"

Vincent came in first. "Time to get up."

Angelo followed Denise in, holding her hand in his. "You put Gianna on the couch? Seriously?"

"I offered her the bed." Nico crossed his arms. "She wouldn't take it."

"Don't blame her," Vincent said. "If that bed could talk, it'd have its own reality show."

"Don't be jealous," Nico returned. "I'm sure your bed will see some action eventually. Despite everything, you're still a Rossi."

"What are you doing here?" I interjected. I was really happy to see them. Having my family around brought back normalcy I'd lost the night before in Jax's bed. I was back to feeling like Gianna Rossi—and not absolutely sure I was the writhing, moaning, clawing woman who'd enjoyed a half-dozen orgasms in a matter of hours. It was as if I were two different people.

And you're mad at Jax for having two sides....

"We're waiting for you to get dressed so we can grab some breakfast," Denise answered. Her hair was pulled into pigtails that framed her pale face. She'd matched her lipstick to the pink in her hair, making her look like some sort of anime super heroine. "I'm starving."

"Something's wrong with you people," Nico muttered. "It's too fucking early for food or anything else."

"It's nine o'clock," Vincent pointed out.

Nico shot me a look and drawled, "As I said."

By noon, we'd eaten and hit the basketball court at Nico's apartment complex. Not to brag, but I was pretty good at the game—enough that I'd gotten a partial scholarship to UNLV for my skills. Of course, I'd learned everything I knew from my brothers.

I had just cleared a three-pointer and was waving off the usual good-natured taunts and ribbing when I caught sight of Jax walking up. I stopped right where I was, admiring his long legs in shorts and his loose-fitting T-shirt. He wore shades and twirled his keys around his finger. When Nico bounced the ball to him, Jax caught it up and dazzled me with his dimpled grin.

"Hey," he said, coming to me first and pressing his lips to my flushed forehead.

"You found us." A hot rush of pleasure surged through me. He'd picked me up and dropped me off at Rossi's, so finding Nico's place had taken initiative and effort.

"I missed waking up to you," he whispered against my skin.

His damned sunglasses made it impossible to read him. I took the ball and backed up so I could breathe.

"Rutledge," Angelo greeted him, bristling.

"Kick back, killer," Denise admonished, rising from the chair her husband had dragged over from the pool area. "Hi, I'm Denise. Angelo's wife."

Jax shook her hand. "A pleasure."

"I've heard a lot about you," she said. "None of it good. I hope you prove the guys wrong."

Jax glanced at me with raised brows.

"Oh, *she* doesn't talk about you at all," Denise qualified, making me smile. The woman knew how to get her digs in.

Vincent and Angelo both reluctantly shook hands with Jax, then Vincent said, "Are we playing or what?"

"I'd like to jump in when there's a chance," Jax said, surprising me.

"Shit." Nico ran a hand through his hair. "Take my spot on Gianna's team. I'm wiped, thanks to some too-fucking-early-in-the-morning visitors."

"Pussy," Angelo muttered.

"Whatev. We were kicking your ass."

"We were going easy on you," Vincent answered, catching the ball when I tossed it his way. "So we wouldn't have to hear you bitch."

"You wouldn't hear me if you'd stayed home."

"Shut up," I told them. "Let's do this."

"There's my girl," Jax said with a smile.

We started the game. Jax was good. Really good.

I've played hoops now and then. Nothing like you. Never gave it the time.

I remembered those words of his from before, whispered into my hair while he cuddled me after sex. Clearly, he'd given it time since we parted.

Had he done so because of me? Was I reaching by making that connection?

Jax passed the ball and I made the shot. If only figuring him out were as easy.

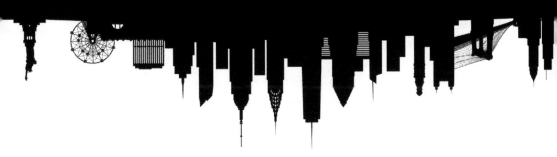

9

MONDAY WAS A day like any other, yet it felt so different. It took a lot of work to avoid thinking about Jax. At least until I got to the office.

I arrived a half hour early, but Lei was already there. She sat at her desk, dressed in a black skirt and blazer embellished with red. Her hair was up, her red-framed glasses perched on her delicate nose. She glanced up when I stepped through the open doorway, her painted mouth set in a hard line.

"Ian got to Isabelle over the weekend and signed her." She pulled her glasses off.

"*What?* How did he know?"

Lei sat back. "That's a good question."

I felt a flutter of unease in my stomach. "I haven't told a soul. No one."

She nodded grimly. "I believe you."

"Would Isabelle leverage you against Ian?"

"It's possible." Leaning back, she gestured for me to settle into one of the chairs in front of her desk. "Ian is better known than I am."

Thanks to the Hollywood-themed eateries she'd envisioned, which Ian had stolen from her. The irony was painful.

"But I don't think so," she went on. "One of the things that attracted Isabelle to working with us is that Savor is headed by a woman. Ian would've had to make an offer too good to refuse."

"I wonder what it was."

"I intend to find out. I'm meeting with Isabelle over lunch to see what I can coax out of her."

I took a seat. "I should talk to Chad. Maybe take him out to lunch."

"Yes, I was going to suggest that." She studied me. "Did you see Jackson Rutledge this weekend?"

I hesitated a split second before answering, feeling as if a trap were closing in on me. "I did," I confessed, "but we didn't talk business. Not even in a roundabout way."

"Do you trust him?"

"I…" I frowned. I trusted him with my body. I trusted him to know how much my family meant to me. Was there anything else? "With what?"

She smiled in a way that said she knew why I'd hesitated. "What are you going to do about him?"

Sitting back, I let the question really sink in. I'd been fielding variations of that same query all weekend, but I hadn't given it much thought. What was I going to *do?* It struck me then that I'd never done anything when it came to Jax. He decided when our relationship began and ended, where we met, and when—and how—we had sex. All along, I'd just gone with his flow.

It was time for me to start making my own rules. Something beyond asking him to say goodbye when *he* decided we were over.

"I'm not sure yet," I answered honestly. But I was going to work on it.

* * *

When I got to my desk, I called the Four Seasons and left a message at the hotel's front desk for Chad to call me. It was still early, and I didn't want to risk waking him up. I needed him refreshed and sharp to go over our business plans.

Isabelle was gone. We needed a replacement. Quick.

I looked through all my notes, considering the chefs who'd caught my attention previously. There weren't that many who specialized in Italian, mostly because my background made it really hard to impress me. Then again, going with another Italian was problematic—it would be hard to spin Isabelle's defection in a way that wouldn't make the new recruit feel like a second choice.

I tapped my pen against my jaw, thinking. "American, European…"

Lei walked out of her office.

"Asian!" I blurted.

She came to a halt, her brows raised. "Excuse me?"

I stood. "Chad represents American cooking. Inez represents European. I think we need to find someone to represent—"

"Asian." Her arms crossed. "Do you have any idea how hard it would be to pull together a dueling menu with that combination?"

"Easier than convincing some chef he or she isn't our last, desperate choice."

Her lips pursed. "Good point. Do you have someone in mind?"

"David Lee."

Lei's mouth curved slightly, her eyes warming with a look of approval. "He's good, but I'm not sure he's ready."

I nodded, very much in agreement with her. "That's why I'm thinking I'll take Chad out to the Asian bistro where Lee works. Introduce them. See how they hit it off. Or not. Chad could steer David along."

"A mentor." She nodded thoughtfully. "I'll let you run with this and we'll regroup after lunch. We'll need to move quickly, but we have the rest of today to decide our plans."

I was grateful for her trust and was determined not to let her down. "Thank you."

Lei smiled. "I like your quick thinking, Gianna. I'm impressed."

Smiling in return, I got back to it.

A beautiful bouquet of starburst lilies in a lovely pink vase arrived shortly after ten. My breath caught at the sight of them being carried down the hall by LaConnie. I knew they were from Jax. They were my favorite flowers, and he knew it.

"Who sent you these, girl?" LaConnie asked, setting them down on my desk. "He might be a keeper."

I wish…. I fingered the card, but didn't want to open it in front of anyone. It felt too personal. "Someone with good taste."

She shot a narrow-eyed glance at me before she backed away.

"I love your dress," I told her, admiring the black sheath she wore that had an electric-blue piping to match her heels.

"Changing the subject won't distract me from wanting to know who sent you those," she warned.

"I'll tell you later," I promised.

She wagged her finger at me. "I'm going to hold you to that!"

When she was a good distance down the hall, I pulled the card from its stake and opened it.

Dinner tonight?

The blunt query was so typical of Jax, I couldn't help but grin. But still, things had to be different the second go-round. He'd insinuated himself into my life so well that I hadn't been able to escape the memories until I'd left Vegas, yet I had barely dipped my toe in his life. When he broke things off again, it would be the same in New York—I'd have memories of him everywhere. But he would be safe from my ghost.

That had to change. This time, I was going to haunt the man the way he haunted me.

I dug my smartphone out of my purse and found the number he'd called me from the night I'd taken Chad to Denise's salon. I texted: **Only if you're cooking. Your place?**

It took five minutes before my phone vibrated on my desk. His reply: **What time should I pick you up from work?**

The surge of triumph I felt brightened my day. **5:30. And BTW...TY for the flowers. Lovely.**

Yes, you are, he sent back.

I typed out a quick response: **Says the most gorgeous guy I know.**

There was another pause, one long enough that I thought he wasn't going to answer. Then he sent, **Skin deep.**

That lingered with me for a long time.

When Chad called me back, I asked him to meet me at Savor's offices. I thought it'd be good to remind him of just how successful Lei was. He showed up just before noon, looking handsome in khakis and a tucked-in dress shirt, with his collar open and cuffs rolled up.

I met him at reception and led him back to my desk under the guise of fetching my purse. I wanted to use it as an excuse to show him around again.

"I'm glad you called," he said, walking beside me. "I'm really starting to have my doubts with all that's going on here."

"I'm sure you are. I mean, how many roadblocks can you hit before you take it as a sign, right?"

"Right." He shot me a grateful smile. "You get it."

"Of course I do. That's why you're going to trust me to tell you if the time comes to throw in the towel." We reached my desk, and I stopped, facing him. "I'm not going to screw you over, Chad. I promise you that."

He shoved his hands in his pockets. "I'm stuck in the middle of a tug-of-war between Ian and Lei, and I can't help thinking that means no one but you is really paying attention to *me*. I could be anyone."

"But you're not anyone. You're one of the most talented chefs in the world today, and I'm going to see that you shine."

Leaning forward, he caught my hand in his. "Thanks."

"Thank *you*. You're giving me the chance to make this happen."

He glanced at the lilies on my desk. "Nice flowers. You got an admirer? Do I have competition?"

"It's not serious."

"Hard to be serious when you're working as much as we do."

"Isn't that the truth?" I caught the handle of my purse and shut the drawer. "I'm married to my fabulous career."

Chad nodded. "I know how that goes. I'm glad we'll be working together so much over the next few months—if everything pans out, anyway. Maybe we can carve out some time for fun. No strings."

My mouth curved. "Maybe. Ready to roll?"

"Have been since I met you, sweetheart."

Laughing, I caught his arm and we headed out.

"Rutledge Capital."

I glanced up as Lei reached my desk. I'd been waiting for her to get back so I could tell her the good news: David Lee was going to work out. He'd hit it off with Chad right away. Plus, when I talked vaguely with David about our plans for Chad, he hadn't been shy. He'd said outright that he was hoping for a similar opportunity to come his way, too.

"What about it?" I asked, rising to my feet.

"According to Isabelle, Rutledge Capital committed to a significant investment in Pembry Ventures. She says she spoke with Jackson Rutledge himself on Sunday and he confirmed it."

A heavy lump of ice settled in my stomach. "Yesterday?" *A weekend Jax had spent in my life. In me...*

I sank slowly back into my chair.

Lei nodded grimly. "Ian offered Isabelle a fantastically lucrative signing package. She would've been a fool to refuse it." She closed her eyes and pinched the bridge of her nose. "So stupid of him! And petty. Ian isn't making smart moves. Neither is

Rutledge."

I'd slid out of Jackson's bed, and he'd slid a knife in my back.

"We can get David Lee," I said hoarsely. I had to focus on the immediate goal. It would happen if I gave it my all. "He likes the idea of a trio. Less pressure and heat while he finds his way."

"Oh," she said drily. "Is he really that humble?"

"It's a strategic move. He'll want to cut loose eventually, sooner rather than later, but we can get a couple years out of him, I think."

She gave an elaborate sigh. "I went ahead and signed Inez before Ian got to her. It's contingent upon a deal with Mondego, but it shores us up."

"So we're back on track." I glanced at the flowers on my desk. If Jax were planning on saying goodbye tonight, he was in for a surprise. I wasn't going to let him just stroll into my life and screw everything up...*again.*

Paybacks were a bitch. So was I, when the situation called for it.

"You okay?" she asked, studying my face.

"I'm good," I said calmly, feeling the chill in my gut spread and numb me. "We should sign David as soon as possible."

"Agreed. I'll take care of it."

"And we should probably take Chad back on a site tour of the Mondego in Atlanta. Let him get the sense that things really are moving forward."

"You want to do that." It wasn't a question.

"I think I could use a few days away."

Lei leaned her hip against the front of my desk. "Away from Jackson?"

"I'm having dinner with him tonight, actually."

Something in my tone must have given my thoughts away, because her lips curved wryly. "That should be interesting."

"You can bet on it." I exhaled the hurt I couldn't contain and let the anger spread. Worry followed swiftly. "You don't have a problem with me seeing him, do you?"

"I haven't forgotten why I hired you, Gianna." Lei headed toward her office. "Don't worry, I'm good and you'll be fine."

I would be. But I wasn't there yet.

Five o'clock rolled around and my excitement ratcheted up. Not just because Chad had agreed to head to Atlanta the next day and I was ready to get out of town. The truth: I was ready to see Jax and deal with him. I had to force myself to slow down when I saw him waiting at the curb for me after work, act as if nothing were wrong in my world and I had time to spare.

He lounged against a black McLaren, a car I recognized because one of Lei's chefs had bought one to celebrate the five year anniversary of his first restaurant. Jax's arms and ankles were crossed, his pose relaxed and sexy. Sunglasses shielded his eyes from the glaring reflections cast by the towering skyscrapers around him. He was dressed in black slacks, a white shirt and gray tie. His dark hair was tousled, like he'd run a hand through it and let his styling efforts go at that.

Women stared at him as they walked by, their heads turning to keep their eyes on him even as their feet moved. Men glanced his way and altered course some, instinctively recognizing an alpha male at rest. Jax always had that effect on people. When he entered a space, he immediately took it over.

Squaring my shoulders, I pushed through the revolving doors and walked straight up to him. I wore a black Nina Ricci sheath. It was an elegant, classic piece that I'd paired with the nude peep-toe Louboutins my brothers had collectively given me for my last birthday.

I looked like the kind of woman who would be seen with Jackson Rutledge. Better yet, I *felt* like it.

Keeping my stride, I marched up to him, fisted his tie in one hand, and stretched up to kiss him. Hard.

A low rumbling sound was my reward, followed by the rapid unfolding of his big body. He got me before I could pull away, catching me by the nape and hip, holding me to him as he deepened the kiss into a full-blown melding of our open mouths.

Standing on the street, with cars and people streaming by, we kissed as if we were alone.

"Hello, gorgeous," he said gruffly when I broke away to pull air into my tightened lungs. He nuzzled his cheek against mine.

I broke free with a quick twist and slapped him across the face.

His head turned with the blow, his breath hissing out between his teeth. Rubbing his jaw, he looked at me with hot eyes. "I'm guessing you're not looking to play rough."

"You fucked me over, Jax. Right after you fucked me literally. Did you take a shower first? Or were you still smelling like me when you made the call?"

"Get in the car, Gia."

"You're an asshole." I tamped down my simmering anger at him. At me. At the entire situation. But mostly at him.

"Always have been," he agreed grimly. He straightened and opened the passenger door, which involved pulling the door out then pushing it upward. "Took you a long time to figure that out."

I stood there a moment, staring at him. He stared back, his eyes hidden behind the damned sunglasses, his mouth an unyielding line.

"Don't lose your confidence now," he taunted softly.

My mind spun as it had all day. Why did he want me to go with him? Why the flowers and the invitation to dinner? "You angling for a kiss-off screw?"

"I'm not ending things. I want you. That's not news."

His brusque, unapologetic attitude made my teeth grind. It was like he was daring me to be the one to walk away.

I slid into the seat and clicked my seat belt into place.

Jax ducked his head down. He looked at me over the rim of his shades. "For future reference, the slap was overkill. You had me down for the count with the kiss."

He straightened and shut the door.

I smiled grimly. In the boardroom and the bedroom, Jackson Rutledge was going to learn a thing or two about playing with me.

Jax pulled into the subterranean parking garage of his apartment building and two valets greeted us. As one of the bow-tied guys helped me out of the car, I was struck again by the financial gulf between Jax and me. I wasn't intimidated by his wealth, but it was possible the disparity was a bigger problem for him.

It didn't improve my mood to think of it.

Reaching for my hand, Jax linked our fingers and led me to an elevator. I'd half expected him to fly us out to Virginia or D.C., and realized abruptly that I had never allowed myself to consider the likelihood of him living at least part-time in New York, too. But of course it made sense that he would have a place in the city, which was the financial center of the country.

The elevator doors closed behind us, and he immediately pulled me into him. I let him. He leaned back against the brass handrail, spread his legs, and urged me to stand between them, his hands running up and down the length of my spine.

It'd been so long since I'd been held with such intimacy and tenderness.

He'd been in New York the whole time....

I closed my eyes and absorbed the warmth of his body, the smell of his skin, the soft caress of his breath against my temple. I'd denied myself the comfort of a man's touch for too long.

"How was your day?" he murmured.

"Busy. How was yours?"

"I couldn't stop thinking about you."

I closed my eyes, holding fiercely to my wrath. It was a harder task than it should've been.

He laid his cheek against my temple. "I'm sorry, Gia."

"For what? Helping Pembry screw the deal I was working on?"

Jax sighed. "You knew the score. We talked about this."

"That doesn't excuse you. I don't accept your apology."

"I don't blame you, but you'll find a way to handle it. This is a minor setback you'll have no problem overcoming."

I met his gaze. "You're damned right."

The elevator dinged, announcing our arrival on his floor. When I turned around and saw a small foyer and double doors, I realized Jax lived in a penthouse apartment. Which explained why the elevator hadn't stopped in between the parking garage and what I now knew to be the top floor.

Grabbing my hand again, Jax led me across gold-veined marble tiles and unlocked the door by placing his palm against a wall-mounted security pad.

"I bet your dates love this James Bond stuff," I said as the thick walnut door swung open automatically. I managed to say the words casually, but envy ate at me as I imagined him with other women.

"What do *you* think of it?" he asked, looking over his shoulder at me.

"Ah, well, I'm a simple girl at heart." My gaze raked over the sunken living room with its snow-white carpet, black-leather-and-chrome chairs and sapphire-blue area rug. A sterile, bluntly masculine bachelor pad.

I frowned. "This isn't you."

The door shut behind us. "No?"

I'd expected warm colors, varied textiles, colorful modern art—decor that reflected the vibrant, slightly rough-around-the-edges, occasionally quirky man I loved.

Stepping deeper into the room, I struggled with a profound sense of disappointment. *Had I really been so wrong about him?*

"Would you like a drink?" he asked quietly, coming up behind me. He stood so close I could feel the warmth radiating from his body.

"Definitely."

His dimple winked at me. "You won't throw it in my face, will you?"

"I'm tempted, I admit," I said dryly.

His hands came to rest on my shoulders. "Remember that night at the Palms?"

My hands fisted. "Low blow, Jackson."

I would never forget standing on the fifty-fifth floor's outdoor sky deck with Jax wrapped around my back and a glass of white wine that we shared in my hand. The city and desert stretched for miles, the glow of the neon lights fading into inky darkness.

What a view, I'd said, leaning into him, feeling happier than I ever had. I was dating the perfect guy, a man who made my toes curl at night and my days bright. *He's going to change my life,* I'd thought. *He's going to change* me, *for the better.*

It seemed ridiculous now. Making changes was my responsibility. Having a great guy was just a bonus.

I started to pull away, but he held me in place.

"I'm sorry," he said again.

I tugged a little and he let me go, freeing me to face him. "Then why did you do it?"

"Why do I do anything?" he said gruffly, his eyes dark and hard. "Because I'm a Rutledge. We fuck people over, Gia. That's just who we are."

"That's a cop-out," I snapped.

"That's the truth."

I walked away, my gaze roaming.

"If you want to walk out," he said quietly, "I won't stop you. But I'd like you to stay."

I paused. Turning, I confronted him, hating how his features gave nothing away. "That's what you want, isn't it? You want *me* to end things. Piss me off, get me to storm out. It wouldn't be a quiet breakup and it'd certainly be a little messy, but quick and final nevertheless. Just the way you like it."

"I'd hate it, but I'm no good for you, Gia." He passed me and moved into the kitchen.

I tossed my purse on one of the armchairs. "I guess I'm a glutton for punishment."

Jax pulled a bottle of white wine out of the fridge, then set it on the counter. The kitchen was as devoid of personality as the living room, with black cupboards and counters, and only a one-cup coffeemaker to show that anyone was in residence. Coming from a family for whom the kitchen was the center of the home, I found Jax's depressing.

He watched me step out of my heels.

When I reached up to release my hair, I warned him, "I'm going to match your backstabbing move and raise you one round of angry sex."

His lips parted when I reached under my dress to shimmy out of my panties. "Gia."

"I can play this game." I tossed my underwear at him and smiled tightly when he caught them. "And I can win."

10

JAX POCKETED MY underwear and came to me, abandoning the unopened wine.

He cupped my face. Lowering his head, he kissed me, his lips clinging sweetly. His hands moved to my shoulders, then down my back, his fingers deftly lowering the zipper on my dress.

I went to work on the knot of his tie, letting the anger simmer and blend with my lust into a raging desire. I focused on him. On us. On the feel of him beneath my hands, the beloved scent that was his alone, the way his breathing deepened and his heartbeat quickened as the hunger grew between us.

I never noticed things like that with anyone else, which made it so much harder to accept that maybe Jax and I weren't meant to be together.

"Did you have this place when you came with me to Rossi's?" I asked.

We'd stayed in a hotel during that trip. If he'd had an apartment in town at the time, it shed a whole new light on his feelings for me. After all, how much could a guy care about his girl if he'd rather bang her in a hotel than his own bed?

"No. I bought this place last year. Gia—" Standing there with his shirt open and parted, his golden torso on display, his body so beautifully hard and defined, his dark eyes so warm and tormented...

I caught his hand and pulled him out of the kitchen. Anticipation thrummed through my veins, along with something darker. And more wicked.

Jax's hand clawed at the sheet, his stomach clenching as I mouthed the plush head of his cock. He was hard and thick, so aroused that precum streamed from the crest to coat my tongue. I fisted him at the root, milking him with my hands and mouth, relishing the curses and moans that spilled from him.

"Jesus," he gasped as I licked along a thick, pulsing vein. Running my parted lips up and down the side, I teased him, kept him on edge, driving him to the point of no return.

"Don't play, Gia," he growled. "Suck me or fuck me. Make me come."

I smiled, my gaze lingering over the tight lacing of muscle that crossed his abdomen. He was sheened with sweat, his gorgeous face flushed and eyes bright. With his gaze on me, I wrapped my mouth around him and sucked, taking him to the back of my throat.

"That's it," he said hoarsely, his neck arching to press his head into the pillow. "God, that's good. Your mouth…"

I owned him in that moment. Jackson Rutledge was mine.

His fingers pushed into my hair, gliding over the damp roots, brushing the strands back from my face. "Ah, Gia. Keep sucking me like that, baby."

He throbbed against my tongue, his flavor and desire intoxicating me. I loved it. Loved giving him so much pleasure his body quaked with it.

"Going to come so hard for you…" he groaned.

Pulling off him, I sat up, then slid off the end of the bed.

"Gia." His heavy-lidded gaze caught mine. "Damn it. Finish me."

"It's tough when you're working toward something…when the excitement builds and you can almost taste it…then someone takes it away from you, isn't it?"

Snarling, he jackknifed upward. "Get back here."

I smiled and snatched his shirt up from the floor. "I think you need to cool off a bit first."

"I think you should get your gorgeous ass back in this bed first." Jax rose from the bed like an orgasmic dream come to life, all hard rippling muscle and golden skin. His cock was thick and long, curved upward and so stiff it barely moved as he walked toward me. He was so perfectly proportioned, so boldly masculine.

It was damned hard resisting jumping on the bed and letting him fuck the hell out of me.

He reached for me, and I sidestepped quickly, laughter in my throat.

The doorbell rang.

Jax didn't care. He stalked me with single-minded determination. I danced away, struggling to thrust my arms through his shirt. The fabric smelled like him. I liked that a lot.

"You should get that," I told him.

"Gia," he said, in a low warning tone. "If you want to be comfortable when I fuck you, you better get on the bed. Otherwise, I'm pinning you to the nearest flat surface."

The doorbell rang again as I darted out of his reach. "Someone's at the door!"

"They can wait." He fisted his cock, stroking it. "This can't."

I feinted to the right, then the left, using moves I'd perfected on basketball courts. It amazed me that he could be naked while chasing me and still look both tempting and formidable. His abs glistened with sweat; his gaze was avid and hot, his body taut with muscle.

He caught me before I crossed the threshold of the bedroom door. His arms locked around me, hard as steel, his chest heaving against my back.

"Jax—"

"Say no if you mean it," he breathed roughly. "Otherwise, I've got to have you, baby."

The note of desperation in his voice swayed me, made me long to give in. Being wanted by Jax was one of the major highs in my life.

"*Jackson.*"

We both stiffened at the sound of Parker Rutledge's voice in the living room.

"I know you're here," he called out. "We need to talk, son." Jax cursed. His hand slid into the open lapels of his shirt and cupped my breast possessively, his grip tightening until my feet left the floor.

"Give me a minute," he yelled before stepping back and kicking the door closed.

I thought he'd let me go, but he turned me instead and kissed me breathless. One hand clenched in my hair, the other gripped my buttock.

When he released me abruptly, I stumbled, my legs weakened by the ferocious passion in his kiss.

He walked to the en suite bathroom and grabbed a black silk robe, belting it angrily. "Stay here."

"Don't you want me to say hi?" I asked, my voice tight.

Jax didn't look at me when he said, "I'm not giving him the satisfaction."

The door shut with a bit too much force behind him and then I heard the sound of him talking. His tone was far from welcoming and I scrambled to get dressed. I wasn't going to hide in his bedroom like a naughty teenager.

By the time I'd finished, I couldn't hear the low drone of conversation anymore. And when I opened the bedroom door, silence greeted me.

I padded out in search of my heels and once I had them on, I felt better prepared to deal with Parker…despite wishing my hair was tied back.

While I waited for Jax and his father to make an appearance, I wandered around the living room, examining it closely for signs of the lover I thought I knew. What I found were only a handful of framed photos, most of them vintage snapshots of a striking blonde whom I assumed was Jackson's mother.

The photos ranged from fresh-faced black-and-whites to more recent ones in color, and the transformation the pictures documented was startling. Youthful softness had hardened over time, had been polished into a glittering facade, then faded. The upturn of pretty lips gradually migrated downward. One candid shot caught her unawares and staring out a window. The look on her beautiful face conveyed a sense of loneliness.

I picked it up, looking at it more closely, and noted another framed picture lying facedown behind it. I slid it forward, then lifted it, stilling when I discovered a photo of Jax and me.

It was a shot Vincent had captured with his cell phone and forwarded to me. He'd taken it during that first and last family dinner with Jax at Rossi's. Jax sat behind me, supporting me as I leaned back against him. We were laughing, his arms around my waist, my arms draped over his. I'd sent the photo to Jax and made it the wallpaper on my phone until it became too painful to look at.

I propped the photo back up and returned the picture of his mother to the shelf, my heart racing along with my thoughts.

Where the hell was Jax?

The apartment was eerily quiet. I went in search of him, my gaze sliding absently past the front door, then stopping on the small security video monitor mounted in the wall beside it. Jax and his dad stood in the foyer, Jax with his arms crossed over his chest and his father with hands tucked into the pockets of his slacks. As alike as they were in physical appearance, they couldn't have been dressed more differently, and yet Jax was clearly holding his own.

I studied the distance between them, the way they stood apart and eyed each other warily. Their family dynamic was alien to me, so far removed from the Rossi warmth that nurtured me.

The Rutledges were demanding. I didn't know all the details of Jax's upbringing but it was clear he'd grown up in a high-pressure environment. He'd made it obvious he didn't hold a high opinion of Rutledges, including himself, but he had chosen his family over me—he'd made sure Ian was able to sabotage the Mondego deal—after saying I was the one person he gave a shit about.

Some long-overdue research was in order.

I took off back down the hall, shameless in my search for answers. I figured he owed me something and I'd snoop for it if I had to.

Turning into his home office, I paused on the threshold, seeing a room more in keeping with what I'd expected of him. Although the overall look was modern and masculine, the space was warmed by neutral walls and honeyed woods, with accents of red and gold. Bookcases hugged the walls, filled with a colorful array of hardcover literary volumes and dog-eared popular fiction paperbacks. There was another picture of me on the shelf, this one upright. I was solo. No Jax.

The photo was recent. No more than six months old.

From across the room, I stared at it, feeling my palms go damp.

He'd been keeping tabs on me.

The questions kept piling up, but one very important answer was made glaringly clear by the existence of that picture. I couldn't decide if I felt joy or pain about it. Maybe it was a mixture of both.

Jax's desk was covered in scattered pages and open folders, but I turned my back on them. I'd seen enough.

I headed back out to the living room where I grabbed my purse and set off toward the door. The men outside seemed surprised when I pulled it open. They stopped talking, and I gave a brisk nod to both of them before striding to the elevator with my head held high.

"Gia." Jax took a step toward me. "Don't go."

"I'll ride down with you, Miss Rossi," Parker offered, coming up to me with a smile that was far too friendly. "It's good to see you again."

"Mr. Rutledge," I replied.

"Call me Parker, please."

"Dad," Jax growled, coming closer. "You and I aren't done talking."

Parker patted him on the shoulder. "We can pick up where we left off later, son."

Jax looked at me. "We're supposed to be having dinner."

"I'll need to take a rain check."

"Don't do this, Gia."

I smiled grimly. "Don't worry, I'll be back."

The elevator car arrived, and Parker gestured me in before him.

Jax caught me by the elbow. "Give me five minutes."

"How about I call you later?" I said, realizing I wasn't even tempted to stay. I was too raw, too confused. I needed some breathing room.

His jaw tightened.

"It's all right, Jackson," Parker said quietly. "I'll show her out."

Jax turned his head slowly toward his father, his features set like stone. "I meant what I said."

"You always do." Parker grinned.

I stepped into the elevator just as the doors started to close again. Parker joined me, but my attention was on Jax, our gazes locked together. His hands were fisted at his sides, his jaw tense and determined. But his eyes…those deep, dark eyes…they made the same promises they always had. I believed them now. I had the proof.

Parker faced me as the car began its descent, smiling. "How are you, Gianna?"

"I've been better. How about you?"

"You make it awkward to say it's been a good day so far."

My mouth curved. "And a good day for your friend Ian, too."

"Ah." His eyes brightened with amusement. "Please don't hold that against Jackson."

I shrugged. "It's just business, right?"

"You're a very practical woman. Certainly one of the many reasons why he's so taken with you. Speaking of which…" He rocked back on his heels. "I'd like to get to know you better, Gianna. Would you and Jax come to dinner with my wife and me? Something quiet at our house in the Hamptons, maybe?"

"I'd like that." I'd like anything that would let me get a better handle on Jax.

"Good. I'll let Regina know." His smile faded a little. "Don't let Jackson talk you out of it. He wants to keep you all to himself."

"Does he?"

Parker sobered further. "He's very protective."

"Is he? What would he have to protect me from?"

"We're men, Gianna," he drawled. "We're not always rational when it comes to women."

I nodded, gathering that Parker was as much of an enigma as his son. It seemed Rutledges were just naturally inclined to be hard to read and cryptic.

The elevator doors opened into the lobby and we stepped out into a meticulously restored pre-war space that exuded luxury and privilege.

"I have a car waiting," he said. "Can I give you a ride?"

"Thank you but no." I didn't even want to contemplate the look on Parker's face if he saw where I lived. Compared to the marble-lined lobby of Jax's building, complete with concierge and doorman, my place would look…not so hot. I wasn't embarrassed by the loft or my family, but I thought it might be wise to not trigger suspicions of gold digging until the Rutledges got to know me better.

"All right, then, if you're sure." Parker hesitated, as if waiting for me to change my mind. When I didn't, he said, "I'll let Jax know the day and time for dinner. I'm looking forward to it, Gianna."

I thought of the man upstairs, high in his tower, a stranger in so many ways and yet one who knew me inside and out. "I am, too."

I heard music blaring in the loft before the freight elevator clanked to a stop on our floor. As I got closer, I recognized the vintage Guns N' Roses riff. "Welcome to the Jungle." Considering my evening with the Rutledges, I found it fitting.

Sliding the door open, I was hit with the full force of Vincent's rocking sound system and the sight of him doing pull-up crunches via a metal pole he'd mounted between two supporting pillars. He was drenched with sweat and gritting his teeth, the slabs of muscle on his stomach tightening as he brought his knees up to his chest. He wore his hair shorter than my other brothers, nearly a crew cut, and it suited his classically Italian features.

I'd read books that compared the hero to a face on a Roman coin, but I guarantee none of them had anything on Vincent. Shirtless, shoeless and wearing only running shorts, he was the stuff other women's dreams were made of. Unlike Nico, Vincent was a serial boyfriend. He had no problem committing, but he never stayed off the market for longer than several months at a time.

"Hey!" he protested, when I turned the volume down.

"You still talk to Deanna?" I asked, referring to the reporter he used to date.

"Yeah." He dropped to the hardwood floor and snatched up the towel waiting there alongside a bottle of water. "Why?"

I set my purse down on the bench by the door and kicked off my shoes. "I need someone to catch me up on the Rutledges."

Vincent scrubbed at his hair, scowling. "The guy's a douche. He doesn't deserve you."

"I won't argue with that." I sprawled across the couch and stared up at the exposed pipes and beamed ceiling. "But that doesn't mean he can't be redeemed."

"Forget the rehab. Find a guy who's smart enough to know what he has from the get-go."

I glanced at him, watching his throat work as he chugged the entire bottle of water. "You telling me you never screwed up with a girl and wanted a second chance?"

"Doesn't count. You're a Rossi. There's no excuse for him screwing up besides being stupid," he said.

"Will you ask her?"

"Fine." He headed toward the kitchen, adding, "Only because I hope she digs up something that convinces you he's bad news."

"Thank you."

"Don't think you're getting the favor for a simple thanks." He tossed his towel over his shoulder and washed his hands. The kitchen was the most finished part of the apartment, with brand-new stainless-steel appliances, chef's cooktop, double wall ovens and a massive workstation island with sink. "I've got a basket of laundry that needs washing."

I sat up. "Are you kidding me?"

"Nope. Better hurry." He grinned. "I'm out of Rossi's T-shirts and my shift starts in two hours."

I'd just closed the louvered doors that concealed the washer and dryer when I heard my smartphone ringing. I ran to my bedroom to grab it, but missed the call. Didn't matter, though, because it immediately started ringing again.

It was Jax.

Taking a deep breath, I touched Answer on the screen and said, "Hey."

"You were supposed to call," he accused.

"So were you," I retorted. "Took you two years to get around to it."

"Jesus." He exhaled harshly. "Why did you leave?"

"It was time. Your dad invited us to dinner."

"We're not going."

I shrugged. "I'll go without you."

"The hell you will! Damn it, Gia. You're swimming with sharks and acting like you're on vacation."

"I'm definitely seeing things I've never seen before. Like those pictures you've got framed in your pad. How long have you been following me? Creepy, by the way."

He cursed. "You're fucking a Rutledge. Surveillance and invasion of privacy come with the territory."

"I wasn't fucking you at the time that picture in your office was taken."

"You were in my office? What the hell, Gia?"

My mouth curved grimly at his inadvertent admission that there were more photos I hadn't found. "I'm going to be in every aspect of your life—get used to it."

Jax was silent for a long minute, then quietly asked, "What do you think you're doing?"

"I'm processing the fact that you're in love with me, Jax." I heard his breath catch and felt a surge of pleasured triumph. "Still, you bailed on me. And now you're sabotaging my work and your own chances with me."

"Gia—"

"I'm on to you, Jackson Rutledge." My voice was low and hard, unwavering. "I'm going to figure you out."

"I'm an open book," he retorted.

"You're a head trip." I ignored the waiting suitcase on my bed and sat at my desk instead. I woke my computer with a shake of the mouse. "And your mystery-man days are numbered."

I hung up, shut off the ringer and started my research.

11

"THAT MAN IS seriously hot. He can take my order anytime."

I scowled at the television in my hotel room as I unpacked my toiletries. God knew why I'd tuned in to a midday talk show, but I certainly hadn't expected to see the man I loved on the screen…or to listen to the glamorous hosts dish about how hot he was.

"Maybe he's going to put voting booths in every Pembry-backed restaurant," the other one said.

Shaking my head, I headed into the bathroom. Jax's investment in Pembry Ventures still stung. I wasn't sure I'd ever forgive him for fucking me over like that. Maybe I shouldn't take it so personally, maybe it was just business, but there were some things you just didn't do to someone you love and screwing up their job—an adored job at that—was one of them.

I was determined to uncover the reason why. And I was going to make him pay. Being in love with him wouldn't change that. I wasn't sure it changed anything.

I'd just hung my makeup bag on the towel rack when the room phone started ringing. Knowing I probably took a lot more time than Chad did to unpack, I expected he was ready to head down to see the construction site of his restaurant in the very same hotel we were staying in. The Atlanta Mondego was being turned into a destination with a capital D, and I would soon have the dust on the soles of my Jimmy Choos to prove it.

Grabbing the receiver off the bathroom wall, I tucked it into the crook of my neck and said, "Hey. You settled in already?"

"Gia, damn it. Turn on your cell phone!"

Jax's deep, sexy voice slid across my senses, bringing with it a rush of heated and beloved memories. Something inside me tingled with pleasure that he'd gone to the trouble of tracking me down. Jackson Rutledge was a busy guy with his pick of women. Following me around the country was entirely unnecessary. And really flattering.

I leaned against the bathroom counter. "News flash—I'm avoiding you."

"Good luck with that."

My jaw tightened. So what if he was an animal in bed? So what if I was happy to hear from him? I was still mad at him. "I'm hanging up now."

"You can't run from me," he said tightly. "And you can't pull that shit you pulled yesterday. We need to talk."

"I agree, but that usually means you tell me I'm only ever going to be a fuck buddy to you and you don't give me any reasons why. I don't have the patience to run around in circles. Unless you've got real answers for me, I'm not giving you any more of my time."

"You're going to give me a hell of a lot more than time, Gia."

A shiver of awareness moved through me. I knew that tone of his. It was his I'm-going-to-bang-the-hell-out-of-you tone. "You wish."

"I'm about to land, Gia. I'll be at the hotel within the hour and you're going to see me."

"What?" My pulse gave a traitorous leap of excitement. My sex drive had been revved since I'd left him the night before. It was all too eager to cross the finish line. "I can't believe you followed me to Atlanta! How the hell did you know where I was?"

"Your sister-in-law."

Denise was going to be hearing from me. She knew better, which meant she'd done it on purpose. "Well, turn around and fly home again. I'm working, Jax. I don't trust you to be around my work."

His sharply indrawn breath told me I'd scored a hit.

"Fine," he snapped. "I'll send a car for you. We'll meet at my hotel."

"I've got stuff to do today. I'll let you know when I have a moment, and I'll find a neutral place for us to meet." A bar, maybe, or even a shopping mall. Someplace where intimacy wouldn't be a problem. Sadly, I couldn't trust myself around him now that I knew how he felt about me.

"My hotel, Gia," he reiterated. "A public place won't save you. We're going to fuck, long and hard, wherever we end up. Better we don't end up in jail and splashed all over the tabloids while doing it, don't you think?"

"You've really got to do something about that ego."

"Baby, I'll crawl on my hands and knees if that's what it takes."

It was my turn to suck in a deep breath. He knew how to get to me, how to open me up and leave me defenseless. I tried to do the same thing to him. "Tell me you love me, Jax."

There was a moment of silence. "Loving each other isn't our problem."

He hung up, leaving me holding on to an empty connection. As usual.

* * *

"It's finally starting to feel real," Chad said, looking around at the construction area. I smiled. "Good."

He reached for my hand and gave it a squeeze. He'd met me at the site, wearing an open-collar dress shirt tucked into loose-fitting jeans. His auburn hair was just barely overlong, with the bangs draping across his brow and framing his stunning green eyes. No doubt about it, Chad Williams was a hunk.

He'd drawn a lot of female attention on the way in, but he hadn't paid any mind to it. I hoped he would stay unaffected at least until the first restaurant opened. I'd seen more than a few chefs get too cocky from attention overload, and their businesses quickly suffered as a result.

"So what happens next?" he asked, turning to face me.

"The Mondego was just waiting for signed contracts to begin serious construction," I explained. "The architect will revamp the initial design to accommodate three chefs. When we agree it works for you, we'll sign off on it and they'll get to work."

"God." He blew out his breath and grinned. "I can't wait to see them."

"We'll get to look at the existing plans tomorrow, which should give us a good idea of how it's going to be laid out. When we get back to New York, we'll bring you, Inez, and David together to start hashing out the dueling menus. It'll be good to come up with some regional variations based on hotel locations."

Chad nodded. "How much say will they have in the whole process?"

"In their menus, a lot," I said honestly. "We picked them for their talent and we need to let them do what they do best. But outside of that, you've got the ultimate say. You're the celebrity chef here. They're riding your coattails for now."

His mouth twisted ruefully. "I hope that doesn't cause any problems."

"I suspect it'll be easier than working with your sister."

"Ha! No doubt."

He joked, but I saw a hint of sadness in his expressive eyes. Things would've been better all around if Stacy had followed through and undertaken this endeavor with him. Jax had contributed to that breakdown between the siblings, which was ironic considering how much he did for his own family.

"Have you called her since the news broke about Rutledge Capital and Pembry Ventures?" I asked gently.

His mouth thinned. "Why? So she can gloat?"

"So you can congratulate her. You know, extend an olive branch."

"She'd be an ass about it."

"Maybe." I put my hand on his shoulder. "But you'll feel better if you do. And later on, when she comes around, you can hold it over her."

That coaxed out a huff of a laugh. "I'll think about it."

"In the meantime, are you hungry?"

"Starved. Let's eat." He held his arm out to me and I took it. "There are a lot of great fried chicken and waffle places around these parts."

"Waffles and fried chicken? At the same time?"

"It's a delicious combination, sweetheart. You haven't lived until you've tried it."

"Sounds like it'll kill me, though. Or at least help me pack on another ten pounds I don't need."

Chad lifted my hand to his lips and kissed the knuckles. "In that case, I'd help you take them back off."

"You are a naughty man, Chad Williams," I admonished, but with a smile. His harmless flirting was a nice contrast to Jax, who was entirely dangerous in every way.

As if he read my mind, he said, "For what it's worth, Lei gave me the heads-up that you've got a thing going with Jackson Rutledge."

I tensed, surprised, then realized Lei was right to have done that. Better to deal with any issues now than to have Chad find out later and feel that we deliberately kept something from him. "We saw each other briefly a couple years ago."

"And now?" He glanced at me. "Is he the guy who sent you the flowers?"

"Yes. Now he's…" I thought of him in his private jet, flying after me. Wanting to see me. Sleep with me. "He's back in my life and involved in my business, which I don't appreciate."

"Which part? The life? The business? Both?"

"My business is my life," I said as we exited out to the front drive and signaled our desire for a cab. "He can't cause any more trouble for you, Chad. You, Inez, and David are set with Mondego. We're rolling ahead."

"Can he cause problems for you? "

"Don't worry about me."

He threw his arm around my shoulder and tugged me close. "Of course I'm going to worry about you. You're my lucky ticket."

I bumped my hip into his. "To what?"

"As if you don't know, Gianna darlin'. Fame and fortune."

I had to admit, the Southern fried chicken and waffles were damned good. I ate more than I should have and felt as if I practically waddled back up to my hotel room. The urge to take a nap was strong, but Chad and I were meeting with the hotel manager at three-thirty and I was worried I'd still be shaking off sleep fog. It wasn't a major meeting, just a courtesy meet and greet over coffee, but business was business.

I opened my laptop and sat at the desk, sifting through my emails. I answered two from Lei about David Lee before opening the one from Deanna Johnson that I'd spotted the moment my inbox opened. I pulled my phone out of my purse and powered it on, punching in the cell number listed in the reporter's signature line. I ignored the notifications of voice mails and texts from Jax.

"Deanna Johnson," she answered briskly.

"Hi. It's Gianna Rossi." Her LinkedIn profile was open in one of the tabs in my browser and I switched to it, looking at her photo. She was a pretty brunette with long hair and dark eyes. She and Vincent had made a good-looking couple when they were dating, their dark coloring making for a visual sync. They hadn't lasted long, but then, Vincent's relationships rarely did. He liked having a steady girlfriend, but with the hours he worked at Rossi's, he wasn't a steady boyfriend.

"Gianna, hey. How are you?"

I leaned into the headrest and stretched my legs out, kicking off my heels. "I'm good. You?"

"Chasing a story, as always." Deanna's voice changed, became more focused. "Vincent says you wanted me to look into something…?"

"Jackson Rutledge."

"Right. That's what he said." She blew out her breath. "Care to tell me why?"

"We've been…seeing each other."

Deanna laughed softly. "An enigmatic millionaire with more secrets than dollars? I know the type."

I pinched the bridge of my nose, knowing it'd be better for my sanity if I walked away. Also knowing I wouldn't. "I just want to get a better handle on him. I need to know if I'm wasting my time even thinking about trying to make things work."

"Probably," she said bluntly. "What are you looking for? I'm not a private investigator, and there are a lot of books out there about the Rutledge family and its various members. Things like ex-girlfriends you can find with a Google search."

"No, that's not what I'm interested in. Maybe you can't help me. Maybe I'm looking for something only he can give up." I sighed. "I don't understand why he'll do anything for his family when he doesn't always seem like them. He certainly spends a lot of time warning me away from them. I thought he was hiding me like a bad habit, but now I feel like he's… protecting me from them."

"If he cares about you that may well be what he's doing. You gotta figure the Rutledges are like tiger sharks—they swim in the same womb but cannibalize each other until only the strongest comes out alive."

I froze, remembering what he'd said to me the night before. *You're swimming with sharks and acting like you're on vacation.*

"Okay," I said carefully, thinking of Jax's father. "Who's the strongest shark in that family, then? Parker Rutledge? "

"Without a doubt."

Jax said his parents had started out as a love match and ended up miserable.… "What do you know about Jax's mom?"

"Leslie Rutledge? Talk about an enigma. Almost never seen in public the last five years before she died, and she avoided the spotlight even before that."

"Jax won't talk about her."

"I can poke around, see what turns up, but it'll take some time. Whenever you turn over a Rutledge stone, security teams come crawling out."

I sighed. I'd been seriously delusional dreaming of a "normal" life with Jax. "I'd appreciate anything you find. And I'll pay for your time, of course."

"Sure thing."

Sitting up, I rolled my shoulders back. I was going to ask Jax outright about his family, but having a Plan B didn't hurt. Especially considering how things had gone for us so far. "Thanks, Deanna."

"Hey, take care, okay? Guys like Jax can really fuck you up if you're not careful."

"Yeah, I know. Thanks. You take care, too."

We hung up and I set my smartphone down on the desk. I was back to running through my email when my cell pinged for an incoming text. Looking at the screen, I saw it was from Jax. My feet tapped a little dance on the carpet before I realized what I was doing.

I know you're thinking about me.

I stared at his message and snorted. "Whatever."

Obviously, you're thinking about me, I typed back.

I dreamt about u 2.

That made me smile. Dreaming about Jax was one of my wayward mind's favorite pastimes. **Hope it was a nightmare about me blowing a major business deal for u.**

A minute later: **It was a wet dream about u blowing me.**

I laughed. He'd changed tactics from our earlier conversation, switching from playing hardball to just playing. Jax knew when a particular strategy wasn't working.

I started typing a reply, but he beat me to it. My phone started ringing. I answered and he spoke before I could even say hello.

"You sucked me so good, baby," he crooned. "I couldn't breathe, it felt so good. Your hot little mouth tugging at the head of my dick, your tongue swirling around me, your tight fist jacking me off. I came so hard for you. And you swallowed it all, Gia baby. Every drop."

For a moment, I couldn't think of what to say, my mind filled with images of me doing just what he said. I loved going down on Jax. Loved the way he felt…how he tasted and smelled. More than that, I loved the way he lost himself with me, shameless in his pleasure. In those moments, I felt the intimacy with him that I craved so much.

"You've always loved sucking my cock," he said silkily. "And God knows I'd spend every minute in your mouth if I could."

I found my voice. "Selfish bastard."

"When it comes to you, yeah." He sighed. "I'm lying in bed, naked and hard, wondering why the fuck you're not here yet."

"Don't you have something to do? "

"You."

I heard the sound of his email pinging in the background and laughed. "Liar. You're working."

We used to play phone sex games with each other, often leading to both of us getting off simultaneously. There was nothing in the world like hearing him say my name when he was coming.

"Guilty," he confessed, unabashed. "Trying to keep my mind off you and failing miserably."

"Probably because what you're working on is the deal that screwed me over."

"You promised me a round of angry sex." He hummed softly, with obvious relish. "I'm waiting for it, baby."

"Not sure you want your dick anywhere near my teeth while I'm feeling this way about you."

Jax laughed and my toes curled. He had the best laugh, deep and full-bodied. "Even threats of bodily harm can't kill this hard-on I've got for you. Come over, Gia."

"Can't. I've got a meeting in a bit." I stood and walked to the window, feeling restless. Pushing the sheer curtains aside, I looked down at the city of Atlanta. *Where was Jax?* It was a question I'd been asking myself every day over the past two years. He hadn't had to ask where I was, though, since he'd had me followed. "Besides, didn't you say we needed to talk? I doubt you'll do much of that when I get there."

He was silent a minute, then, "You've got a great family. I've always known where I stood with them, good or bad. They don't bullshit and they don't waste time on petty crap. They're good people."

"Thank you," I murmured, taking that to heart. I was proud of my family, proud to be a Rossi.

"My family isn't like that, Gia. Don't be fooled by Parker's charm. He only gives the time of day to people who are useful."

"Jax, I don't have anything."

"You have me," he said grimly.

"Are you saying your dad would use me against you? "

"Maybe. Or he'd just use you, period. It could be anything, babe. Just trust me, there's an angle."

I absorbed that for a moment, trying to wrap my head around a father and son who didn't trust each other. "Is he the reason you stayed away the past couple of years?"

Is he the reason you're determined to leave me again?

"I stayed away because it's the best thing for you."

I hated that non-answer. "Yet here you are. Give me a good reason why I should see you, Jax."

"Because you want to."

"I suggest you come up with something better than that."

He exhaled in a rush. "Because *I* want you to. Because I need to spend time with you. You make me feel…human. Being with you makes me feel like I'm not a complete piece of shit."

I closed my eyes, my hand lifting to my chest to rub the ache in my heart. I wanted to know why he always put himself down, why he thought he wasn't good enough for me. I knew I was going to make a go of it just to try to get those answers. Still, I was honest and told him, "Being with you makes me feel lonely. It reminds me that I want to find someone to be steady in my life. Someone I can depend on."

"I wish I was that guy," he said quietly.

"Yeah. Me, too."

12

I INTERRUPTED MY sister-in-law the instant she answered the phone. "Traitor!"

Denise paused in the middle of reciting the name of her beauty salon, then said, "So he called you, eh?"

"He's here!" I sat on the edge of my bed with a groan.

"He's in Atlanta? Are you serious?" Denise whistled. I heard a squeak in the background and could picture her sitting on the hot-pink stool behind the front counter of her shop. "He's got it bad for you."

"I can't believe you ratted me out like that. Don't you think if I'd wanted him to know where I was, I would've told him? "

"Come on. I've never seen you look at a guy the way you look at him. You can't blame me for wanting you to be happy."

"He deserves to stew a bit, Denise. He deserves to miss me and wonder what I'm doing."

"Ah, I feel you. Sorry."

I kicked out my legs, my gaze dropping to my pedicure. "No, you're not."

"I'm a *little* sorry," she amended. "So, are you two going to kiss and make up?"

"It's not like that."

"So tell me what it's like."

"Boy meets girl, boy ditches girl, boy pops up again two years later, boy screws girl and then almost screws her big business deal, boy wants to screw girl again—maybe both ways—but this time, boy says up front that he'll be ditching girl again at some point."

"Hmm." Her chewing gum bubble popped loudly. "If I hadn't seen the way boy looks at girl, I might tell you to kick him to the curb."

"Probably the smart thing to do. So what's your alternative?"

"Screw him senseless. Rock his world. Show him what he'll be missing. Make it hurt when he decides it's time to walk away so he won't go through with it."

If only it were that easy. "I think that's an asinine plan."

"Maybe." She laughed, and I smiled reluctantly. "But that's a fine piece of prime male ass, Gianna. There are worse things a girl can do than spend a few hours in bed with a hot guy who's in love with her."

She was saying what I'd wanted to hear—some excuse to go forward instead of cutting my losses and running. "You're an enabler, Denise!"

"Whatev. If Jackson's bad for you, think about how good sex is. It's great for the complexion, good exercise, an awesome mood booster—"

I rolled my eyes. "Hanging up now."

"Love you!" she said quickly.

"Love you, too." I killed the call and stood for a moment, lightly tapping my chin with the end of my phone.

I loved Jax enough that it was impossible to just walk away, even for my own self-preservation. Jax loved me enough that walking away was the only end he'd consider. Maybe Denise was onto something. Maybe instead of pushing back all the time, I had to love him with everything I had. Really make him feel it, so he'd miss it when it was gone, enough to bring him back to me.

Problem with that, though, was that he'd screwed me businesswise. And I couldn't let it go. That was a cut that ran deep.

Chad and Rick, the hotel manager, hit it off right away. I enjoyed listening to the two talk with their Southern drawls, charmed by both men and entertained to boot. But when Rick extended an invitation to dinner, I declined after Chad accepted, not wanting to cramp his style. I figured it was important for him to feel connected on his own, without me hovering all the time. I wasn't his babysitter, and I didn't want him to feel as if I didn't trust him to handle his business on his own.

When I got back to my room, I called Lei.

"Gianna," she said when she picked up, knowing it was me from the office's caller ID. "How are things going in Atlanta?"

"Chad's feeling good," I said. "He's been comfortable and relaxed, and really excited. The visit did what we'd hoped."

Perceptive as she was, she asked, "And you? Are you feeling good, too?"

"Jackson followed me down here." I didn't share that personal detail with my boss, or dish like I would with Denise or one of my girlfriends. I would with Denise or one of my girlfriends. I told her because there was no way around a possible conflict of interest. I wasn't going to let Jax jeopardize my job any further.

"Did he?" Her tone was thoughtful. "Well… How do you feel about that?"

"I'm not sure. No," I amended, "that's not true. I'm pissed off that he's made an already complicated relationship more complicated by investing in Pembry Ventures. Not just that, but he called Isabelle directly to solidify her defecting. I can't trust him, Lei."

Every time I thought about what he'd done, I got angry all over again.

"That's a fatal flaw."

"I know it." The thing was, I couldn't shake the feeling that Jax had deliberately moved to put a wedge between us. But I couldn't decide if that motivation made him less dangerous or more so. "I need you to tell me if I'm risking my job."

"You know you are. I'm not going to fire you over who you date, Gianna. That's your business. But if he happens to make another move that looks like he got a tip from you— whether it was done deliberately or not—I'll have to let you go, because then we're talking about my business. Got it?"

My stomach knotted. "Got it."

"All right." Her voice softened. "What's on the agenda tomorrow?"

I told her. While I spoke calmly and steadily, I couldn't shake the fear that had taken root. I'd planned my whole future around my job and I didn't have a Plan B.

"Let me know what Chad thinks of the architect's renderings when he sees them. And take care of yourself, Gianna. You're not just an employee to me. I think you know that."

I nodded, even though she couldn't see me. "I do. Thanks, Lei."

We hung up and I threw my phone on the bed. A headache was building and I loosened the clip that rolled my hair into a neat chignon at my nape. I really hated Jax at that moment. I didn't know how to deal with all the emotions he'd been stirring up in me since he had walked back into my life. I kept shifting from wanting to heal whatever was wounding him to wanting to hurt him myself.

Ping. Incoming text.

When I saw *Going crazy waiting 4 u* from Jax, I let it all explode.

I called him. Everything that was wrong in my life was his fault and he needed to know that.

"Tell me you're in the lobby," he said in greeting, his voice husky.

I didn't screw around. "I love my job. It's the most important thing in my life, and I'm in danger of losing it because of you."

It took him a second to switch gears. "Fuck. Gia—"

"If you love me at all, you'll tell me right now if this is going to end with me jobless. You can get easy pussy, Jax. You don't need mine."

"Jesus." He exhaled roughly. "I've done what business I intend to do with Ian Pembry."

It was another non-answer. I was sick of them. He gave them for damn near everything.

I hung up and tossed the phone onto the bed. I started undressing, wanting to take a shower and scrub the day off.

My phone started ringing. *Click.* Time to shut that sucker down for the night.

I took my room phone off the hook, too, before he could start in on me that way. I'd come to Atlanta for some time away from Jax, and I needed it, despite how my body protested the idea of being denied him.

"I don't need him to have an orgasm," I scolded myself aloud. Of course that didn't address what I really loved about sex with Jax—the man himself.

Twenty minutes later, my hair was wrapped up in a towel on my head and I was on the phone with room service. An impatient, angry rap on the door startled me enough to make me jump.

I knew who it was before Jax said, "Open the damned door, Gia."

My jaw clenched. There was no way in hell the hotel had given out my room number. It irritated me to no end that Jax had the connections to circumvent the rules everyone else lived by.

I returned my attention to my call. "You know what? Make that a bottle of Ste. Michelle instead of a glass, please. Thank you."

Jax knocked with even more impatience.

I hung up and glared at the door. "Fuck you," I snapped.

"You're acting like a child." Even muffled through the door, his voice resonated with fury.

"Get a clue, Jax. I don't want to see you."

"That's too damn bad. You can't stay in there forever, Gia, but I can put a guard on your door who'll make sure that when you come out, you come straight to me. It's your choice how you want this to go."

Narrow-eyed, I slapped the security bar back and yanked the door open. Jax immediately crowded me, forcing me back into the room. I caught barely a glimpse of a guy in a suit behind Jax's big frame, then Jax kicked the door shut behind him.

I backed up quickly, my gaze darting down the length of his body. He was dressed in black slacks and a matching vest, his gray shirt and tie not softening the dark vibe. His hair looked as if he'd been running his fingers through it, the longer strands falling over his forehead in sexy disarray. His brown eyes were hot as they catalogued my appearance, his irritation evident in the scowl that furrowed his brow.

He'd said I was sexy as hell when I was mad at him and I understood what he meant when confronted by over six feet of angry, bristling masculinity. The angles of his gorgeous face were tight, his jaw rigid, the sensual curve of his lips firmed into an unyielding line. He looked dangerous and fiercely sexual.

"I'm getting real tired of you cutting things off," he said, clenching his teeth.

"Boy do I know that feeling."

He glanced at the ceiling as if he were praying for patience. "Is Yeung giving you a hard time?"

"No." I crossed my arms, wishing I were wearing more than the hotel-provided robe, which was a thin shield for my nakedness underneath. "She's actually been remarkably forgiving, all things considered."

He watched me back carefully away. He filled the entryway of the room, blocking the exit, the closet, and the bathroom. The Mondego was a really nice hotel, beautifully decorated with understated elegance, but this suite was nowhere near as fabulous as the one Jax had taken me to in New Jersey. "My deal with Pembry has nothing to do with you."

"I don't believe you."

His brows rose. "*You* don't? Or Yeung doesn't?"

"Me. I'm sure you had a few reasons why you did it, but I'm also pretty sure I was *one* of the reasons. And since it's worked out so well and made me seriously consider how much of a liability you are, I can't be sure you won't pull something else that makes me hate you. That's what you want, isn't it? You want me to end things because you can't."

His face revealed no expression, but something in his eyes changed. "Why would

I want to do that?"

"Because you're afraid of me. Especially the way you feel about me."

"Am I?"

"That, or your dad has you running scared. Which is it? "

"I've told you what he's like," Jax said softly.

That stopped my retreat. "I guess I have more faith in you than you have in yourself. I think you can take him on, Jax. I trust that you'd watch out for me."

He laughed and it was a horrible, humorless sound. "You think I'd protect you from the big bad wolf?"

I stared at him, shocked, never having seen this bitter side of him. The next thing I knew, he had me in his powerful grip, his body curling into me and his face close to mine. He was impossibly beautiful. The most stunning man I'd ever seen. And he was seriously pissed.

"I *am* the big bad wolf, baby," he growled. "You want to be with me? You want to be my girlfriend? You want to go to parties with me…events…have dinner with the family?"

"Yes!" I lifted onto my tiptoes. "I'm sick of being your booty call, Jax. You've got dozens of women for that. I deserve better!"

"Dozens? I've damn near been a monk since I met you! Two women, Gia. *Two*. And since you fucked two guys, you've got no room to talk. I'm entitled to those two, as pointless as they were."

I gasped, horrified that he'd watched me close enough to know how many men I had slept with since we'd been apart. "You want the whole deal?" he snapped. "Fine. Your life is about to change completely. Your privacy is a thing of the past. You're going—"

"As if I had any privacy! My God, you've been stalking me for years. Are you—?"

"Gia, every questionable thing you've ever done is about to become tomorrow's news. Your brothers' lives are up for grabs, too. And that goes for your parents and friends, too. Go out in public and the photographers will follow. From how you vote to what you're wearing, everything is fair game."

I swallowed hard.

"You're going to move in with me. You'll be safe in my apartment, but I can't say what your brothers will have to deal with. Or your sister-in-law. There'll be security with you at all times. And I don't want to hear about how inconvenient it is to constantly have someone with you, someone you'll have to report your schedule to."

"You can't scare me," I whispered, but it was a lie. My heart was pounding with anxiety. I had always been incredibly protective of my family. Whenever they were threatened, I came out swinging.

"Oh, I will," he warned darkly. "You've had nothing but the best of me so far, but if you want it all, that's what you'll get. The good and the really fucking ugly."

"Bring it on," I challenged, getting angry again. He was deliberately being an ass.

"I travel a lot. You're going to have some late nights that will bore you to tears, only to get up the next day to go to work. I'll tell you what to wear, what to say, how to act. It's what I do, Gia. Image is everything in politics and business, but you've already figured that out, haven't you? You've laid a lot of the groundwork for me. Sometimes, I barely recognize you."

I rebelled, yanking myself away from him. "Thank you, Jax," I said, my voice dripping with sarcasm. "You've made the decision really easy for me."

His mouth curled in a cruel smile. "Scared you off, did I?"

I was so frustrated with his crap, I wanted to scream. We'd never been nasty to each other. More than anything, I was desperate to put distance between us.

"I'd face all that and more for a guy who really loved me," I told him coldly. "But I'm not putting up with this shit from a jerk."

He looked ready to smash his clenched fist through the wall.

I waved toward the door. "Please leave, Jax. I don't want to look at you right now." Another lie. I would never get tired of looking at him. But I was tired of dealing with him. I'd wanted a break for a reason.

"I give it to you straight and you flip." He scrubbed a hand over his face and cursed.

"No," I corrected. "You wanted to scare me straight and you're getting what you wanted. I'm settling for a fuck-only arrangement, but I'll do so on my time, not yours. I'll call you when I want you, so don't bother calling me—I won't answer. And stop popping up where I am. It's creepy."

"Damn it." Jax stepped forward, reaching for me. I backed up quickly. "Don't touch me."

His dark eyes bored into mine. "You might as well tell me to stop breathing. What the fuck do you want from me, Gia? I'm trying to give you what you're asking for, and it's still not enough."

"Damn right! You set up all those pitfalls and didn't leave me any way out. Why would I want to take the first step?"

"Living under a microscope is part of my life! I can't change it."

"You could've said something like, 'Listen, Gia, sharing my life won't be easy, but I love you. I'll do the best I can to make sure our private life is worth the public hell.' Or something like that!"

"Jesus." He made a frustrated sound. "This isn't a goddamned romance novel! I'm just a guy trying to give in to what you want so I can have you."

As if. He knew what I wanted and he was fighting it all the way. "Well, now you can have your life *and* me—when I'm in the mood." I held up a warning hand. "Not now. Believe me. I'll call you when I get back to New York."

"Fine. Whatever." He pivoted and strode to the door, his back stiff and shoulders rigid.

There was still a part of me that wanted to cave, to drag him back and tell him to stay, to sleep with him and feel that incredible intimacy and sensual closeness I'd never felt with anyone else. But we had a lot of thinking to do and we needed time—and space—to do it.

Jax yanked the door open and stepped out to the hallway. I swallowed the words stuck in my throat and reached for my smartphone on the bed, using it as a distraction to avoid watching him leave.

I heard the door shut and closed my eyes, breathing out a shaky exhalation. We weren't going to recover from this. This was going to change what we'd had. Forever.

"I…"

My lungs seized in surprise at the sound of Jax's voice.

"I love you. Okay? I love you so much it's driving me crazy."

I reached for the desk chair, trying to support my weakened knees. I'd wanted to hear him say the words, but now that I had, they didn't sink in. I didn't realize how upset he was until his hands gripped my upper arms and he buried his face in my neck.

"I want you in my home," he said softly. "I want to wake up to you, go to sleep holding you, to come home from work and eat dinner with you. I want what we had in Las Vegas, but things were different then. I had you all to myself. It's not going to be that way now."

I reached up with my right hand and set it over his left. "I get it. I can deal with it."

"I hope so," he murmured, turning me around. "Because I'm not going to be able to let you go after this, Gia. For better or worse, you're mine."

13

"IF YOU'RE STILL trying to scare me," I whispered, overcome, "you'll have to do better than that."

Jax laughed softly, huskily. "I'm scared enough for both of us."

He cupped my face, tilting it up to kiss me. The moment his firm lips touched mine, love pierced my heart, making it ache. I caught his waist, pushing up onto my tiptoes to deepen the kiss. Heat and hunger slid through me, provoked by the beloved smell of him…the feel of his warmth and hard body… the taste of him.

He groaned, drawing me closer. I'd been starved for him for so long that appeasing my craving seemed impossible. My tongue tangled with his, licking into his mouth, my mouth slanting across his with unabashed ravenousness.

"Come here." He tugged at the tie of my robe, pushing it open and then down to where my elbows were bent.

I let him go only long enough to allow the sleeves to slide off so the robe dropped on the floor.

"God." He pulled me into him, molding my naked body fully against him.

The buttons of his vest pressed into my skin, driving home the realization that he was clothed, dressed for work in a way I'd never seen when we were together in Vegas. Turning my head, I looked into the mirror on the wall and shivered at our reflection—Jax, so formal and dark, a dangerously sexy businessman; and me, naked and shameless.

"Look at us," I whispered, watching as his gaze found us. Watching the lust tighten his face into primal masculine beauty.

His chin nuzzled against my temple, his eyes closing. "You're so beautiful, baby. So goddamned hot you burn me up. I'm so afraid of fucking this up. Of looking at you one day and finding that you've lost that light in your eyes you have when you're looking at me."

"Jax." He'd always made me feel as if no other woman had ever compared to me. But as thrilled as I was to finally have him, the pain he'd put me through still throbbed like an unhealed wound. "You hurt me," I told him softly. "You broke my heart."

His forehead touched mine. "I hurt us both. I wish I could say it won't happen again, but I have no idea how this is going to play out or how you'll take to living my life with me."

"I'm sure I'll make mistakes, too." I started on the buttons of his vest, freeing them one by one. "We just have to love each other."

He tilted his head and took my mouth again, kissing me with such tenderness my eyes stung. His hands slid up my torso, splaying under my breasts with his thumbs beneath the curves. The pads stroked the sensitive undersides, making my nipples harden. I whimpered, begging for a more carnal touch. The deep-seated ache in my core was painful, my sex already wet and ready.

It had always been that way with Jax, as if my body recognized his as the one it'd been built to take.

Jax exploded into motion, picking me up effortlessly and laying me on the bed. The towel wrapped around my hair loosened and fell off. He positioned himself over me, his hands planted at my sides. He ran the tip of his nose up my cleavage. "Tell me you have a condom."

I bit my lip, regretting that I had to shake my head.

His eyes closed again and he took a deep breath. "I'll keep my clothes on."

"Jax…" There was a plea in my voice, because I couldn't imagine not feeling him inside me. So hard and long and thick.

His head lifted and I shivered at the raging lust in his dark eyes, knowing exactly how it would feel to have it unleashed on me. "There's no way I'd pull out," he said, his voice guttural with desire. "No way."

I opened my mouth to say it was okay…that I was on the pill…that I wanted to feel him come inside me without anything between us…but the doorbell rang, followed by a quick "Room service."

I moaned.

A pained look crossed his face. Then he laughed softly. "Saved by the bell."

"Wait—"

But he was already grabbing my robe off the floor and draping it over me. "Don't move," he ordered.

He got the door, barred the server from entering, and took care of everything in the hallway. When he reappeared, he was carrying the tray in one hand, deftly balancing the bottle of wine, wineglass, and a dome-covered meal.

Setting it all on the desk, he glanced at me as I sat up, my legs stretching out in front of me. "You're killing me."

"You deserve it."

Jax's mouth curved wryly. "I don't doubt it. Still, there's only so much a desperate man can take. I have to get out of here."

I pouted. "Spoilsport."

"Get your sexy ass back to New York, and I'll give you all you can take." He ran a hand through his hair, restoring order to it. "I'm going to start making the arrangements for your return."

My brows rose. "You have to make arrangements to fuck me?"

"No, for you to move in. And I have to let you eat so you have the strength for everything I'll do to you while fucking you." He grabbed me as I pushed to my feet and gave me a quick, hard kiss. "And if you're ready to go raw with me, we do it right—in our own apartment, in our own bed."

I swallowed hard. "I have to talk to my brothers. My parents."

"We'll do it together."

"You're moving fast for a guy who just had his hand forced."

A softness came over Jax's face. "I've thought about this for a while. Tried to plan it in my head…come up with a way to make it work…."

"Maybe it won't be as hard as you think."

He brushed my damp hair back behind my ears. "The media is going to love you, Gia," he murmured. "You're a walking wet dream. You've got sex appeal, baby, and a body that won't quit. They're going to take a look at you and see me looking at you, and they're going to imagine hot, salacious monkey sex. And *that's* news."

I shoved at him. "Be serious!"

"They're going to get it wrong, and think I'm just having a good time with you. They'll start speculating right away on how long it'll last. They'll pair us with other people, inventing news just to have an excuse to publish another picture of you."

I'd seen it before, with other couples. But Jax and I were different. We weren't celebrities. I was nobody, and even though he was a Rutledge, he worked behind the scenes of the political circles that had made his family so well-known.

"You don't believe me." He rubbed his temple against mine. "You'll have to trust me. I've seen what can happen. I've seen the stress rip people apart."

A niggling suspicion spurred me to ask, "Someone you cared about?"

"Yeah."

"What happened?"

Jax pulled back and I saw that he'd shut down. "She checked out," he said tonelessly. "I'm not going to let that happen with you."

My fingers flexed into his lean waist. It was hard thinking about Jax loving someone else. It was harder still thinking about his former lover hurting him so deeply that he'd pushed me away to avoid becoming vulnerable again.

He kissed my forehead. "When are you coming home?"

"Day after tomorrow."

"All right. See if we can't get together with your family that night. We'll get you moved in the next day."

I felt as if I was standing on the edge of a cliff, about to jump, without any idea of where I might land. "You're making my head spin."

Backing up a step, he winked. "Just returning the favor, babe."

"You're miles away."

The sound of Chad's voice snapped me out of my thoughts. I looked at him sitting in the seat next to me on the plane and offered an apologetic smile. "Sorry."

"Should I be worried?"

I shook my head. "It's personal."

His brows rose. "Good for me, maybe. Not so good for you it looks like. Wanna talk about it?"

I debated just how personal I wanted to get with Chad, then asked, "Have you ever lived with a girlfriend?"

"Not really. There were one or two who spent a lot of time at my house, which was convenient as far as sex went, but wasn't great for privacy or hanging with the guys. I figure I'll save that kind of commitment for marriage. Why do you ask?"

"I'm just thinking I agree with you about the commitment level."

The amusement in his eyes faded. "Rutledge asked you to move in?"

"Something like that." Told *me was more like it, but…*

He took a second. "I may have a problem with that."

"Oh?" I twisted in my seat to face him more directly.

"You've known this guy a couple years, you said. But he only starts putting the heat on after you start working with me? He helps to break up my deal with Stacy, then follows that up with nabbing Isabelle. Now he's wanting to share digs with you, the gal that's got all my info and knows all my plans?"

Taking a deep breath, I processed what he'd said. "The day before yesterday, you seemed easier with it."

"I've been doing some thinking."

Okay. *Crap.* I felt like I'd been blindsided. "I don't think it's personal. In fact, I know it's not. Jax always says business should never be personal."

"It's personal to me," he shot back. That hit home. I'd said something similar to Jax when he'd thrown that line at me. "And it's personal to Stacy. She's not just going to want to succeed—she'll want to be better than me. Have more than me. She's going to want to prove that I made the wrong decision, and he's on *her* side! Pembry's got a lot riding on her. They're going to want to keep her happy."

He wasn't wrong, damn it all.

"It works both ways," I pointed out quietly. "I'm going to know what he's into, too."

I hadn't really thought of my relationship with Jax that way before, as a situation that required tiptoeing around issues. Hadn't wanted to. I wanted things with us to be real and straight and beautiful. But everyone I worked with wasn't in sync with that hope, including Jax. Of course, Jax expected the hits to come from the outside, but no matter what, it seemed as though I needed to be a little more realistic about what being with Jax was going to entail.

You're swimming with sharks….

Chad assessed me. "No offense, Gianna. But Rutledge might be out of your league."

"Oh, he is for sure. That doesn't mean I can't handle him. That said—" I took a deep breath "—if you want someone else to spearhead your projects with Savor, I'd understand."

His lips pursed. "I hate to say it, but that might be best."

I'd planned on heading straight into work after landing at LaGuardia, but decided to stop at home first instead. My conversation with Chad had rattled me and I really felt as though I needed some time to pull myself together before going in to face Lei.

I slid open the large metal front door to the loft and found two of my brothers on the couch, playing a video game.

"Catch that one, dude," Angelo snapped, jerking his controller to the right. "Come on! Fucker's about to take me out."

"Hang on." Vincent surged to his feet, frantically hitting buttons. "I've got six of them on me."

I paused on the threshold, feeling so grateful to be home. "Behind you!" I shouted to Angelo as a zombie lumbered up to his avatar.

Both guys jumped and two pairs of dark eyes swung toward me.

"You scared the shit out of me!" Vincent complained, hitting Pause on his split screen.

"Hey," Angelo greeted me, returning his attention to his game. "How was Hotlanta?"

"Hot," I said wryly, turning to pull the door closed behind me. The apartment smelled like bacon, and I could see the remnants of breakfast on the counter and sink. The guys were too used to having dishwashers take care of things at Rossi's.

"You got the day off?" Vincent asked, strolling over. Dressed in shorts and nothing else, he reminded me why my high school friends had been so eager to come over to my house all the time.

"Nah. I gotta show up," I said. "Just wanted to drop off my stuff."

"Get your ass back over here," Angelo muttered. "I'm getting slaughtered by these freaks."

Vincent rolled his eyes. "Damn. I was hoping you'd take over the game, Gianna. You and Nico are the ones who like this shit."

"Not right now. Hey, before I forget, thanks for putting me in touch with Deanna."

"Sure." He grinned. "Thanks for doing my laundry."

I deliberately bumped his shoulder as I passed him on the way to my room. Our apartment was mostly one large massive space, but we'd put up some walls to block off bedrooms for a semblance of privacy. They were more like giant cubicles than actual rooms, but it worked for us while we were renovating the place.

It didn't escape me that I was thinking about leaving a place where I was totally safe and secure to live with a lover who I hadn't entirely trusted just forty-eight hours before.

I sank onto the edge of my bed and gripped my knees with damp palms. I was giving up a lot to be with Jax, and I couldn't think of anything he was really risking to be with me in return.

My smartphone started ringing. Without looking, I dug into my purse and pulled it out. Seeing Jax's name on the screen wasn't a surprise. "Hello."

"Hey, babe." His voice was deep and low, intimate. "Glad you're back."

"Amazing how much everything can change over just a couple of days."

"What's wrong?"

It was wryly amusing that he knew me so well. Maybe Chad was right to be worried about me being an open book. "What isn't wrong?"

His tone turned brisk. "Be more specific."

"Chad Williams has some understandable concerns about me, his project leader, sleeping with the enemy. Shacking up with you seems likely to be a deal breaker."

"Who's shacking up?" Angelo asked, scowling at me from my bedroom doorway. He was the shortest of my three brothers at an even six feet tall and he had the longest hair, the dark waves framing his handsome face and brushing his shoulders. A lot of hearts had broken when he'd married Denise.

"Fuck," I muttered, wishing I could just hit a reset button and start the day over. "Get out!"

"I'm not in," my brother argued. "You left the door open."

"Well, close it!"

"Are you back together with that asshole?!"

I pushed to my feet. "Did I ask you?"

"*Gia!*" Jax barked through the phone.

"Hold on," I told him, glaring at my brother. "I'm on the phone, Angelo. Close the door and mind your own business!"

"Is that Jax you're talking to?" He barged into my room as if he had the right. "Let me talk to him."

"Excuse me?"

"*Gia! Damn it, talk to me,*" Jax snapped.

"I'm a little busy right now," I snapped back. "I'll call you later."

"*Don't you—*"

I cut Jax off by hanging up, tossing my smartphone on the bed as Angelo made a grab for it. "Have you lost your mind?" I yelled at him.

"Rutledge certainly has if he thinks you're moving in with him!"

Vincent's interruption drew both of our attentions to the doorway. "What's going on?"

"Get him out of here!" I told him, waving my hand at Angelo.

"Rutledge wants Gianna to move in with him," Angelo said, facing Vincent and crossing his arms.

Vincent's brows rose. "You got a ring?"

I threw up my hands. "I don't believe this! It's the twenty-first century. Did you know that?"

"The rules haven't changed," he said, crossing his arms, too. "He wants the milk, he's got to buy the cow."

My gaze narrowed. "Did you just call me a cow? And for your information, I'm not a virgin! I've had sex. More than once!"

Both Vincent and Angelo plugged their ears. Angelo hummed loudly.

"You're both ridiculous!" I scolded them. "I'm an adult. I can do what I want."

Vincent dropped his hands. "And you want to live with that guy? Really?"

"Maybe. It's my decision."

Angelo crossed his arms again. "You'll break Dad's heart."

"Oh, my God." I rubbed my temples, fighting a growing headache. "You're going to pull a guilt trip on me now? For what it's worth, Jax wanted to sit down with you all and talk this out."

"So what?" Vincent scoffed. "We're supposed to give him props?"

"I do," Angelo said unexpectedly. "Takes balls to face a girl's brothers and family and say you want to live with her."

Vincent shook his head, his jaw hard. "If he wants you around that bad, he should put a ring on it."

"Before she knows what she's getting into?"

We all turned to find Jax standing in my bedroom doorway. He was dressed for work, looking dashing in a slate-gray suit, white shirt, and black tie. I realized he must've been on his way when he called me. Despite everything, I got a little thrill from that.

"The security in this place is nonexistent," he pointed out tightly. "Jesus. I just walked right in!"

Vincent raised his fists. "I've got security for you, right here."

I snatched up my phone and my purse, and headed out. If everything was going to implode at home as well as work, I figured I might as well go to work.

"Gia." Jax caught my upper arm as I moved to pass him. "I've got this. Don't stress."

"Easy for you to say," I told him, my chin lifting. "You don't have anything on the line."

His jaw tightened. "I love you. I've got everything on the line."

14

LEI WAS ON the phone when I got to work, pacing in her office while talking into a headset. She waved in greeting and offered a quick smile, which only made me feel worse about my news.

Because she was busy, I went to my desk and started going through my voice mail, taking down messages for Lei and making notes to return calls that had come in for me. Usually being at work soothed me, but I was too edgy. My feet tapped restlessly beneath the table.

"Gianna."

I looked toward Lei's office and found her leaning against the doorjamb. She was dressed in crimson pants and a white silk shell, her black hair pulled back in a simple ponytail. She looked younger than her years, and delicate, but her dark eyes gave her away—Lei could be as delicate as a saber-toothed tiger.

"How's Chad?" she asked.

Standing, I put my hands on the desk to anchor myself. "He's very happy with the Mondego, and the plans, and the progress. He's happy with the choices of David and Inez, too. But…he's not so happy with me."

"Oh?" Her eyes widened. "What happened?"

"Jackson Rutledge. More precisely, the fact that Jax has asked me to move in with him."

"I see." She straightened. "Why don't we talk in my office?"

I followed her, feeling a bit like I was being called into the teacher's office for a lecture.

Beyond the floor-to-ceiling windows of Lei's expansive office, Manhattan was laid out for viewing pleasure and awe. Glittering spires with architecture designed to impress overshadowed buildings that were centuries old. Wooden water towers on matchstick stilts were everywhere, features of the cityscape as distinctive and beloved as any other landmark. Blue rooftop pools and green terrace gardens marked the apartments of the wealthy. Giant cranes reminded you that the city, already teeming with life, was still growing.

The metal-and-glass jungle was a gourmand's paradise. New York was known for its fantastic food and its great chefs, and Lei was a driving force in the world I loved so much. It was a hard blow, feeling as though I was disappointing her.

"A week ago," she began, "you hadn't heard from the man in two years."

"Lei, I'll be honest. I've heard enough from everyone— including myself. I've never felt more pressure to stay away from something in my life. If only people were so helpful when I'm on a diet!"

She leaned against the front of her desk, her hands gripping the edge. She didn't crack a smile at my poor attempt at humor. "Well, I moved in with Ian over time. It wasn't planned. I just spent more and more nights with him until it seemed ridiculous to keep paying rent on my own place."

Lei paused as if she was thinking of how best to say something I might not want to hear. Then she came right out with it. "Just be smarter about it than I was. Have some sort of legal agreement between you, so you're not fighting over petty crap while your heart is breaking."

My hands clenched. "You're so sure it's going to end badly."

"I shouldn't have to point out to you that it took ten years for Ian to backstab me. It took Jackson less than a week to pull a similar move on you. Come on, Gianna. You're not naïve."

"I learn from my mistakes," I said, wishing my voice didn't sound so defensive.

"I'm not saying you shouldn't take the risk. Taking risks is what gets you the greater rewards. I'm just telling you to mitigate those risks. You're talking about a merger here, but you're not considering the most basic of precautions?"

Suddenly, I felt very foolish.

Lei saw that and gentled her voice. "Jackson has already cost you the Mondego project. Don't let him take anything else from you."

The rest of my day went on as usual, but I was miserable the whole time. I was seriously torn between saying goodbye to Jax and saying goodbye to the life I'd built without him in it. The easiest thing was to forget he'd come back at all, but after wishing for something for so long, it was excruciating to let it go now that it was in my grasp.

Shortly before three, my phone rang and I answered it with as much enthusiasm as I could muster.

"Gianna," Chad greeted me, sounding a bit breathless. "Can I talk to Lei?"

My eyes closed, knowing he was going to ask to work with someone else. I'd been hoping the delay between his return to New York and his call meant he'd changed his mind, or at least decided to wait it out a bit more before pulling the trigger. "Let me see if she's free. Hang on."

I got up and walked to the open door of her office. She was working on her computer, her brows drawn together in a frown above her crimson glasses. I knocked lightly.

She looked up at me. "Yes?"

"Chad Williams is on the line for you."

She pulled her glasses off and nodded. "Put him through."

I went back to my desk and routed the call, then tried to focus on something else besides the low murmur of Lei's voice. It was all too easy to think about Jax instead, remembering the way he'd sounded when he last told me he loved me.

He'd consumed me from the moment I first laid eyes on him. I didn't know how to give him up. I also didn't know how to live with him. He wasn't going to integrate into my life easily. I was going to have to change everything to accommodate him.

Why couldn't I have fallen in love with someone simple and easygoing? Someone who brought a little fun into my life instead a whole slew of problems.

"Gianna."

I looked up as Lei stepped out of her office, her lips pursed thoughtfully. "Yes?"

I steeled myself for the blow. When would I ever have the chance again to spearhead a project that had the magnitude of the Mondego deal?

"Chad just got through with a meeting with Jackson Rutledge," she said.

My back stiffened and my stomach roiled. Crap. Was Jax screwing me over again? "Why?"

"Jackson offered to make a three-million-dollar investment in Chad, for a 30 percent share."

My mouth fell open. *"What?"*

What did that mean? Was he trying to steal Chad? How could he, when Chad was under contract with Lei?

Lei frowned. "Basically, Jackson is offering to guarantee that he's not going to sabotage Chad, to the tune of a few million dollars."

I stared at her, trying to process that news.

She shrugged. "Chad's going to have his lawyers look over the paperwork, but he's sending it to me, too. Wants to make sure there's no conflict."

Nodding slowly, I glanced at my drawer, thinking about the smartphone sitting inside it.

"He didn't say anything about wanting to work with anyone else," she added. "There's no reason to, if the offer is legit."

"Right." I said the word, but I was still trying to fully grasp the ramifications of what Jax had done.

"I take it you told Jax about Chad's concerns?"

Pushing slowly to my feet, I nodded. "I didn't know anything about this, though. I swear."

"I can see that on your face." She studied me for a moment longer. "Looks like Jackson's clearing a path to you."

"Yeah." It was crazy. What was the catch?

It was just depressing having to ask myself that question. How could I love him more than anything when I was constantly second-guessing him?

My desk phone rang and I answered, grateful for the distraction from Lei's examining gaze.

"Gia." Jax's voice sent me skidding into deeper turmoil. "We're going to sit down with your family tonight after the restaurant closes. I've got a lot of work to do, so I'll meet you there. A driver will be waiting for you after work and he'll stay with you until it's time to take you to the restaurant. He'll take care of loading up the things you'll bring to the penthouse to get you through 'til the weekend, when we can grab the rest. Let me—"

"Jax. Jesus. Will you *slow down?*" I slumped in my chair, feeling exhausted.

He was quiet for the length of a heartbeat. "It's taken two long years to get here."

"Yeah. Two years of nothing. Not a single word from you. And now, all of a sudden, you're bulldozing your way through my life and I'm feeling wrecked. Wiped out. I can't think. Can't figure out anything."

"What's to figure out?" he shot back, sounding annoyed, which only irritated me further.

I sat up, but lowered my voice, hating to have such a personal conversation at work but unable to hold back. I'd been simmering for hours and was finally boiling over. "What took you so damned long! Why now? Why are you fighting for me *now?*"

"Because you're finally fighting for me!" he snapped. "You were happy with the way things were in Vegas. You wanted that to go on, probably thought we'd do that for a year or two, see where things went. And that wasn't going to happen, Gia. We were living on borrowed time. Too much longer and someone would've caught on, and started hounding and exploiting you while I was thousands of miles away. I let us go on too long as it was."

"You could've talked to me about it!"

"What were you going to do? Leave UNLV? Move to Virginia with me? Were you ready for that then, when you're not now? I don't fucking think so."

"You never gave me the chance!"

"Bullshit. You've had plenty of chances, Gia. I waited for you to decide what we had was worth fighting for. Not a day went by when I didn't hope you'd call or just show up. You never even left me an angry voice mail. You called a few times, sent a few emails, then nothing. You gave up."

"So it was some kind of test?" I snapped, incensed. "You broke my heart to test me?"

"Maybe. And don't think it doesn't piss me off that I had to come back to you to get you to finally say you wanted more."

"You're an asshole!"

"You're goddamned right I am! I never claimed otherwise."

My eyes stung with hot tears and that was the last straw for me. I was at work. I wasn't going to break down at my desk, not when anyone could just walk by and see me crying. "I have to go."

I hung up. Lei had gone back into her office at some point, thank God. I stood for a minute, shaking with anger and hurting. I couldn't believe Jax was blaming me for the time we'd been apart.

Closing my eyes, I took deep breaths and forcibly put it all away. I locked up every emotion I felt and focused on the job at hand.

"Fuck you, Jax," I whispered as I lowered into my chair.

Then I buried myself in work.

A black Mercedes waited for me at the curb after work. I knew it on sight because the driver who waited beside it had that coiled, dangerous look to him, despite the crispness of his black suit. His bearing screamed personal security and his eyes locked on me so fiercely, I felt it even through his mirrored shades.

Had Jax deliberately picked someone who'd intimidate me? Another scare tactic. Another test.

I'd been seeing a lot of new sides to Jackson Rutledge lately. Had I been in love with a mirage this whole time?

The driver gave a brisk nod in greeting and opened the back door. I slid inside and melted into the butter-soft leather seat. Closing my eyes, I longed for home. I wanted to sprawl across my bed and call my friend Lynn in Vegas. She'd been there when I first met Jax and through the weeks that followed. If anyone could help me put things into perspective, it was her.

The engine rumbled to life and the car pulled away from the curb. Knowing we were facing a slow drive due to rush-hour traffic in Manhattan, I went over the past several days in my head, gathering my thoughts so I would be at least partially coherent when I talked to Lynn. I didn't get far before I realized we were descending into an underground parking lot. Opening my eyes and sitting up, I recognized Jax's apartment complex.

"I thought I was going home," I said to the driver.

"I was told to bring you here."

I almost argued, but knew it wasn't the guy's fault. Jax was the one getting on my nerves. And if he wasn't smart enough to let me settle down some before seeing him, he'd get what was coming to him.

One of the valets opened the door for me and I climbed out. The driver led me to the elevator, punched in the penthouse code, then left me to take the ride up myself.

The elevator doors slid open on the penthouse floor, revealing Jax waiting for me in the private foyer. The sight of him hit me hard.

He'd shucked his suit jacket at some point and unbuttoned his vest. His tie was loosened and the top button of his dress shirt was undone, exposing the golden column of his throat. He'd rolled up his sleeves, displaying powerful, veined forearms.

He was dressed like a businessman, yet exuded the potent virility of a man in his prime. Lust shimmered on the edges of my anger and frustration.

"Put your palm on the pad," he ordered, jerking his chin toward the security panel beside his front door.

Clenching my teeth, I walked past him, my heels clicking across the marble. I slammed my hand against the glass and it beeped three times. "Gianna Rossi recognized and saved," a computerized female voice said as the front door swung open.

I stalked into his apartment, tense and ready to fight. I heard him shut the door behind me.

I waited for him to say something, but he just passed me, his stride confident and sexy as hell. He carried himself like a man who liked to fuck and knew he did it well. That subtle sexual arrogance had always turned me on. Mad as I was, I still wasn't immune.

Stopping at the metal-and-glass console in front of the wall of windows, he poured amber liquid from a crystal decanter into a squat tumbler. He took a drink, his back to me.

The silence stretched, weighting the room. I dropped my purse onto one of the black leather armchairs and crossed my arms, studying him, waiting for him. Still he stood there as if he was in the room alone.

Finally, I said, "I thought you had to work late."

"I need to," he said evenly.

"Then why are we here?"

He exhaled harshly. "What was it you said in Atlanta? Something about what we've got is worth dealing with all this crap."

"Don't act like I've got any say or control over what's going here." I crossed my arms. "You're running your own show and I'm just getting dragged along for the ride."

Jax faced me then. "I fix problems, Gia. You know that."

"It's not just that! It's not just about Chad and my family. It's always been this way with us. You say when and how and where and how long. I have no input. No control."

His face tightened. He took a step toward me. "Is that what you think? Christ, Gia, you've got me by the balls!"

"If that's true, that's not what I want. I want us to be a team, Jax. I don't want either of us to feel like we're at the mercy of the other."

He set his glass down on the coffee table as he passed it on his way toward me. "I'm completely at your mercy," he said softly, his eyes so dark they appeared black. "All day I've been feeling like every step I take to get closer to you is only pushing you back. I can feel you pulling away from me…wanting distance. I can't stand it."

"And I've felt like I'm dealing with a stranger. I don't know who you are when you're like this. I can't help wondering if I ever really knew you. And if I didn't, who the hell am I in love with?"

"Baby." He cupped my face in his hands and lowered his lips to mine. He brushed his mouth across mine, from one side to the other. Once, twice. Then his tongue licked across the seam, his breath warm and moist, his taste flavored by the liquor he'd been drinking.

I moaned and tilted my head, trying to deepen the kiss. One of his hands slid around to cup my nape, while the other moved downward to cup my hip. His touch was hot, sending goose bumps racing across my skin. He squeezed gently and my breasts swelled, growing heavy and tender.

Inhaling deeply, I breathed him in. Felt my body stir in response, recognizing Jax as the one thing it desperately wanted and couldn't resist. I reached up and pushed my fingers into the thick silk of his dark hair, drawing him closer.

"You know me, Gia," he whispered against my lips. "You love *me*."

"Jax—" I pressed against him, leaning into all that hard, flexing muscle. "Have we made too many mistakes?"

"Probably." His mouth moved along my jaw and down my throat, suckling softly. "But there's something we've always gotten right."

His arm wrapped around my waist and he rolled his hips, grinding the rigid length of his erection against my belly. My sex clenched, hungry for him.

"We can't stay in bed all the time," I pointed out, remembering the weekends in Vegas when we'd scarcely untangled ourselves from each other.

Jax scooped me up, cradling me as if I weighed nothing. "Two years apart and we're still in love. It's got to be easier when we're together."

"It's not working that way so far." Still, I kicked my shoes off.

He headed toward his bedroom. "Which is why I'm moving on to the part where I remind you why it's all worth it."

15

AN HOUR BEFORE, I would've said the chances of Jax getting laid were nonexistent. Right at that moment, however, with his gorgeous face taut with lust and his eyes soft with something far more tender, I wanted nothing more than to forget everything but the way he could make me feel. I wanted him to remind me of what we'd once had, what I'd clung so tightly to , what I hoped to have again.

He placed me on the bed and came over me, putting one knee on the comforter. He brushed a loose tendril of hair off my cheek, then his gaze drifted downward to where his other hand was gliding up my thigh and beneath the hem of my skirt.

"I want you naked," I told him.

His mouth, that wickedly sexy mouth that could drive me insane, curved in a smug smile. "Do you, now?"

I stretched, knowing it would entice him. When he growled low in his throat, I returned a smug smile of my own.

Catching me behind the knee, he pushed my leg up and to the side, riding my skirt up and exposing my garters and matching panties.

He licked his lips. "Baby…I'm going to love watching you get ready for work every morning."

It struck me then that we would be sharing everyday moments like that moving forward, and I wanted them. I wanted the man I'd had so briefly. "You've still got too many clothes on."

Jax straightened and shrugged out of his vest, letting it drop to the floor. He yanked at the knot of his tie, then pulled the loosened silk down one side to fall to the carpet, as well. When he went to work on the buttons of his shirt, I pushed up onto my elbows to watch.

A low hum of pleasure escaped me.

Jax paused, his brow lifting. There was a gleam in his eye that made my legs shift restlessly. The man knew he was hot as hell, knew how much I liked looking at him.

"Don't stop," I told him.

"I love it when you look at me like that." He freed another button.

I caught my lower lip between my teeth. He'd always been fit and leanly muscular, but he was harder now. More defined. Golden skin stretched over ridges and slabs of muscle. I wanted to run my fingertips over every inch of it...lick him like a favorite dessert...make him feel how much I loved him.

He shrugged off the shirt and I moved, rising up onto my knees to reach for him. He groaned when my hands smoothed over his shoulders then down his biceps, squeezing and caressing.

"How is it possible?" I wondered aloud. "You're more delicious than you were before, and you were a god back then."

"Baby." He sealed his mouth over mine and stole my breath, his tongue licking and gliding.

Greedy, my hands ran all over his chest and abs, tracing every plane and groove. "You're so hard," I breathed, wanting to feel all that warm, silk-covered marble pressed against me.

"The sexual-frustration workout." He caught me by the wrist and pressed my hand against his straining erection, grinding into my palm. "Pushing my body to exhaustion because I couldn't have you, and the wet dreams were killing me."

I cupped him, stroking from root to tip. "Not always frustrated," I muttered, thinking of the women who'd had him, the women who'd had what was mine. "At least on two occasions."

Fisting my ponytail, he pulled my head back to look up at him. "Always," he said fiercely. "You've ruined me for other women, Gia."

"Good." I kissed his shoulder. "You're still dressed."

"You finish it." He tugged the band out of my hair, his fingers sifting through it. My eyelids grew heavy, my senses drugged by the sexual hunger radiating off Jax. The feel of his fingertips kneading my scalp sent bliss radiating through me. Every word he spoke...every move he made...was designed to seduce me.

And it was working.

I fumbled with the hidden closure of his tailored slacks, pushing the halves aside to discover black boxer briefs. His cock was so hard and ready, the wide crown peeking above the waistband. Shiny with precum, it beckoned me, inciting me to push the underwear down below his hips.

A soft, needy sound filled the air between us. Jax was gorgeous everywhere. Gorgeous, big, and hard. Standing there with his slacks undone, his cock shamelessly exposed and mouthwateringly erect, his body ripped and powerful, he was the most erotic thing I'd ever seen.

I wanted him inside me.

He lowered the zipper of my skirt, then went to work on the buttons of my blouse. All the while, his lips were at my throat, his tongue gliding along my fluttering pulse.

"I'm going to lick you up," he promised, his words a whisper of air against my damp skin.

I wrapped my hands around him, finding him hot and wet. He was so aroused he was dribbling precum in a steady stream. His virility was a potent aphrodisiac, making me as hot and wet as he was. My sex was slick with wanting, tightening hungrily, aching to be filled with the thick shaft I was stroking so lovingly.

Lifting my fingers to my mouth, I tasted him, feeling as if I became intoxicated by his rich, heady flavor.

He watched me, cursing softly. His hands tightened on the silk of my blouse and buttons popped off and rolled onto the floor.

"I wanted you naked," he muttered, grabbing me by the waist and flipping me around, folding me facedown over the edge of the bed. "Next time."

Shoving my loosened skirt up my hips, he exposed my ass. He cupped the back of my knee in his hand and pushed my leg up onto the bed, opening me. Then his hands were on the twin curves of my buttocks, squeezing them. His breath gusted hot and quick over my sensitive skin, his teeth scraping and gently biting.

"God, you were made for fucking," he said gruffly. "You were built just to drive me out of my mind."

One finger slid beneath the lace of my thong, running below it from the small of my back to the damp flesh between my legs. His knuckle brushed against my sex, and I quivered, gasping as a tremor shook my core.

The lace snapped in his grip, and I jolted, shocked by the sharp, quick tug against my skin and the harsh sound of the material rending. He blanketed me, his feverishly hot body covering my back, his hands pushing underneath me to cup my swollen breasts. His cock lay hot and thick between the cheeks of my ass, and he thrust, pushing the steely length between them.

The sensation of being overpowered, helpless, had me primed to come. A man so ragingly aroused he was tearing my clothes off had me spread for the taking. Jax's desire was dizzying and irresistible. As much as I loved his body, he loved mine. Maybe more, which seemed impossible, but he always managed to make me feel that way.

"Don't wait," I begged, my hips rocking back against him.

"What do you want, baby?" he crooned, massaging the tight points of my nipples with clever fingers. "Tell me what you need."

I was panting, writhing, teased by the feeling of his heavy sac resting against the wet lips of my sex. "Fuck me, Jax. Fuck me hard."

He nuzzled against my temple. "You want this?"

With a shift of his hips, the broad head of his cock was notched into the clenching opening of my body. Pressure built as the crown pushed inside me, spreading me for the penetration of the hard shaft to follow.

I moaned and squeezed my eyes shut, trembling. He was everywhere. In every breath I sucked in…over every inch of my skin….

"Tight, baby," he ground out between clenched teeth, withdrawing and pushing deeper. Slow, easy thrusts that worked him into me with every lunge. He groaned and gripped my desperately circling hips, holding me down as he fucked his way deeper. "Tight and creamy… Jesus, you feel amazing. I'm going to come so hard for you. I'm going to fill you up with it."

My fingers clawed into the comforter. My eyes opened blindly, my lips parted to suck air into burning lungs. I fought against his hold, wanting him harder, faster. I caught movement in the corner of my eye and saw us reflected in the dressing mirror affixed to the inside of his walk-in closet door.

The clutch of my body tightened, trying to pull him in to where I needed him. Jax's head turned to follow my gaze and he stilled, taking in the sight of him hunched over me, his slacks barely clinging to his upper thighs.

It was a lewd and decadent picture. Me, pinned and still fully clothed, my sex opened and penetrated by his massive cock; and Jax, firm buttocks tight with the force of a thrust, his biceps thick and flexing from the kneading of my breasts, his back glistening with a fine sheen of perspiration.

His mouth curved wickedly. "You like watching me fuck you."

To prove it, he withdrew and thrust again, his entire body tightening as he sank farther into me. I whimpered. My sex sucked greedily at his cock; my nipples tightened painfully against his palms.

"Oh, yeah, you do," he crooned in a darkly seductive voice. "I'm going to mirror the ceiling, Gia baby. You're going to watch me worship this sexy body of yours every day and night. You'll never forget why you're putting up with the world outside our bed. It's going to be seared into your brain. Every time you close your eyes, you'll see me riding you until you can't come any more."

I climaxed. I couldn't stop it. I cried out as the tension finally broke, pleasure arching my spine into a tight bow against his chest.

Jax growled and lost control, fucking me hard and fast, surging deep and erupting with a vicious curse. His teeth sank into my shoulder. He came inside me, chasing my orgasm with ragged groans, his body shaking violently with the force of his ejaculations.

It was too much. I couldn't see, couldn't think. My nails raked across the comforter, instinctively trying to pull me away from the flood of sensation, away from the spurting cock still plunging inside me, making me take more…feel more…when I couldn't possible withstand it.

Jax kept me with him, trapped and possessed, a willing prisoner to the endless need between us.

Jax undressed me, washed his semen away with a warm washcloth, and arranged me on the bed. I was limp and breathless the whole time, and slightly irritated that he could move and think while I was a brainless mess of post-orgasmic endorphins.

"You suck," I told him when he finally sprawled on the bed beside me, gloriously naked.

He propped his head in his hand and grinned, his fingers running lightly down my cleavage to circle my navel. "Guess you missed the ten minutes it took for me to be able to stand up."

"I'm taking you down for the count next time," I grumbled.

"Mmm…" Leaning over me, he pressed his lips to mine. "I'm just happy there's a next time. Lots of next times. You've got two years to make up for."

My eyes narrowed. "I'm not taking the blame. You walked. Whether or not I followed, you're the one who bailed."

"So *I* have two years to make up for." He slid over me, kneeing my thighs open and settling between them. "I better get started."

Reaching up, I brushed his hair back from his forehead. He was even more breathtaking after sex, his face softened and seemingly younger, his eyes bright and his smile boyishly charming. He looked happy and it twisted my heart to think I'd made him that way without even really trying.

Turning his head, he pressed his lips to my palm. "I love you."

"Jax." My eyes stung. "I used to dream about you saying that to me."

"I told you a lot," he confessed, "while you were sleeping."

That hurt worse than thinking he'd never felt that way about me at all. "Will I ever understand why you put us through hell?"

The light in his eyes dimmed. His smile faded. "I'm afraid you will."

Tension gripped his big frame, and I regretted bringing it up. I wrapped my legs around his hips, hugging him close.

"Let's agree not to bring anything but us into our bed," he murmured, running his nose along my cheek. "I want us to have someplace where it's just you and me, a place where we can remember why nothing else really matters but what we've got."

I nodded, my hands stroking up and down his back. Burying my face in his throat, I breathed him in, letting the familiar and beloved scent of his skin ground me in the moment. "I'm game for that. But I'll warn you right now that if you don't start including me, we won't make it as far as this bed to begin with."

His mouth curved against my skin. "You drive a hard bargain, Miss Rossi."

"You're damn right."

His back tightened beneath my hands. He started pushing inside me with a serrated groan.

"In all fairness," he said gutturally, "I can, too."

Drowning in one of Jax's robes, I sipped a glass of wine and watched him slice cold cuts and cheese. His massive Sub-Zero refrigerator was bachelor barren.

"You ever live with a woman before?" I asked him.

"No."

I nodded, admiring him in loose-fitting pajama pants. "Aren't you worried it'll feel like an invasion of your privacy?"

He glanced at me, his dark eyes piercing from beneath the locks of his disheveled hair. "No."

"This place is pretty…sterile. You don't think it might drive you a little nuts to see my shoes kicked off here and there, or my purse on the chair, or—"

"Your panties on the rug because I yanked them off to fuck you?" He straightened. "No, I'm not going to mind. You having second thoughts?"

I took another sip of the crisp Riesling before answering. "I'm just worried that you're thinking about me so much that you're not thinking about how this is going to affect you."

He set the knife down and picked up his own glass. Dangerously casual with those assessing eyes. "What are you afraid of, Gia?"

I thought about the best way to say what was on my mind. "I know you're worried about what we're going to deal with outside this apartment. But I'm more sketchy about what's going to happen right here. It's all fun and games until you start feeling irritated by the day-to-day reality of living with someone."

Jax leaned back against the counter, crossing his ankles and wrapping one arm around his chest. Holding his wineglass aloft, he looked relaxed and at ease, which wasn't the case at all. He'd honed in on me, stripping me bare with that jaded gaze.

"Like the way you splash water everywhere when you're washing your face?" he drawled. "How you leave dishes in the sink because you're still pulling clean ones out of the dishwasher one at a time as you use them? How you've got phone charger cords stuck into outlets in every room, so you don't have to go far to plug the damn thing in? How I'm going to be tripping over those shoes you kick off all over the place?"

I blinked. "Um…yeah."

"Just because I like staring at your ass, babe, doesn't mean I wasn't paying attention to the rest of you while we were together in Vegas." His mouth curved. "That said, if you're really worried about pissing me off, we can establish terms for what you'll do for me when it happens."

Rolling my eyes, I muttered, "You're such a guy."

"You're just now noticing that? Gia, your observation skills need some work."

I had to fight to keep from smiling. "Are we going to eat or what?"

"Are you going to quit worrying?"

"After a while, I hope so." I ran my fingers up and down the stem of my glass. "We've been together six weeks total over the course of our relationship. You wouldn't be asking me to move in under normal circumstances—it's too soon. You can tell me that it's not a big deal to you and you're ready, but I'm going to have to see it to believe it."

"Fair enough." He straightened. "Maybe, under 'normal' circumstances, we would've bounced back and forth between each other's places for a few months, keeping up the pretense that we weren't rushing things along, but we never would've spent a night apart. We don't have that much self-control."

"Maybe," I conceded. "But you're not a guy who likes having his hand forced."

"I had options." Setting his glass on the counter, he rounded the breakfast bar, approaching me with a slow, deliberate pace that made my toes curl. "I could've walked. I could've beefed up the security of your loft, or put you up someplace, or just let you fend for yourself."

He stopped in front of me, tugging the belt of my robe loose and exposing me. He licked his lips, his eyelids becoming weighted with arousal. He set his hands over my knees, pushing my thighs apart. Cool air caressed my sex as his thumbs slid along the inside of my thighs. "I could've taken your offer to be the guy you call when you get lonely for this."

I wrapped my legs around his hips and lured him closer. "Maybe I wouldn't have called."

"Would you be that cruel?" Jax untied the drawstring of his pants and freed his heavy cock. Fisting it, he primed himself for me.

I was riveted, entranced by the sight of his large hand stroking his thickly veined erection. "I would've held off as long as I could."

"I would've sexted you, called you, hounded you…. No way I'd suffer alone." His lips brushed across my forehead and he breathed, "Can you take me again?"

"You really are making up for lost time, aren't you?"

"Can't help what you do to me." He ran the wide crown through the lips of my sex, nudging my clit. "The minute you showed up at that bar in Vegas, I was a dead man walking."

My hands curled around the seat of the bar stool. "Liar. You were trolling. Half a dozen guys painting the town for a bachelor party. You were out to get laid no matter what."

"I was," he concurred, grinning. "So were you."

"Picked up the hottest guy in the bar," I said breathlessly, squirming as he teased me with languid strokes of the velvety head of his erection.

"I scored the hottest girl ever." His tongue licked across my parted lips in a blatantly erotic tease. "You had me so worked up. Embarrassing as hell to be sporting a major hard-on for hours."

"It was impossible to miss." I smiled, remembering the rush. "You're so big."

"You want it?"

I nodded. "Wanted it then, too. Took you home with me, didn't I? Figured I was too easy, but I couldn't resist you."

Jax notched himself into my wet cleft with a low groan. "I would've chased after you for days if that's what it took. I couldn't imagine not having you."

Tightening my legs, I pulled him closer, shivering as he slid inexorably into me. I moaned his name, awed by the vulnerability I felt every time he took me.

"Gia. Baby." He cupped my nape with one hand and gripped my hip with the other, holding me steady as he rolled his hips, urging slick tissues to let him sink deeper. "Feel that? I'm pushing into you but it feels like you're sliding into me. Every fucking time, it's like you're slipping under my skin."

"I want to." My nails dug into his back, my fingers flexing. "I want to own you, Jackson."

"Witch," he bit out between clenched teeth, his jaw tight. "I thought I was going to take you to bed, bang the hell out of your insanely sexy body until sunrise, then head home with a smile. But you chewed me up and wrung me out. I couldn't've crawled out of your bed if I'd wanted to and would've begged to stay if you'd tried to kick me out."

"Ha! Tells me what a player you are." I gasped as he filled me too full, a wild joy spreading through me. "I had no clue. You had me thinking you regularly medaled in marathon fucking."

His gaze was soft on my flushed face. "I was a starving man, baby, living on junk food and scraps, and you were my first real home-cooked meal. I needed you, Gia, and I haven't stopped."

"I need you, too." So much. Too much. Just being in the same room with him made me feel alive.

Cupping my ass, he lifted me and carried me to the couch. He spread me out, never leaving me, rising above me like a golden god.

"Don't forget that," he said hoarsely. Shaky fingertips brushed my hair away from my forehead. "When things get rough, don't forget I need you."

I saw the worry in his eyes, the worry he told me not to feel, and my heart twisted in my chest. Then he started moving inside me, riding me with strong smooth thrusts, and I let him sweep me away.

16

"THERE'S SOMETHING WRONG with your view, man," Nico said, as he set a box of my stuff onto the breakfast bar and headed toward the windows. "Too much sky, and you can't spy on your neighbors."

"I've got all the view I need right here," Jax shot back, catching me around the waist as I entered his apartment—*our* apartment—behind my brother.

"Gag," Vincent muttered, walking through the open front door, carrying my suitcase and a duffel bag. "Where do you want this?"

"You can just put it down," I told him, squirming as Jax nibbled at my neck. It was a gorgeous Saturday afternoon, perfect for being out in the city. Moving didn't qualify, but I wasn't complaining. And neither was my family, which I considered a minor miracle.

Jackson Rutledge could sell sand in a desert. He never once said we were heading to a lifetime commitment, yet he'd managed to convey an earnest and passionate desire to be with me when we sat down with my family after Rossi's closed on Thursday night. I think we both understood that my family heard wedding bells, but he didn't seem pressured by that expectation. For my part, I was working hard not to get my hopes up.

Lei had wished me well at work on Friday when I told her what was happening, but she'd been notably subdued. That was hard for me, because I'd come to seek and depend on her approval.

"Looks like I arrived right on time."

I felt Jax stiffen at the sound of his father's voice. His hold on me loosened and he straightened, freeing me to turn around and face Parker Rutledge.

"I brought beer," he said, holding up a twelve-pack. His smile was wide, his face startling in its resemblance to his son's. He thrust his hand out to Vincent and introduced himself, then glanced at me. "There she is, the woman who's got my son smiling nonstop lately. It's good to see you again, Gianna."

"Hello, Mr. Rutledge."

"Parker, please." He ripped open the top of the twelve-pack and handed a beer to Vincent, then stepped down into the living room to shake hands with Nico. "Saw the other Rossi downstairs in the lobby. Sounded like he was making a bet with the doorman."

I shot a look at Jax and saw his face had hardened into an inscrutable mask, his attention on his father, watching as Parker passed a beer to my older brother.

"Let's plan for all of us to get together sometime this coming week," Parker said, taking in everyone with a sweeping glance. "Your parents, too, of course. And my wife, Regina."

"The Rossis are as busy as we are," Jax said tightly. "Possibly more so."

"I'm sure they are. American entrepreneurship at its finest." Parker set the case of beer down on the coffee table and pulled one out for himself. "But surely we can work something out. Family is family, after all."

Nico's dark, thoughtful gaze met mine. He shrugged. "Sure. Why not?"

Jax holed up in his home office after everyone left, leaving me to put my stuff away wherever I wanted. We didn't talk about it, but I was pretty sure he'd had different plans for our Saturday before his dad showed up. It tripped me out how Parker Rutledge blew into a room like a ray of sunshine and his son turned instantly arctic.

What *was* the story there? Why was it that every time his dad popped into our lives, it automatically put a wedge between us?

I was unpacked within an hour, leaving me hanging around an unfamiliar place with nothing to do. I debated watching TV, then decided to surf online for movie showtimes and dinner reservations. I was damned if Parker was going to ruin my first weekend living with Jax.

Dropping onto the couch, I propped my bare feet up on the coffee table and set my laptop on my knees. I'd scarcely typed in my password when Jax appeared.

"Hey," I greeted him. My smile faded when I saw the tightness around his eyes and mouth. "Everything all right?"

"Sure. Why?"

"Your hair's a sexy mess." The dark locks were wild, as if he'd been shoving his hands into them to release inner tension, something I would have been happy to do for him.

Giving me a sheepish look, Jax ran a hand over his hair to smooth it. "I was just thinking—you up for one of those mind-numbingly boring affairs I warned you about?"

"I'm up for anything that puts you in a tuxedo."

His mouth softened into a wry smile. "All right, then."

I snapped my laptop closed and set it on the coffee table. "I'll need to go shopping, though. When is it?"

"Tonight."

My brows rose. "You couldn't give me more warning?"

"Just found out about it," he said grimly. "We can have a stylist come here with some choices for you."

"Seriously? How important is this thing you're asking me to?"

He leaned into the wall in what might have seemed like a casual pose if he wasn't so edgy. I could almost see the agitation radiating from him. "I'm outing you as my girl. But before you get it into your head that I want you looking any particular way, let me tell you that I'd take you out just the way you are right now."

Pushing to my feet, I glanced down at my basic white ribbed tank top and tan capris. "Shut up."

"Baby, that killer body of yours makes everything sexy." He crossed his arms, settling in. "I just don't want you running all over town."

"I can find something off the rack, unless you have a problem with that."

"Takes all the fun out of it for me. We bring someone here, I get to watch you dress and undress. We hit the stores, they'll kick me out of the dressing rooms."

My lips twitched with a repressed smile. "Pervert."

"Guilty as charged."

"You do this sort of thing often?" I asked as casually as I could manage. It hadn't escaped me that most guys wouldn't have a stylist on call for their girlfriends.

"Get kicked out of dressing rooms? Not as a rule, no."

I told myself to drop it. "Well, that's a good thing. Anyway…I'll just head out for a couple hours, let you work."

"And stew all afternoon over whether or not I play dress-up with all the chicks I fuck?" he asked, straightening.

"I don't want to talk about your sexual conquests." I grabbed my purse off the armchair and looked around for my flats.

"You just want to be mad at me for stuff you're making up in your head."

I glared at him. "Don't pick a fight with me just because you've got issues with your dad."

"This has nothing to do with him."

"Really? Because I get the impression damn near everything in your life has something to do with him."

"Not you," he said quietly. Dangerously. He closed the distance between us. "Stop changing the subject and spit it out, Gia."

"It doesn't matter, Jax. I knew you were a player when I met you. I'll get over it."

"I had my moments," he agreed. "They never included giving a damn about how the women I nailed felt about anything, let alone the clothes they were wearing."

My chin lifted. "Why are you always so quick to make yourself sound like a class A prick?"

He shrugged. "Just calling 'em like I see 'em."

"No, you're trying to paint a picture of yourself that has nothing to do with reality. You can't keep telling me that I know you, while insisting that you're really an asshole." I dropped my purse back down. "It's like you're trying to convince you and me both that you're something you're not."

"More like reminding us both of what I am," he stopped in front of me, "what I've got inside me just waiting to come out."

"I think your dad reminds you of that."

"You're fixated on my father."

"Just calling 'em like I see 'em," I shot back.

Jax stared down at me for a long minute, his body tense and the air between us strained. "What you're *not* seeing is that he and I have a lot more in common than just our faces."

"So, let's talk about it."

"I don't want to talk about it."

"You just want to fight."

He reached up and rubbed the back of his neck, his biceps stretching the sleeve of his T-shirt. He growled. "What I want is to fuck you bowlegged."

"Jax." I laughed, I couldn't help it. His frustration was palpable and his response to it was so typically…*male*. "You're lucky I grew up with three brothers, you know. I'm used to chest thumping."

"And driving me insane."

"You're doing that all by yourself, what with your self-confessed multiple personality disorder." I touched a finger to my jaw. "Wait. I get it. You're a twin. There's two of you!"

Closing his eyes, he rubbed his temples with his fingertips. "Jesus."

"If I sleep with both of you, does that count as cheating?"

His hands dropped and he looked at me. "Are you in love with both of them?"

I reached out and touched his chest. "I'm in love with you." With a sigh, Jax hugged me and pressed his lips to my shoulder. "Image is everything in politics. Sometimes, I'm asked to help others with theirs. That's why I know a few stylists."

I pushed my hands up beneath his shirt to touch his bare skin. His soft shiver and low moan sent my heartbeat skipping. "Good to know."

I wanted to know more, but for the first time in our relationship we had time to let things grow and develop. I gave myself the right to enjoy that.

* * *

There were a handful of things in life that made me catch my breath in wonder—Jax in a tuxedo topped the list.

I watched him cross the ballroom with a champagne flute in each hand, his stride fiercely elegant and unmistakably sexual. The D.C. hotel was filled with men and women who were political and financial scions wielding tremendous power. Enormous crystal chandeliers cast light that glittered off priceless jewels and glossy, perfectly coiffed locks. Crystal glasses clinked against each other, and the hum of conversation sounded like a swarm of bees.

In the midst of it all, Jackson Rutledge stood out from the crowd.

His hair was nearly as dark as his tuxedo, his skin lightly tanned, his eyes framed by arrogantly slashed brows. The beautifully tailored tux hugged his broad shoulders and emphasized the length of his legs.

Discreetly, I licked my lips. *Mine.*

Jax would've caught my eye no matter what, but it was the look in his eyes that set my heart racing.

"I still love that dress," he said, handing me a flute and bending to kiss my shoulder.

My lips curved against the mouth of the glass. The muted gold gown had been the first one I'd tried on and he'd voted for it on sight, shaking his head at the three dresses I had tried on after it. A smooth column of lined silk poured down my body, held in place by thin beaded straps at my shoulders and back. I'd been wary of the color at first, but the gown did a splendid job of hinting at my curves, instead of hugging them.

"Thank you."

He turned to face the room, his hand coming to rest on my hip in a blatantly possessive display of ownership. "In a couple of hours we can fly back to New York. Or we can grab a room here in the hotel."

"Or join the mile-high club. After all, what's the point of taking a private jet if we don't get naughty in it?"

His fingers flexed into my flesh. "And once again, I have an erection in public. Thank you very much."

I laughed and leaned into him. "What do you need to do here?"

"Not sure." He took a drink. "Once Parker shows up, I'll have an idea."

"He relies on you a lot, doesn't he?"

Jax shrugged, but I saw the tightness around his mouth again. It was soon echoed by a corresponding tautness to his big frame, and when I followed his gaze, I saw why. Parker and Regina Rutledge had arrived. The two stood near the entrance to the ballroom, surrounded by those who wanted to rub shoulders with a Rutledge. There were several of them in attendance, but Parker was the wizard behind the curtain whom everyone wanted to see.

He looked over at Jax and me, smiling when he caught my eye and then glancing at Jax. A silent bit of communication passed between them.

"Gimme a second, babe," Jax murmured, then he walked away, striding easily through a crowd that parted for him.

I watched him until he reached his father, studying both men for body language.

"Well, you cleaned up nicely," a familiar voice said beside me.

Turning my head, I looked at Allison Rutledge, formerly Allison Kelsey. I raked her with a glance, noting the changes. I'd barely seen her the night I escorted Ian, so I took the opportunity. She was thinner than she had been in Vegas and she'd been slender then. Polished and perfect in a brittle way, she appeared to have hardened and grown more jaded. There was a world-weariness in her eyes that echoed what I occasionally saw in Jax.

But she was still as beautiful as ever, with dark hair cut into a sleek bob that framed delicate features and big blue eyes. Her aqua-hued gown was a lovely contrast to her porcelain skin.

"Hello, Allison," I said, turning my attention back to the two darkly handsome Rutledge men across the room.

"That's a beautiful dress." She examined me. "Gretchen must be partial to it. She suggested it to me, as well, but it's not my style."

I took another sip of champagne to hide how I felt at the unexpected mention of the stylist's name. So, Gretchen was an ace in the hole for the entire Rutledge family. Nice to know. "You might be surprised to hear that it wasn't my first choice, either."

Her smile was anything but friendly. "You're smart to let Jackson dress you. But then you're obviously smarter than I gave you credit for, or you wouldn't be here."

"Can you go be a bitch somewhere else?" I said, waving my hand carelessly. "This is my space and you need to see your way out of it."

"If I remember correctly, you're not a woman who likes pretense and bullshit, so I'm not shoveling any your way. We have to get along, after all. Might as well start now."

"We don't have to do anything." My gaze flicked over to her. "I suggest we do our best to avoid one another."

Her brows rose as if she were surprised, then she laughed, the sound as melodious as her voice. "That's not how this works, Gianna. You and I are going to be best friends, as far as public knowledge goes. We'll have lunch and shop together. Ted and I will have dinner with you and Jackson. We'll go to ball games and exhibitions. All sorts of things where we'll smile at the camera and look tighter than sisters."

"You've had too much champagne."

"I'll let Jackson explain it to you." Her eyes were suspiciously bright, which got my back up.

"Explain what?" Regina Rutledge asked, joining us.

"Ted's upcoming mayoral bid. Jackson's outdone himself this time."

My hand tightened around the stem of my glass, alarm bells ringing.

Regina's mouth curved, but her voice came cold and sharp. "I think you should leave Gianna to Jackson. He's very protective."

"I get the hint." Allison looked at me. "I'll plan for us to have dinner in the city soon. Enjoy yourself, Gianna. And again, you look stunning. That dress was made for you."

She glided off and I rubbed my nose with my middle finger, discreetly flipping her off before dismissing her and looking away. Parker still had Jax at his side, his hand resting on his son's shoulder as they spoke to a white-haired gentleman whose face was vaguely familiar.

"Don't pay her any mind," Regina said, stepping into my line of sight.

Her blond hair skimmed her shoulders in stylized waves that were reminiscent of the heydays of Hollywood starlets. "She's jealous. She has a Rutledge, but…" She lifted one shoulder in a careless shrug. "Ted isn't Jackson or Parker."

I silently agreed with that. "It's nice seeing you again," I said instead.

Her mouth curved. "You and I are lucky women. Trust me, Jackson's stamina won't fade with time."

My brows lifted. Even though Regina was nearer to my age than her husband's, she was still Jax's stepmother. It felt weird talking to her about sex with our men.

Jax appeared in front of me, taking my flute and passing it to Regina. His dark eyes hot on my face, he caught my hand and pulled me into him. "Dance with me."

He led me onto the dance floor, his arms coming around me. "You're the most beautiful woman here."

"Flattery will get you everywhere." It was heady being in Jax's arms in public, nearly as heady as being held by him in private. "I have to say, though, that I'd rather not work with stylists who are also working with Allison. I don't like her, Jax."

His fingers stroked over my back. "She's not one of my favorite people, either, but she's married to Ted. She's family."

"I'm done with her treating me like I'm the scratching post for her claws."

"She can be a raging bitch," he agreed, "but she has those claws for a reason. You'll need them, too, Gia."

I treated him to a sulky stare. "I know you think I'm not strong enough to deal with your life, and I'm going to prove you wrong. That said, I am *not* going to go out of my way to spend time with people who give me grief."

"So, the part about us acting as a team…that only applies to things you choose?"

"That's not fair! I would never ask you to just suffer quietly while people insult you. I respect you more than that!"

A muscle ticked in his jaw. "It's not about respect, Gia. I shouldn't have to tell you that I'm going to talk to Allison about how she approaches you—that should be obvious. But whether we like her or not, we've all got to work together."

"I don't have to do anything for her."

"Then do it for me," he snapped. "This is my life. I was very clear about how unpleasant some parts of it may be for you."

I was startled by his vehemence. "You don't like this any more than I do. I *know* you don't. You don't want to be here, at this party. It'd be different if you were asking me to hang in there because of something that's really important to you, but that's not the case!"

"I made my bed, Gia," he said tightly, his face hard and remote. "And you made the decision to lie in it with me."

I shook my head, trying to reconcile the Jax in front of me with the one I'd first met. That Jax had been fun-loving, larger than life, a hedonist in many ways. "I don't understand you. Life is short, Jax. Why spend time doing things that don't make you happy?"

"Doing you makes me very happy."

I shoved at his shoulder. "Be serious. This is important. I really need to know."

He didn't answer me for a minute, long enough for one song to end and another to begin. I felt a change move through him, the quickening of his breath and a tightening of his hold on me. "The time for me to make a different choice came and went a long time ago."

"That's a cop-out. You're not even thirty. Your whole life is ahead of you and nothing is behind you that you can't fix."

Jax looked over my shoulder, his gaze distant and unfocused, as if he were seeing something I couldn't. "Sometimes you can't go back," he muttered. "You just have to face the consequences and own your mistakes."

"You don't have to keep making new ones." I cupped his cheek, returning his attention back to me. "We're starting over, Jax. We've got a second chance to get it right. Let's not waste energy on people and situations that just drag us down."

He heaved out his breath, then pressed a quick hard kiss to my forehead. "Let's get out of here."

17

"YOU LOOK FANTASTIC," my best friend, Lynn, said, checking me out. "I haven't seen you look this good since Vegas."

"Considering that was a couple years ago, I'm not feeling too hot about that compliment." I was teasing her and she knew it, just as I knew I *was* looking pretty good lately.

Three weeks of living with Jax had led to me dropping about five pounds—the honeymoon diet without the honeymoon. Jax was insatiable and I was eating better because of it. There was a greater incentive to make smart food choices when you knew someone was going to be seeing you naked every day.

She laughed and glanced around Rossi's. "This place looks great, too."

Business at both Rossi's locations was brisk, due in part to media mentions of Jax and me. Because I'd made an effort to avoid hearing anything about Jax while we were apart, I hadn't realized just how often his name made the news. He'd said the gossip blogs and social media hounds would love me, but he hadn't mentioned how much they loved him. The public wanted him in office. He was young, gorgeous, a Rutledge, and he had just enough ruthlessness to put him on the right side of edgy.

"The eye candy is delicious as always," Lynn went on, her attention drifting to Vincent, who was working the bar.

He looked up, caught her eye, and winked.

"Be still my heart," she said, tucking a stray lock of her red hair behind her ear and blowing him a kiss.

I groaned. "He's got a big-enough head already."

"Wouldn't I like to find out?"

"Eww." I rolled my eyes. I'd suggested we meet at Rossi's because I wanted to relax without worrying about someone snapping a picture of me. I'd gotten used to having a bodyguard around all the time, but at Rossi's I had the added eyes of my family watching out for invasions of my privacy.

She shot me a sympathetic look. "Is it really bad?"

"It's not terrible. I'm not a celebrity or anything. But there always seems to be one or two photographers lurking around."

"Stalker rat bastards."

I shrugged, having accepted them as part of my life. Whenever I got irritated, I reminded myself that Jax had broken both our hearts to protect me from the attention. If I'd learned anything over the past three weeks, it was how happy being with Jax could make me. I couldn't remember ever being happier. "I just have to be careful, that's all."

Twisting on her bar stool, she faced me, her long legs kicking playfully. Dressed in a long floral maxi and jean jacket, with a ton of bracelets and necklaces that she made—and sold—herself, she rocked bohemian elegance. "How is Jackson, anyway? I mean, on an ordinary day. He seems so...intense in interviews."

"He is. But he can also be playful. And funny. He makes me laugh every day."

She grinned. "Look at that smile on your face. Almost makes up for his conservative politics."

I rolled my eyes, not wanting to get into a discussion about Lynn's liberal views. I left that to my dad, who loved to talk to her about their similar stances on issues. "That's not to say he can't be stubborn, irrational, frustrating—"

"A man."

"Yeah."

"So...speaking of politics."

"We weren't," I said firmly.

She gave me a toothy grin. "*I* was. You manage to get the tribe all together in one place yet?"

"Not yet." My feet tapped on the brass foot rail. "Shooting for a brunch this Saturday. It's the only time we could get everyone together."

"God. You're going to have to give me all the details. Wish I could listen in. That's going to be a hell of a brunch."

She wasn't wrong. In most ways, the Rossis and Rutledges were two different breeds of family.

I took a bite of a crostini, then glanced at my smartphone as it buzzed on the bar. The text message from Jax made me smile. **Bring home lasagna.**

Lynn glanced at it, too. "Girl, don't tell me the romance is over already."

My phone vibrated again. **I've got the gelato to lick off your body….**

She laughed and I laughed with her.

"I need a boyfriend." Her gaze slid over to where Vincent was shaking up a drink. "Or a booty call."

I distracted her from my heartbreaker of a brother. "How's work?"

"Busy." She played with her long necklaces. "Internet sales are really picking up. If my rent and taxes keep going up, too, I may close the store and just focus on the online business."

"Really? But you love that store!" I knew how hard Lynn had worked to open it, and how much she'd wanted to prove that her jewelry making and pottery weren't just worthless hobbies.

She shrugged, but I could see it bothered her. "Wouldn't be so bad to set my own hours and have more time to come up with new concepts. I could also travel to more conventions and shows, which might be better for me."

I wanted to keep her thinking positively. "I could use more of your business cards. I wore your amethyst earrings to a party last week and got a ton of compliments on them."

"Yeah?" She brightened. "That's great. Thank you."

I gestured for Vincent to refill our beers, while Lynn pulled some business cards out of her behemoth of a purse.

"How's work going for you?" she asked when she handed them over.

"Good."

"You still love it?"

"I do, yes." I smiled at Vincent as he set two fresh, full glasses in front of us and took the others away.

"What aren't you telling me?"

I shot my best friend a narrowed glance. She was too perceptive. "Nothing."

"And your boss is totally okay with you and Jackson?" she prodded.

Sighing, I picked up another crostini. "We don't talk about it. Which is okay, because she's my boss and not my friend, but still…."

"You think she's got a problem with it?"

"I'd say she's taking it pretty well, considering I'm living with the guy who is doing business with the man who screwed her over. She still trusts me with sensitive information. But there's…something between us that wasn't there before." And that bothered me. A lot.

"What are you going to do?"

"What can I do?" I chewed and swallowed, chasing the toast down with a swig of beer. "I figure she's waiting to see how it all shakes out. After enough time passes, maybe she'll feel better about the whole thing."

Lynn wrinkled her nose. "Have you talked to Jackson? "

"Can't. He's a fixer. He'll want to step in and smooth things over, and that might make things even more uncomfortable."

"That's probably the best endorsement you could've made for him in my eyes. Every gal wants their best friend to end up with a guy willing to slay their dragons." She winked. "And lick gelato off them."

Laughing, I turned my head and glanced around the packed restaurant. Walk-in patrons waited in the foyer by reception, while tables were turned with brisk efficiency thanks to my dad's insistence on a robust service staff. Families mixed with couples and groups, while a popular television star enjoyed the illusion of anonymity at her favorite table. A camera flash caught my eye, luring my attention to what looked to be a birthday party. Above the din of conversation and the clattering of silverware, an Italian tenor sang about love and loss through the speaker system.

Contentment slid through me, as it always did when I was at Rossi's.

"Did hell just freeze over?" Lynn asked, bringing my gaze back to her.

"Huh?"

She gestured with a jerk of her chin and I followed. Blinking, I took in the sight of my dad standing beside Ted Rutledge, who had his arm tossed across his shoulders. Ted was dressed in a suit and tie, while my father wore his usual white chef's coat, black pants, and red Rossi's apron. Giovanni Rossi remained a striking man, with a full head of salt and pepper hair, and a strong jaw. A photographer snapped their photo.

"Hard to tell from here," she said. "Is that a campaign button on his shirt?"

I looked at my dad first, then at Ted. Sure enough, Ted had something pinned to his jacket.

"Second time he's been in here this week," Vincent said behind me.

When I looked at my brother, I saw the muscle ticcing in his jaw.

"I didn't know anything about this," I told him.

"Yeah?" His brown eyes were hard. "Can Jackson say that?"

Lynn took off around eight, but I decided to stay and wait until closing, so I could talk to my dad. I also decided to head back to the loft with Angelo and Vincent.

Because I didn't want to get into it with Jax when I was tired and cranky, I sent a text letting him know I wasn't coming home, and then dropped my phone back into my purse. I sipped at a glass of anisette decorated with a lemon twist. After seeing my dad with Ted, a liqueur was calming.

I felt Jax enter the restaurant before I saw him. I'd always been attuned to him, but it had gotten more intense since we started living together.

"Gia." His hands slid possessively over my hips, his warmth radiating into my back.

I glanced at Vincent, who was scowling at us, and spoke over my shoulder to Jax. "What are you doing here?"

"Picking you up." His arms encircled my waist. "You didn't really think I was going to let you spend the night somewhere else?"

I finished my drink. "I didn't realize I was a prisoner."

He stiffened at my tone, then whispered, "If we're going to fight, we'll do it at home."

"I don't want to fight, which is why I wasn't coming home."

Jax stepped back. "Let's go."

"You're not listening."

Spinning me around in my seat, he bent over me. "You haven't said anything yet worth listening to."

"Excuse me?" I glared at him, trying to ignore how sexy he looked in a black V-neck sweater and loose-fitting jeans.

He set his hands on the bar on either side me, caging me in. "I'm not leaving you here to drink and stew over whatever's got you pissed off, and I sure as hell am not sleeping alone."

"Back off, Jackson," Vincent ordered, coming up to us.

Jax's head snapped up. "You're her brother and you're watching out for her, I respect that. But she's my girl and I love her, and you need to respect that. Don't stick your nose in our business."

"She doesn't want to go, she doesn't have to go."

"Don't talk around me like I'm not here!" I said crossly, shooting both of them a warning look. "I don't appreciate Rutledges coming in here and yanking my family and me around. You said you wanted to protect us from the public eye, not drag us out in front of it!"

I saw when Jax understood what had me riled. Then his face closed off and gave nothing away. "And you're welcome to hash it out with me—at home."

"It's late and I have to work tomorrow. Plus, I want to talk to my dad about this Ted thing, whatever it is. Obviously I don't know because no one saw fit to tell me."

"*I've* talked to your dad about this," he said, sounding so condescendingly reasonable he made my teeth grit. "And I don't want to hear about it being late when you're sitting here drinking."

"News flash, Jackson: I'm old enough to drink a glass of liqueur. And anything else I feel like drinking."

"Are you mature enough?"

"What the fuck does that mean?"

He reached down and grabbed my purse from the hook beneath the bar. "Getting drunk isn't helping anybody."

"I'm not getting drunk!"

"Good." He gave me a tight smile. "Then you've got no reason to stay."

"Jax—"

"We should both stop talking now." He leaned down until we were at eye level. "There is no scenario where I walk out of here without you."

"Gianna," Vincent said. "You want me to deal with this?"

"I've got it." I slid off the bar stool, suddenly very much in the mood to fight. At least if Jax was dealing with just me, it would be somewhat fair. If my brothers got into it with him, fists would start flying. "I'll call you later."

Jax jerked his chin at Vincent in a silent goodbye, then set his hand at my elbow to lead me out. He dismissed the bodyguard who'd been hovering by the entrance, then steered me into the cool night air toward a sleek, sexy car waiting in a no-parking zone.

I checked the vehicle out while Jax opened the passenger door for me. It wasn't the kind of car a person rented. It was, however, the kind of car that suited Jax perfectly.

That impression was solidified when he got behind the wheel and the engine roared to life, then pulled away from the curb with crisp agility and a powerful purr.

Jax didn't say anything further on the ride back to the penthouse, allowing the tension between us to thicken and grow hotter. He handled the expensive sports car with commanding ease, completely relaxed amid the chaos of Manhattan streets and aggressive, swerving cabbies.

It wasn't until we got into the elevator at our apartment building that I broke the silence, unable to bear the weight of his stare. "What did you talk to my dad about?"

"Having Rossi's featured as a thriving and expanding small business."

"Featured in what? "

"Various materials."

I crossed my arms. "Political materials?"

He arched one of his brows. "What else? "

"Why didn't you tell me?"

"Because we don't talk about work—yours or mine."

The elevator doors opened and he gestured me out ahead of him. I cleared us through the security system and entered the penthouse.

"I think we need to straighten something out." I tossed my purse on the armchair. "My understanding is that your work is in finance."

"And you work with Lei Yeung," he countered, shutting the door behind us. "Doesn't stop you from getting into your family business, does it?"

I rounded on him. "I would never have a conversation with your dad without telling you!"

"You can't say that yet." He pulled his sweater off, revealing the gorgeous chiseled bare torso I couldn't help eyeing. "And why aren't you equally pissed at your dad for not saying anything?"

He had a point, which irritated me. I hated how I suddenly felt like I was being irrational. "What are you doing?"

He headed for the hallway. "Getting ready for bed."

"I'm too pissed to sleep with you!"

"Sweetheart," he tossed over his shoulder, "I feel the same way."

I kicked off my heels and went after him, following him into the bedroom. He toed off his shoes and shucked his jeans, magnificently naked in an instant.

He'd been commando beneath those jeans.

My brain scrambled for a minute, then I fought back by getting naked, too. "I don't want my family being used."

"I don't want my girlfriend making assumptions about my motives." Jax yanked the covers back and slid into bed.

"You're the one who keeps telling me that your family can't be trusted!"

He settled against the headboard. "But you didn't get mad at my family, did you?

You got mad at me. And instead of asking me about it, you decided to drink and close ranks."

"I wouldn't have to ask you about it if you told me in advance." I headed into the bathroom. "But whatever. You're always right, aren't you, Jax?"

"Seems to me I'm always in the wrong," he muttered after me.

I turned on the shower and scrubbed my makeup off while the water heated. When I stepped into the stall, I took my time, dragging out the shower as long as I could in the hopes that Jax would fall asleep and stop talking.

Closing my eyes, I stood beneath the spray. Jax was a man who cowed other dominant men with a single glance. He talked around others, refused to cede any ground whatsoever, and he was a painfully sharp strategist. I respected all those things about him. I was attracted to and aroused by his self-command. But I really hated how he could retreat behind that rigid control and put me on the outside; shutting me out and dealing with me like an opponent.

I couldn't imagine living the rest of my life being treated that way.

"Am I going to have to drag you out of there, too?" Jax said, opening the floating glass door and standing amid the steam that surged eagerly around his bared body.

"Go away," I told him wearily, shutting off the taps. "I'm sleeping in the guest room tonight."

His jaw tightened. His chest expanded on a deep, slow breath. "I…" He paused. "I'm sorry."

Nodding, I pushed him back and stepped around him. "Thank you for that. I'm sorry, too. We both handled this badly."

I shrugged into the terry-cloth robe hanging on a hook, then wrapped my hair up in a turban to wring it dry. "Goodnight, Jax."

He followed me through the bedroom, grabbing me by the elbow when I approached the door to the hallway. "Don't be like this. I said I'm sorry and I meant it."

Stopping, I looked at him. "I know you did, and I meant it, too. But it doesn't fix a fundamental problem we're having with the way we communicate. We don't talk about family. We don't talk about work. We hang out together and fuck, which makes us more friends with benefits than anything, doesn't it?"

He pulled me closer, stepping into me at the same time so that he was pressed up against me. "I love you, Gia. More than I've ever loved anything. You know that."

I sighed. "And I love you enough that I couldn't get over you, even after I thought you'd dumped me like trash. But that means you can hurt me real bad, Jax. I'm having a hard time living on the periphery of your life. And if being with you hurts worse than being without you, I've got to decide what's the best thing for me to do."

"You're the center of my life." His hands went to my shoulders. "There isn't a moment that goes by when I'm not thinking about you."

"That may be true, but you've got a unique ability to cut me off, and I'm not sure I can live with that."

"You're cutting me off now," he accused. "You cut me off earlier tonight."

"So once again, we're both handling this badly. Maybe that's a sign. Listen, I've got to get some sleep. We can talk about this tomorrow. Okay?"

He cupped my nape. "Sleep with me. I'll keep my hands to myself if that's what you want."

I ached to do what he asked, but I also worried that we'd just be putting a Band-Aid on something that needed a lot more work. "I want to sleep in the guest room."

I pulled away and left the room, feeling his eyes on my back as he stepped out into the hallway after me. Surprisingly, I fell asleep quickly, despite having damp hair and a painfully tight chest.

Sometime during the night, I felt Jax slip into the bed with me. I rolled to my side, hugged my pillow, and went back to sleep.

18

IT WAS A relief to arrive at work the next day.

I woke up next to a brooding and uncommunicative Jax. The rest of our shared morning had been thick with tension. On the walk to the subway, I texted my dad, asking him to call me when he could, then I scrolled through my email. Adrenaline surged through me when I saw Deanna's name. I'd nearly forgotten about the favor I had asked of her. Once reminded, I couldn't help but hope for news.

"Please have something for me," I muttered to myself as I arrived at my station and hurried up the steps to reach the street. I was damned near desperate to have something—*anything*— that would give me insight into the man I loved.

Unfortunately, her email only read to call her, and I reached Deanna's voice mail when I tried. I didn't hear back from her before I reached Savor, where I had to silence my smartphone and tuck it away.

"Good morning," I greeted Lei when she arrived.

"Good morning." She tilted her head to the side. "Everything all right?"

I blinked, startled by the question. "Everything's great."

She hesitated, then said, "Come into my office."

I followed her, taking a deep breath in preparation for whatever might be coming my way.

Lei bypassed her desk and settled into one of the gray club chairs in the seating area, looking younger with her hair hanging straight and loose, even with the wicked cool streak of silver. She waited until I took the matching chair before beginning. "Things have been…strained between us the last few weeks. I really regret that."

The tension left my shoulders. "I do, too."

"I'm concerned for you…and I have my reservations about Jackson…but really—" she swiveled her chair to face me directly "—the problem is with me. I'm projecting my own experience onto you."

"You mean Ian."

Her red mouth curved without humor. "It must be obvious that I loved him. He was my whole world. If you'd asked me then, I would have told you that he'd never betray me. That he didn't have it in him. I would've told you he loved me too much to do anything like that."

"What happened?" I had never broached the subject before, but now that she'd opened the door, I was dying to know what had helped shaped my boss into the woman she was today.

"We were working on a deal. The negotiations had been tough, but I had the advantage and Ian let me run with it." A thoughtful wrinkle appeared on her otherwise smooth forehead. "Unfortunately, sometimes I get so focused on the hunt itself that I forget to pay attention to my prey."

She looked out the windows at the Manhattan skyline. "I was too confident and I pushed for too much without giving enough in return. Worse, I made the man on the other side of the negotiating table feel insignificant and powerless. Somewhere along the way, he decided he'd do anything to put me in my place."

"What place?"

"*Behind* Ian, instead of beside him. I think Bruce was insulted that Ian had him doing business with me. I don't think he ever saw me as Ian's partner, just Ian's piece of ass, so that's what he used against us."

"How?"

"He kept setting up recurring meetings with me, telling me he needed clarification on different points or wanted to discuss alternatives. We met in the restaurants of the hotels he was staying in at the time, just as you and I did with the Williams twins at the Four Seasons. It wasn't until later that I understood he'd been creating a paper trail to prove he and I had been having an affair."

"Oh, Lei." I felt a little of her remembered suffering; her tone of voice carried so much pain. "What did you do?"

"Nothing, and maybe that was the wrong choice. Ian is prone to jealousy, so he's especially vulnerable in that regard. I refused to confirm or deny his accusations because I was so hurt that he'd given them any credence at all. I told him to figure it out for himself, and apparently I was tried and convicted."

"Jeez. I'm sorry."

She shrugged off my sympathy, but gave me a rueful smile. "It's been over a long time now."

I drummed my fingers on the armrests of my chair as I warred with myself about discussing Jax with someone who didn't trust him. I valued Lei's opinion, but it wasn't objective when it came to Jackson Rutledge.

In the end, though, I told her *because* of her bias. I wanted an extreme, worst-case-scenario opinion.

Lei sat forward as I spoke, and by the time I finished, she'd set her elbows on her knees and her chin on her hands. "So he's withholding information from you. People keep secrets for two main reasons—to protect themselves or to protect someone else. Do you have any thoughts about which direction Jackson is moving in?"

"I'm not sure. With everything else we've faced, I could see him trying to…shield me from something. But this… I can't help feeling like he didn't want me to know my family was being used to further a Rutledge agenda."

"If that's the case, it probably won't be the last time. How do you feel about that?"

"Pissed. How can he say he loves me, and then do things that I have a problem with?"

"That's a question you have to ask him. Sooner rather than later."

Lei had just reaffirmed what I already knew, but it was still valuable to have my position confirmed.

Now I just had to prepare myself for what I'd do once I got the answer.

When my lunch break rolled around, I checked my smartphone and saw I'd missed a callback from Deanna. I headed to one of Savor's conference rooms for privacy, passing LaConnie, who was arranging a new display of branded spices and seasonings on the shelf behind her reception desk.

She waved as I passed, and I complimented her on the kick-ass red pantsuit she was wearing.

I was smiling when I entered the same conference room where I'd taken Jax when he visited Savor. That memory helped alleviate some of the nervous anticipation I felt when I dialed Deanna's number.

"Gianna," she greeted me. "Glad we got past the game of phone tag."

"Me, too. How are you?"

"Excellent. Hang on. Let me move somewhere more quiet." A moment later, the background noise of multiple people talking at once disappeared. "So I looked into the Rutledges, focusing on Leslie Rutledge as you suggested. You've got great instincts—I hit a gold mine with that one."

"Oh?" A shiver of unease slid down my spine.

"The family had her committed to a sanitarium for a few months. It was after she was released that she disappeared from public view. There were some rumors back then, nothing concrete, but now I've got a reliable source."

My gut twisted. I started pacing.

"I can't confirm what kind of mental illness she had," Deanna went on, "but the real story here is that she was expendable. She had a problem and they packed her up, out of sight."

"You don't know that!" I thought of the photos of Leslie in Jax's living room. He hadn't forgotten her.

"Uh, yeah. I do. Just a minute." The receiver was muffled, then, "Anyway. More details will emerge after the story breaks. They always do."

I straightened, panicked. "What do you mean 'after the story breaks'?"

"It's news and about to be public knowledge."

"That wasn't the deal!"

"What deal?" Deanna shot back. "We didn't have one beyond you paying me for my time, which I won't be collecting on because this is going to pay off in other ways."

"You can't run this story!" I hissed, circling the conference table with angry strides.

"It's already done, Gianna. Your name isn't mentioned, so don't worry about that. Listen, I've got to go. I just wanted to give you a head's up and say thanks. Take care, all right?"

She hung up and my smartphone disconnected before I'd even lowered the phone from my ear.

* * *

I left the conference room in a rage, so pissed I could hardly see straight. I was as furious with myself as I was with Deanna. How could I not have foreseen the possibility that she'd use the information she found?

"Your man knows how to treat you right," LaConnie said as I passed her again. "I just set another delivery on your desk."

Cringing inwardly, I felt the weight of guilt on my shoulders. The sight of pure white lilies next to my phone damn near closed off my throat.

I plucked off the attached card.

I'm waving the white flag of surrender.
I love you, baby. We'll talk tonight.

Jax had signed the card, but his signature blurred amid my anxious tears.

Worse than the violation of his privacy, I feared that such personal revelations about his mother would hurt him deeply. Her pictures in the living room of our home told me he had cared for her, but his reluctance to talk about her suggested the topic was painful.

And now the world would know about her, and I was directly to blame.

I touched a velvet-soft petal. "We've screwed up something perfect," I said softly.

Sinking into my chair, I started to plan how best to tell him what I'd done.

I had a good handle on how I wanted to open the subject of Deanna's story when the elevators on the penthouse floor opened and I stepped out into chaos.

I paused, shocked. The front door was open and through it I could see a dozen people in suits, pacing in my living room with smartphones pressed to their ears.

The queasiness I'd felt all day worsened until I thought I might be sick right there in the foyer.

When I crossed the threshold into the apartment, I looked for Jax. I couldn't find him, but Parker was there in front of the entertainment center, his gaze on the photos of his late wife. He would have stood out from the melee on sheer presence, but unmoving amid the frenetic swarm of visitors, he riveted me.

He turned his head toward me. I watched as the recognition of my presence set in. He started toward me.

"What's going on?" I asked, although I feared I already knew the answer.

"We're trying to put out a fire. I'm sorry we've taken over, but Jackson prefers to handle some issues from his home office."

"Is there anything I can do?"

His mouth, so like Jax's, twisted wryly. "I could use a drink. Something strong, preferably."

"Okay." I looked around him to the console by the window where crystal decanters held the world's finest liquors. I frowned when I saw only a vase of flowers atop it. "I'll get you something."

"Thanks. I'll put your purse in your bedroom," he offered, holding out his hand for it.

As he set off down the hallway, I maneuvered through the men and women wandering around the sunken living room. Bits and pieces of conversations washed over me.

"...confirm the source..."

"...should consider possible defamation and slander liabilities..."

"...a declaration of war against the Rutledge family isn't wise..."

My hands were shaking when I opened the doors of the console. The crystal decanters were tucked neatly inside, but they were empty. I made my way back to the kitchen, where I discovered an empty wine fridge.

Confused, I faced Parker when he returned. "Looks like we're out of everything."

"I couldn't find anything, either."

"I'm sorry. I'll call the concierge. Is there anything in particular you'd like?"

He touched my arm. "I'll take care of it. Why don't you hole up in your room and get out of this mess?"

"I feel like I should help somehow."

"Just take care of my son," he murmured. "Leave this to me."

My mouth opened to say something, but nothing came out. I didn't know what to say. I ended up nodding and heading down the hallway, passing my room and going to Jax's home office instead. He was alone in there, standing in front of the window with his arms crossed as he barked at someone through a headset.

"We need those records. Yes, I understand that and I don't give a shit.... Don't think whatever this is won't blow back on you, too. Right. I'll be at this number." He tapped the earpiece, then pivoted abruptly, stilling when he saw me standing in front of his desk. "Gia..."

He fell silent. Shoving a hand through his hair, he cursed softly. He looked worn and edgy. He'd ditched his jacket and tossed it over a chair in the corner. His vest was unbuttoned, as was the button at the throat of his shirt. His tie was loosened and the shadow of evening stubble on his tight jaw gave him a dangerous appeal.

"Hi," I said quietly.

"Baby." He sighed. "I'm sorry about this. Something's come up and we've got to get a handle on it."

"What is it?"

"We got a tip today about an article that's supposedly going out tomorrow, and I'm trying to get details about the reporter and her piece."

I swallowed hard. "Deanna Johnson."

Jax froze. "You know her?"

"She used to date Vincent."

"Fuck." He scowled. "I need all of her contact info—email, mobile and home numbers, address."

"All right." I stepped closer. "Jax, we have to talk."

"I know, and we will. But I can't right now."

"This is my fault."

He came to me and pressed a kiss to my forehead. "No. I should've talked to you about Ted and—"

His smartphone started ringing on his desk.

"I have to get this." He tapped his earpiece. "Rutledge," he answered briskly, then, "That's a start. How quickly can you get them to me?"

He turned his back to me, and I clenched my fists. I left the room to fetch my smartphone to get the information he'd asked for. I was just going to have to blurt it out before he cut me off. I hated to blindside him like that, but he needed to know.

With my cell in hand, I headed back to his office and closed the door behind me. He was off the phone and sitting at his desk, reading something on his monitor.

"I have the information you wanted." I walked up to him. "Deanna's written an article about your mother. About how the family had her committed to an institution."

His head snapped back as if I'd hit him physically. "You talked to her?"

I swallowed past the painful lump in my throat. "Weeks ago. And again this afternoon. I'm so sorry, Jax. I should never have contacted her. I had no idea…"

He stared at me, unblinking, his body so still I knew I'd knocked his legs right out from under him. "Sit down," he ordered, with dangerous softness. "And tell me what the fuck you're talking about."

I practically fell into the seat in front of his desk, my knees shaking from the way he looked at me. His dark eyes were like a shark's, hard and lifeless. "Remember when I said I was going to do some research and—"

"You went to a goddamned reporter?" He surged to his feet and slapped his palms down hard on his desktop. "Are you *insane?*"

"I contacted Deanna as a friend. *Before* you talked to me about never having privacy again!"

"Do you realize what you've done? How much damage this might cause? My mother's disease was *never* supposed to become fodder for the fucking media!"

"Jax…" I stood, then flinched when he shoved away from his desk so violently he knocked his desk chair over. "I know this is terribly personal—and painful—but a lot of families are impacted by mental illness. People are going to understand and—"

"She wasn't crazy, Gia," he said coldly. "She was a drunk."

The venom in his voice took me aback.

He faced the window. "She couldn't handle the pressure."

That single statement told me so much. My eyes burned as memories coalesced in my mind and were refracted back with a clarity I'd lacked before. "Alcoholism is an illness, Jax. You said it yourself."

"She was weak." His arms crossed. "She married the wrong man for what she wanted."

"They loved each other. That's what you told me before."

He shrugged. "Parker is trying to change the world. She would've preferred him to just change the light bulb or a channel on the television."

"She didn't like politics?"

"She didn't like the life that goes with them." Jax faced me. "Agendas require allies and allies require compromises. She didn't like some of the compromises that had to be made. Alcohol was liquid courage for her. She used it as a crutch."

I deflated into my chair, overloaded by the emotional highs and lows I'd bounced between all day. I wanted nothing more than to crawl into bed with Jax and hold him, but I knew he'd never let me help. That stung.

"Jax… When you said someone you loved had been torn up by the stress, you were talking about her, weren't you?"

He flinched, and I finally felt like I had a shot at understanding him. I certainly understood why he'd been such an ass about the drink I'd had at Rossi's…and why there was suddenly no alcohol in the apartment. If he thought the situation with Ted and my dad was enough to drive me to drink, he'd worry about how future—more stressful—incidences would affect me. And I couldn't forget that we'd met in a bar…

"She was a lot like you," he said in a tone that wasn't complimentary at all. "Her family…her expectations of what a relationship with my dad would be like. She thought that being politically aware and active was a choice, instead of a responsibility."

I felt the need to defend Leslie Rutledge, a woman I would never meet but still sympathized with. It wasn't easy living with the rules Jax set but didn't always share. "If she was kept in the dark like me, I don't blame her for not being on the same page with the rest of you."

"My dad told her everything, that was his mistake. He wanted her approval, but all he did was alienate her. Sometimes the end justifies the means, and the means can be ugly."

I took a shaky breath. "You're so angry with her."

"I have a right to be! She tried to make me choose between her vision and my father's. No one should be forced into that position, least of all a teenager." He rolled his shoulders back. "I can't get into this with you now. I've got to do…something. Damage control. If that's even possible."

"What can I do?"

Closing his eyes, he bowed his head. The defeat in his posture broke my heart, but his next words cut me wide open. "You should go stay with your brothers tonight. And pack a couple days' worth of clothes."

Pain made me lash out in self-defense. "Did you cut your mom off like this, too? Is that how you deal with the people who love you when they inconvenience you?"

"For all of her faults," he bit out between clenched teeth, "she never sabotaged us!"

"That's not fair! I made a mistake, Jax, and I can't begin to tell you how sorry I am. But I made it because I love you, not because I wanted to hurt you."

He opened his eyes. "This whole relationship has been a mistake."

The flat finality in his voice sent ice coursing through my veins. "You know what, Jackson Rutledge? Fuck you.

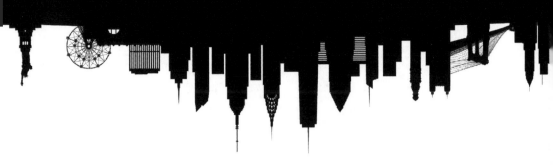

19

"I GET WHY you did it," Nico said, "but I'd be seriously pissed if a chick I was seeing sicced some investigator after me."

My brother's voice and the background sound of a busy evening at Rossi's anchored my nerves.

"We're not seeing each other," I argued, staring at the half-packed suitcase waiting at my side, reminding me that things were in a precarious place with Jax and me. "We live together."

"That's worse. You have to ask a woman outside of your relationship for news about the guy you're shacked up with? That's some whack shit, Gianna. I'm gonna ask you again: is this really the way you want to be living?"

I scowled at him through the phone. "No, of course not."

"Then get the fuck out of there and hook up with a decent guy who gives you what you want."

"I tried that. It didn't happen for me."

He snorted. "Try harder."

"Can you stop being so negative for a minute and help me find a way out of this mess? Why is it that guys are always trying to problem solve when we just want to vent? Then, when we do want solutions, they've got nothin'?"

"The solution to being with the wrong guy is to leave. There. Solved."

I growled. "I'm thinking the problem is Deanna."

"I never liked that bitch," Nico said, startling me. He didn't often speak in a derogatory way about women—our mother had raised my brothers to be gentlemen. "Vincent never liked her much either. He just put up with her because she was crazy in bed. Liked some kink and bondage."

"Eww." I shook my head. "TMI, Nico. Seriously. And it's kinda uncool that you guys are sharing that level of detail with each other. Whatever happened to privacy?"

"Hey, I didn't ask to see those photos she was sexting to him. Told him to take it into his room. Anyway, he should've warned you about her. She'd told him once that she started her career by sleeping with prominent *married* men, and then using pillow talk and extortion, if necessary, to get leads out of them."

I stared at the closed bedroom door, frozen by a flash of an idea.

"So…" my brother went on, "should I head up there this weekend and help you move your stuff out?"

"Not yet." I stood and walked to the bag where I kept my laptop. "Let me call you back."

"If I can't answer, I'll call *you* back."

With half my focus on something else, I still couldn't miss how wonderful Nico was. I had a lot of blessings in my life, but my brothers definitely topped the list. "*Ti amo, fratello.*"

"Love you, too."

Shoving my phone into my pocket, I grabbed my laptop out of its carrying case and sat on the bench at the foot of the bed. I surfed to the cloud and sent up a silent prayer asking for Vincent not to have changed his password since he'd given it to me once months ago.

He hadn't.

I had a hard moment of indecision, weighing my options. Either way, someone I loved was going to get hurt.

In the end, the public nature of Deanna's threat won out.

I got into Vincent's account, clicked on the photo album that synced with his phone, and immediately wanted to scour my eyeballs. There were some things a girl just didn't want to think about her brothers knowing. Or doing.

I downloaded all the racy photos of Deanna—wondering why Vincent had kept them after their breakup—and then I sent her a text telling her to call me ASAP for info she'd want to hear.

With shaking hands, I started unpacking. Jax didn't believe I was strong enough to share his life and it was up to me to prove him wrong. I could do that. I *would* do that. And then he wouldn't feel like he had to hide things from me because I couldn't handle it.

I heard Jax's voice outside the door, growing louder as he approached. "I get it, Dad, but I'm going after Gianna now—"

The door opened and Jax strode in, pausing midstep when he caught sight of me. Parker was fast on his heels, but he stopped when he saw me, his mouth closing before he said whatever he'd been about to say.

With a nod of acknowledgment, Parker caught the doorknob and pulled the door shut. Jax locked the door.

My smartphone started ringing. Deanna's name appeared on the screen. Holding Jax's gaze, I answered with a curt "Gianna Rossi."

"What's up?" Deanna asked, sounding distracted and impatient.

"Hello to you, too, Deanna."

Jax's gaze narrowed.

I took a deep breath, knowing I needed to pull off the bluff of my life. "I'll make this quick—either you kill the Rutledge story or I post X-rated pictures of you on every revenge porn site known to man."

Jax's nostrils flared on a sharply indrawn breath.

"Bullshit," Deanna hissed.

"Is it?" I asked. "You want to take that chance?"

"Those photos are private property!"

"*You're* throwing privacy in *my* face?"

"Two totally different things, Gianna! The Rutledge family gave up any expectation of privacy when they decided to take a stab at controlling this country."

"You're taking it too far."

"And you're not? There are laws against revenge porn. You post those pictures, and it'll come back on you *and* the Rutledges. *You'll* be the enemy then."

"There are laws against extortion, too," I said tightly, "but that didn't stop you. There are ways of finding out who you're squeezing for information, just as there are ways to hide how those pictures of you make it online."

My lies were spinning into a clusterfuck, but I couldn't stop.

She sucked in her breath. "I don't know what you think you've got on me—"

"I've got enough." My hand fisted around my phone. "Kill the story, Deanna, or I kill your reputation—your choice."

"I can't pull the story! It's too late."

"That's too bad for you." I hung up.

Jax stared at me. "What are you doing?"

"Not sure. I'm winging it." My phone rang again and I answered.

"How can you do this?" Deanna's voice was laced with panic. "One woman to another, how can you?"

I couldn't ask myself that same question, because I'd back off if I did. I had sent Jax suggestive pictures before. Nothing as extreme as Deanna's, but still…I'd be mortified if any of them ever got out. "Give me another choice."

"This isn't your business! Jackson Rutledge is a big boy. Let him fight his own battles."

"I would, if I weren't responsible for this mess to begin with."

Jax started toward me.

Deanna groaned. "You're going to take me to the mat for a guy who won't tell you jack about himself? Do you think he'd care if the situation were reversed? He'd distance himself so quick your head would spin. Don't think he wouldn't!"

She'd picked the wrong time to throw that scenario at me, because the look in Jax's eyes at that moment was fierce with love. Right then, I was pretty sure he'd do anything for me.

"This conversation is over," I told her, needing to end it before I wavered. Yes, she was an opportunistic bitch, but what I'd threatened to do didn't put me on higher ground. "You know the deal."

I hung up a split second before Jax grabbed me and crushed me so close I could hardly breathe.

"Jesus, Gia." His lips pressed hard against my temple. "I wasn't expecting you to— I didn't want— *Fuck.*"

I hugged him back, holding on tight. He was right; I hadn't fought for him the first time we broke up. I wasn't going to make that mistake twice. "We'll get through this. Right?"

There was a plea in my voice. I hated hearing it, but I had a knot in my stomach that wouldn't quit. I had a horrible feeling that the worst was still ahead of us.

Jax leaned his head against me, his entire body heavy with weariness. "I'm sorry, baby. I was pissed off at everything and everyone *except you,* but you were the easy target. I was an ass."

"I'm sorry, too. I don't know what I was thinking when I asked her for help."

"This life… It's an adjustment. I'll have to teach you how to deal with it." His lips brushed my cheek. "I should've talked to you. When you needed answers, I should've been the one to give them to you."

"Next time," I said, praying for it to be that easy. Eventually, we'd run out of mistakes to make. I had to believe that.

A sigh left me. What we'd had in Vegas…it'd seemed so clear. So true. Now everything was murky, clouded by our family ties. I grieved a little for the innocence our relationship had lost along the way.

But mourning what we'd lost didn't stop me from appreciating what we still had. When I was in Jax's arms, I felt like I was right where I was supposed to be. The only other thing that came close to giving me that feeling of homecoming was Rossi's.

I knew what it felt like to lose it. Now I had to learn what it would take to keep it.

Pulling back, Jax looked at me, his hands gliding up and down my back. "I was coming after you. If you'd left, I would have been bringing you home now."

I nuzzled into his touch, wanting to comfort him and wanting comfort in return. I could feel the strain in his body, the tension pulled tight and ready to snap. "I might've made you work for it."

His hands lifted to my neck, his fingers kneading into the knotted muscles. I moaned, melting under his expert touch.

He lowered his head, and his voice came deep and low. "I'll work for it now."

Even though I saw the kiss coming, it still knocked me out. The seal of Jax's mouth over mine was tight and greedy, laced with a wildness I hadn't tasted since we'd been together in Vegas. His tongue stroked fast and hard into my mouth, licking deep with devastating sexuality. The message was clear before he spoke.

"I want you," he said softly, tracing my lips with the tip of his tongue. "There are a dozen people on the other side of these walls and I don't care. I can't be quiet when I'm fucking you…they'll hear me when I come inside you. They'll see it on my face when I step outside. I couldn't care less. If I'm not buried deep in you within the next ten minutes, I'm going to lose my mind."

"Jax." My phone started ringing. I switched it to silent mode and dropped it, not caring where it landed. Then I fisted Jax's hair in my hands, holding him in place as I ate at his mouth.

I loved kissing him. The feel of his lips, so firm yet soft. The rough sounds of pleasure he made. How ravenous he was for me. He made me feel like he couldn't live without me.

He caught one of my wrists and dragged my hand down to his erection, wrapping my fingers around him. He was hard as stone and deliciously thick. Then he pulled my hand up to his chest and pressed it flat over his pounding heart. "Gia…"

I lost it.

We tore at each other's clothing, yanking off buttons and ripping through delicate threads. I was desperate to get at him, my lips and teeth catching every inch of golden skin that they could reach, my hands pulling and tugging at every scrap of material that got in my way.

In a distant part of my mind I heard my phone vibrating, but I didn't care. Neither did Jax. With everything on fire around us, we focused only on each other.

He urged me back until I tumbled onto the bed, shrugging off his ruined shirt before following me down. His skin was hot to the touch, burning me even through my bra and slacks. Kissing me deeply, he cupped one of my breasts in his hand, kneading covetously before shoving the lace cup aside to touch my bare skin.

I gasped into his mouth, my nipple hardening against his palm. I fumbled with the hidden button of his tailored pants, growling when he settled on me and trapped my hands.

"You first," he muttered. Clever fingers circled my nipple and rolled it, sending delight arrowing to my core.

The next moment, that mouth I adored was on my breast, wet heat surrounding my tender nipple. His tongue lashed at the hardened tip, his cheeks hollowing on a drawing pull. His hand was between my legs, rubbing my aching cleft through my slacks, teasing me by grinding the length of his erection against my thigh.

His scent and heat surrounded me, his hands and mouth moved all over me. I wanted some control, but he was too fast, sliding lower before I could catch him.

His gaze snared mine as he tugged my slacks and panties down my legs.

Sitting up, I pulled off my blouse and unhooked my bra. My phone was vibrating nonstop, setting a driving urgent pace. Jax rolled to his back and opened his fly, lifting his hips to shove his pants and boxer briefs out of the way. He came at me like that, too impatient to strip all the way.

I spread for him, lifted my arms to him, and cried out his name when he pinned my hips down and shoved half his cock inside me.

Lowering his head, he groaned in my ear. "Let me in, baby."

Wriggling, panting, I pulled at him. My nails dug into the rigid muscles of his back, my calves tightened on his thighs. I grew wetter by the moment, turned on by the helpless way his hips swiveled, his body mindlessly seeking a deeper connection to mine. I could've used more foreplay, but I was quickly catching up, my sex clutching at him in rhythmic pulses.

"That's it," he gasped, pulling back an inch and thrusting again. "Take my cock."

I moaned when he slid deeper, my hips fighting his hold, needing to arch upward.

Suddenly, he was gone, leaving me aching and empty. Then his mouth was there between my legs, licking, circling my clit, and fluttering over the throbbing bundle of nerves. My hands fisted in the sheets, my back arching. I went from not quite ready to orgasm so quickly the climax took me by surprise.

Heat spread over my skin like a fever. Shivers of pleasure wracked my body. I sucked in air, squirming away from the delicious torment of Jax's talented tongue. He gripped my thighs in both hands, holding me down, making me take the rapid-fire shallow plunges. It was a wicked tease that left me desperate for the steely length of his cock.

The moment he moved to slide over me again, I wrapped my legs around him and twisted, taking him beneath me. He lay sprawled magnificently, golden and hot and wild-eyed. Sweat glistened on the hard ridges of his abdomen and heat burnished his cheekbones. His sinner's mouth was wet from me and red from our kisses.

God, he was crazy sexy. And the way his hands gripped my hips as he pulled me over him made me insane with the need to ride him. To take what I needed. To own him.

I caught him in my hand and positioned him, holding his erection upright so I could slide over him. He was so damn hard, my mouth watered. I looked at the long, thick penis in my grip and licked my lips, wanting to taste him.

"Later," he growled, lifting his hips to notch the wide head in place. Goose bumps swept over my skin at how hot he was. He was burning up, and taking me into the fire with him.

He yanked me down and I moaned, so wet and ready from the miracle of his mouth that I took him to the root in one easy glide. His neck arched, his back bowing upward from the bed with a pleasured hiss released from between clenched teeth.

"*Gia.*"

My throat burned. Knowing I gave him what he needed… seeing it level him… nothing else affected me the same way.

Jax jackknifed up in a ripple of honed muscle and buried his face in my throat. "I love you."

"Jax…" I pushed my fingers into his hair, cupping the back of his head to hold him close.

"I want to take off with you," he muttered. "Go away and tell everyone else to go to hell."

I tightened around him. "For how long?"

His teeth sank gently into the skin of my throat. "Forever."

"Okay." I rose onto my knees, letting him slide from me. "Let's go."

The next moment I was on my back and Jax loomed, his mouth curving in a dangerously sexy smile. "Let's finish what we've started first."

"I don't ever want to be finished," I told him softly.

He cupped the sides of my face and held my gaze. He swallowed, and it seemed like he was going to speak. Then, he lowered his head and kissed me, telling me without words instead.

Sitting cross-legged on the bed, I watched Jax get dressed. He was quiet, his thoughts clearly taking him far from me.

"Jax."

"Hmm?" He glanced at me and the blankness in his eyes slowly sharpened into full awareness. His fingers paused in the act of buttoning his shirt. "You okay?"

As rushed as he'd been to get inside me, once he had, he'd slowed way down. He'd made love to me. Slowly. Sweetly. As if he, too, wanted to remember how things used to be between us.

I turned the question back on him. "Are you?"

His chest lifted, then fell. "Yeah. I've got to take care of some things, but I know what needs to be done. You, however, are out of it. Okay? No more, Gia. I'm not going to let you—"

A shout from the living room interrupted him. The tone was angry and caught his attention and mine, until it became recognizable.

I stiffened. Anxiety set my heart racing. I slid from the bed to get dressed. "It's my brother."

A quick glance at the clock told me it was the busiest shift of the night for Rossi's. My nerves frayed. There was no good reason why Vincent would abandon the restaurant to make the trip to Jax's.

Jax shoved the tail of his shirt into his pants. "I'll take care of it."

"No. This is my problem."

"The hell it is." He slipped into his oxfords and strode toward the door. "You've dealt with enough today."

"Jackson—" The latch clicked shut behind him, leaving me scrambling to make myself presentable.

Vincent shouted again, sounding angrier than before. To be quick, I pulled on a pair of yoga pants and a sports top. I made it out to the living room in time to see everyone clearing out. Jax stood by the couch rubbing his jaw, while Vincent stood on the last step leading down into the sunken living room, his hands clenched at his sides. He was dressed for work in a Rossi's T-shirt, his handsome face set in harsh lines.

"Vincent."

He rounded on me. "You wanna tell me why I'm getting crazy calls from Deanna at work?"

I crossed my arms, shielding my heart from the coldness in his gaze. In all of my life, none of my brothers had ever looked at me that way. "Did she tell you what she's been up to?"

"She's a reporter, Gianna. Writing news pieces is what she does."

"Is that the bull she fed you? What she's doing is wrong."

"And *you're* right?" he shot back, taking a step toward me, which had Jax stepping forward, too. Vincent's head whipped toward him. "Back off, Rutledge. You put her up to this!"

Jax nodded grimly. "I did."

My mouth fell open. "That's a lie! He had nothing to do with it."

"The fuck he didn't!" my brother said curtly. "You would never have done something like this if it weren't for him. How did you know about the pictures?"

There was no way I was bringing Nico into this. "I have the password for your cloud account."

He stared at me as if he'd never seen me before. "And you used it? How long have you been invading my privacy?"

"Just tonight."

"I don't believe you."

That cut me deep and hurt. Badly. "It's true."

"You could've called me. I could've tried talking to her. You didn't have to—"

"It wouldn't have worked," I told him flatly. "I would never have threatened her if there'd been another choice."

"So you went with abusing my trust and putting me in the middle without giving me a heads-up? You cut me out, Gianna, instead of coming to me for help. That's not the way our family works and you know it." He jerked his chin at Jax. "That's the way *he* handles dirt, not you."

"There wasn't enough time, Vincent!" I argued, hating myself for the pain I saw on his face. Something precious had been destroyed and seeing the loss was breaking me into little pieces. "I was going to tell you."

"Too late." He faced Jax. "Congratulations, douchebag. You ruined the perfect girl." He stalked toward the door.

"Vincent. Wait!" I rushed after him, frantic to mend the first real rift I'd ever had with one of my brothers. I'd never been so scared. My heart was beating so fast I felt lightheaded.

Jax darted in front of me, grabbing me by the shoulders and holding me in place. "Let me deal with this."

I opened my mouth to argue, then noted the spreading bruise on his jaw. Shock froze my feet in place. "He *hit* you? "

"Don't leave," he said, as if I hadn't spoken, his attention going to the door when it slammed shut behind my brother. "Understand? Wait for me to come back."

He went after Vincent.

And almost two weeks later, I found myself still waiting for him to come home.

20

"HE'S JUST BEING stubborn." Angelo shook his head and took a long drink of his soda. "You know how Vincent gets."

"He misses you," Denise agreed, shoving a cluster of French fries into a pool of ketchup. "Try calling him again."

"He hangs up as soon as he hears my voice." I slid my chair closer to the table so that a woman could squeeze by behind me. The diner near my work was packed and we'd been lucky to snag seats.

"But thanks to caller ID," Denise said, "he knows it's you before he answers. He could just let it go to voice mail if he really didn't want to talk."

I picked at the bun of my hot dog, struggling with a lack of appetite. I'd been on the outs with Vincent for nearly two weeks, and the Rossis had finally decided enough was enough. My mother had called the day before, and Nico had followed up that night. Angelo and Denise hit me up at work to meet them for lunch. I half expected my dad to show up for dinner.

"Gianna." Denise set her hand over mine. "Come by the loft and see him. Work this out. You're both miserable."

"Better yet," Angelo caught my eye, "move back in. You shouldn't be living alone in Jackson's apartment."

That was the only upside to fighting with Vincent: it'd given me a reason to stay in the penthouse even though Jax had been staying away.

"Is Jackson still calling you?" Denise asked, dunking more fries.

I nodded. "Every night."

He'd tell me he missed me. He was working hard and didn't want to bring it home. But he didn't say more than that, leaving me in an odd place. Had we broken up and he just couldn't say it? Was he calling just to see if I'd moved out so he could move back in?

That wouldn't explain why he spoke to me like a lover who was away on business.

Angelo's lips tightened. "I know you don't want to hear it, but this is for the best, Gianna. He was changing you into something you're not. It was never going to work out."

At night, when I was lying in bed alone, my thoughts followed the same path to the same conclusion. Deanna's story had never materialized, but whatever she'd said or done to get the story pulled at the last minute got her fired. I had a hard time living with that.

"I love him," I said. "As much as you love Denise. You might be surprised what you'd do if someone was threatening to spread her personal business all over the place."

"No, I wouldn't be. I get that part of what you did. But Jackson's world is different and you know it. It's not the life for you," Angelo insisted, looking for a moment like our father did when he was breaking hard news to us.

I spent the rest of the afternoon at work thinking about what I needed to do to get my personal life back on track. Professionally, things were rolling along smoothly. Chad was comfortable with me again and working well with Inez and David. The design of the launch restaurant had been decided and construction was well under way. Lei stayed on top of things, but didn't smother me. I still went in to work grateful every day and I shared that gratitude with Jax. The wariness I'd once felt about discussing my work with him was gone. I trusted him to want good things for me.

It was weird in a way. The mess with Deanna had made some parts of our relationship feel stronger than ever and yet we were apart again. I couldn't figure that out.

I headed to Rossi's after work. My family was right; it was time to fix things with Vincent.

He was working happy hour at the bar when I came in, but he spotted me straight away, scowling for a moment before returning his attention to the drink he was mixing. His serving style wasn't the same as Nico's. He didn't flirt shamelessly, but he got the same number of girls following him with their eyes everywhere he went. The dark and broody thing worked for him.

I snagged an empty barstool and watched him work. There were a few contenders trying their hand at capturing his attention, but he was eyeing me, I knew, even though he didn't spare me another glance. The same couldn't be said about our parents, who couldn't stop looking our way every few minutes.

When Vincent neared to serve a beer to the guy sitting on my right, I broke the ice and said, "I'm sorry."

He sucked in a deep breath and straightened his spine. Then he grabbed the five spot tip off the bar, rapped his knuckles on the polished wood in thanks, and dropped the cash in the tip jar. "I'm taking ten," he told Jen, the gal working the bar with him.

"Got it," she said, giving me a smile.

Vincent met me on the other side. "Office," he said, gesturing me ahead of him with an impatient wave of his hand.

It was impossible not to be reminded of Jax when I entered the back office, but I pushed the memory from my mind and faced my brother.

I got to the point. "I need you to forgive me."

He crossed his arms. "I did that a while ago."

"You did?" I blinked through the rush of relief that had me leaning heavily against our dad's desk. "Then why won't you talk to me?"

"To punish you. Plus, I don't want to hear any excuses about what you did. If being with Jax means losing who you are, you need to get out."

"He didn't have anything to do with how I handled Deanna. I don't know why he told you that."

"Because he knows he did." Vincent held up a hand to cut me off. "I'm walking out of here if you don't understand this real quick: you dealt with the situation like a Rutledge, not a Rossi, and you learned how to be like that from him."

I let that sink in. Then I took a second to glance at the family portrait on the wall, before finally nodding my agreement. "You're right."

"Of course I'm right." He ran a hand over the top of his head, then made a sudden grab for me, enfolding me in a hug.

I started bawling. I hadn't expected it, hadn't even known it was bottled up in me until I was wrapped in love and safety again.

Vincent cursed and gripped me tighter. I knew he hated tears and had a hard time dealing with crying women, but I couldn't stop and it felt so good to let go.

"Cut it out," he muttered, with his lips at the crown of my head.

"I missed you," I sobbed.

"For fuck's sake. I was right here."

"I miss Jax, too. He's been gone for *days.*"

His chest heaved with a sigh beneath my cheek. "I know."

I pulled back, my breathing reduced to stuttered inhalations. "I d-don't know what to do."

Vincent's jaw tightened. "Stop crying for one thing. Then stop worrying about Jax. He's getting his shit together."

"What? What does that mean? How do you know that?"

He stepped back. "He told me."

I frowned and wiped at my cheeks. "Why would he tell you that and not me?"

"Because I'm probably one of the few people who won't try and talk him out of it."

"Can you speak English, please?"

He snorted. "I'm not smoothing the way for him, Gianna. It's his deal, and however it goes, it'll be up to him to lay it out for you."

"You're irritating me, Vincent."

"Good. You deserve it." He tossed an arm around my shoulder. "I've got to get back to the bar. I'll make you a drink."

"I wish you'd make sense instead," I complained, bumping into him so he stumbled a step.

"Watch it."

We returned to the restaurant and my steps slowed. I recognized the head of pure white hair from across the crowded room. As if he felt me staring, Parker Rutledge turned and found me. When he visibly relaxed, I knew he'd come to seek me out.

I couldn't help but be worried. Was something wrong with Jax?

"Holler if you need me," Vincent said, squeezing my shoulder before returning to the bar.

I watched Parker approach and hoped my eyeliner and mascara hadn't smeared. I ran my hands over my skirt, wishing I'd taken a minute to freshen up in the ladies' room. Jax's dad was dressed in a sharp black suit and pale blue tie, and he looked ready to conquer the world. I was afraid I looked defeated.

"Gianna." He pulled me into a brief hug. "I've been hoping to speak with you."

"Is everything all right?"

"I'm afraid not. Can we talk?"

"Sure." Because he looked and sounded so serious, I asked, "Would it be better to go to the penthouse?"

His lips twisted ruefully. "Jackson gave me strict orders not to bother you at work or home, although I confess I was about to anyway if you hadn't come to Rossi's tonight."

I glanced over at the bodyguard who went everywhere with me. Had he tipped off Parker? Not that I cared either way.

I caught my mother's eye and gestured at an empty table, letting her know I was taking it. She nodded and crossed it off the seating chart.

"I have to talk to you about Jackson," Parker began the minute he settled into the chair. "He's making a terrible mistake."

My hands flattened on the table. "How?"

"He can't just walk away. The game is in his blood. But more than that, he has a responsibility to this country. He has what it takes to shape the world in profound and necessary ways."

Clearly, Parker thought I was up to speed on what Jax was doing, and I figured it might be better not to tell him I was clueless. So I puzzled it out as best I could and tried not to get too excited about the possibility that Jax was thinking about stepping away from the family business. So to speak. "I'm sure he's doing everything he can."

"He can't say that until he runs for office."

"Oh." I'd never even considered *that* possibility. A game changer. The little spark of hope I felt quickly died. "I didn't realize he wanted a career in politics."

He leaned forward. "Jackson told me how you handled that reporter. You're an asset, Gianna. You're what he needs to reach the next level. With you at his side, he could make it all the way to the White House."

The very idea scrambled my brain. "The White... Are you kidding?"

He sat back. "Don't you believe he could do it?"

I stared at him, blown away by the grandeur of his dreams for his son. "Jackson can do anything he wants. He's amazing."

"Agreed."

"As long as I'm part of his life, I'll support him in whatever he chooses to do." I took a deep breath. "But..."

He studied me. "But what?"

There was no easy way to say it. "Do you know that he blames the stress of a public, political life for his mother's alcoholism?"

Parker straightened abruptly, his shoulders rolling back. "He's stronger than she was."

I couldn't disagree with that. "I think he's more worried about me."

"I know," he agreed, with an emphatic nod. "That's why you have to speak to him. Tell him you can handle it. Make him believe it."

My gaze moved to the bar and met Vincent's. His earlier words about being one of only a few people who wouldn't talk Jax out of "it" abruptly made sense. "Do you know where he is?"

"D.C. I can get you there."

I looked at him. "I'm ready whenever you are."

I'd expected to end up at the Rutledge mansion, but found myself knocking on the door to a high-rise apartment instead. Not too long ago, I would never have thought I'd be used to flying by private jet, but my life was different now. I was adjusting as quickly as I could. Still, one thing I had never learned to deal with was living without—

"Jax," I said, when the door opened and he stood in front of me. My heart gave a little leap. He looked edible. The bespoke three-piece suit he wore didn't soften the edge created by the shadow of stubble on his jaw and the slightly too-long hair. His gorgeous face was leaner, his gaze intensely focused. He didn't say a word, just grabbed me and kissed me as if he'd been dying of thirst and I was a cool glass of water. I wrapped my arms around his neck and opened my mouth, letting him lick and thrust, whimpering as he ate at my mouth with erotic ferocity.

The nervousness I'd felt on the flight dissipated into oblivion. Whatever he was doing by staying away from me wasn't because he didn't want me anymore.

He pulled me into the house and kicked the door shut, pinning me against it. "I've got to take a call in a minute," he muttered against my lips. "Then I'm going to fuck you for a really long time."

I hit him on the shoulder. "What the hell are you doing in D.C.?"

"You know. That's why you're here." He released me and backed away. "Did Parker send you?"

"He provided the means. I came because I wanted to."

"He'll get the hint eventually." He turned away from me and pointed at a set of double doors to the left. "Bedroom's in there. Get naked and wait for me."

I bit back a smile at his arrogance, knowing he was baiting me on purpose. "Dream on."

He glanced my way when he reached a desk set up in the living room. The apartment was considerably smaller than the penthouse in New York and barely furnished. There was a sofa and coffee table, but no television or artwork. Only the desk had anything on it, and it was littered with pens and loose papers.

"I've done nothing but dream of you the past two weeks." He picked up his smartphone and leaned back against the front of the desk. "I've always seen white picket fences in your eyes when you look at me. I was positive I wasn't that guy. I was wrong. One of these days, when you're ready, I'll give that dream to you. And you're going to give me a gorgeous little girl or two with your dark curly hair and smiles that slay me."

My chest tightened. "Jax…"

His phone rang and he answered it. "Dennis…No, you heard right, which is why I wanted to touch base with you about reaching out to Parker going forward…No, he won't be bringing me up to speed. I'm out." He looked at me. "I'm getting married. Yes, that's a good thing…Thank you. Good luck in the next election, Senator."

I watched him kill the call and set his phone on the desk.

He crossed his arms. "You're still dressed."

"I don't sleep with engaged guys." I fought to stand still while excitement pounded through me. There was something different about him. Something that reminded me of the Jax I'd met in Vegas. I liked it. A lot.

"I didn't say I was engaged—" his mouth quirked up on one side "—yet. Didn't say I wanted to sleep, either."

"You're awfully sure of yourself."

"You're crazy about me."

"Or just plain crazy." I crossed my arms, too. "Is this where you've been?"

"Mostly."

"And you couldn't tell me that?" We were standing across the room from each other, but I felt a powerful pull, as if he were actually tugging me closer.

"Made myself a promise not to bring any more crap to our doorstep for you to deal with. I had to see my way clear first."

"Clear of what, exactly?"

"Everything except you and Rutledge Capital."

I rubbed at my chest. "I didn't ask you to do that."

"No, but it had to be done. And I wanted to give you time to fix things with your family and to decide whether or not you can forgive me for putting you in that position." Scrubbing at his jaw, he said hoarsely, "Watching you deal with Deanna… Seeing you and Vincent hurting like that… It shredded me, Gia. I hated myself for putting you through that."

"It's all right now. We worked everything out."

"I'm glad. But it wouldn't have been the last time." He shrugged out of his jacket. "All that bullshit I was feeding you about being strong and dealing with it? Famous last words. I said the same things to my mother the last time we spoke, and I think they killed her. They killed the hope in her that she could save me from the life she hated."

"No." My heart broke at the guilt and shame I saw on his face. "Don't beat yourself up like that."

"I deserve it." He rubbed wearily at the back of his neck. "I'll find a way to live with it. I was young. Thoughtless. High on my own self-importance and so certain my dad was a goddamned national hero. I didn't care that his ambition was destroying our family."

He looked at me fiercely. "I'm not doing that to us. Nothing is worth losing you again. Nothing."

I swallowed past the lump in my throat, loving him more in that moment than I ever had. "Not even the White House?"

Jax laughed, his dark eyes sparkling with humor. "He told you about that dream, huh? That was never going to happen. I think Parker looks at me and deludes himself into thinking that he's looking in a mirror."

I could believe that.

"I'm not going to live the life he wants, Gia. I'm going to live the life he should have had. I'm going to marry a sweet girl from a great family, and I'm going to keep her sweet and protected and happy. We'll have a few kids, a couple dogs, and the occasional barbecue with her overprotective brothers."

"Is that enough excitement for you?"

"Absolutely. Especially if I can get you out of those clothes."

I walked over to him and placed my hand on his chest, feeling his heart beating strong and steady through his vest. "I want you to be happy. I don't want you to make sacrifices for me that you'll regret."

Setting his hand over mine, Jax pressed his lips to my forehead. "The only time I've ever been happy is when I'm with you. As for the rest of it…I felt like I needed to own those words I said to my mother, otherwise what was the point of saying them and causing her that pain? No one can say I'm not stubborn," he said with a rueful twist to his mouth. "It's too late to fix what I did to her, but it's not too late to avoid making the same mistake with you."

Closing my eyes, I leaned into him. Did he realize that with all the talk of picket fences and children, it was his raw honesty that bound me to him tighter than vows ever could? "I love you."

His mouth curved against my skin. "I know. And I'll never doubt it, not after this."

"Your dad is going to have a hard time letting you go," I warned, pulling back to study him.

Jax shrugged, but his jaw was set with determination. "Just so long as *you* don't let go."

"Don't worry." Lifting onto the tips of my toes, I nipped his lower lip with my teeth and smiled when he growled. "I'm stubborn, too."

Epilogue

"I HAVE TO keep telling myself it's real," I said, glancing at Lei.

She grinned and gently clinked her champagne flute against mine. "As real as that enormous diamond on your finger."

As I did several hundred times a day, I extended my hand and admired the five-carat emerald-cut engagement ring Jax had wowed me with. His proposal had been the single most exciting moment in my life, although the opening of the first Trifecta restaurant was nearly up there with it.

I dropped my arm back to my side and turned my attention to the three chefs who were the stars of the party. Chad, David, and Inez stood together as a single unit, talking with the VIPs who'd been invited to the exclusive soft opening of the Atlanta venue.

"Chad looks awesome," I pointed out unnecessarily. Lei was a red-blooded woman, after all. She knew a prime piece of male eye candy when she saw it. "I'm so proud of him."

"I'm proud of *you*," she said. "We wouldn't be here now, if not for your dedication and hard work."

"Thank you for giving me the opportunity." Seeing the smile on Lei's face sent a bright sense of accomplishment tingling through me. A lapel pin in the shape of Trifecta's logo accented her figure-hugging red sheath dress. With her hair down and her eyes bright, she looked young and fresh.

"I feel sorry for her," she murmured, gesturing discreetly with a slight tilt of her chin.

I followed her gaze and saw Stacy Williams hovering on the fringes of the crowd, her attention on her brother. "I wonder when her first restaurant will launch."

"Good question. I haven't heard anything."

The pretty redhead didn't look happy. I didn't know if that was because her brother had shot out of the proverbial gate before she did or because Ian was spending the evening at Isabelle's side. By all appearances, Ian had a new favorite.

"Does it bother you that he's here?" I asked, searching the room until I found Jax talking with a man I recognized as the host of a Food Network TV show. Taking a deep breath, I enjoyed the sight of my man, which still hadn't lessened in impact even after months of living together. He wore an elegant black sweater and dress slacks, and I was looking forward to stripping him out of both in just a few hours.

He caught me staring and winked.

"Ian?" Lei shook her head. "I would've been surprised if he hadn't come. You should say hi to him."

"Will you?"

She grinned. "When he breaks down and comes to me, yes. I'll offer him a drink, too. It's the least I can do."

Lifting my flute in a farewell toast, I took her advice and started mingling. Eclectic fusion music pumped through the hidden speakers, an audible reflection of the menu. The food was garnering raves and the excitement was high. Opening a new restaurant was always a momentous occasion. Like Lei, I lived for the high.

Soon Vincent would be launching his own Rossi's. So much to celebrate. Life was getting better every day.

"Congratulations, Gianna. This is quite an accomplishment."

I stopped and faced Ian Pembry. My mother would call him "dashing." I thought of him as arresting, with an undeniable charisma.

"Thank you," I said, holding out my hand to him. "I'll pass the kudos along to the chefs."

He kissed my knuckles with firm, dry lips. "I know exactly how much work goes into a successful launch like this. Take the praise—you deserve it."

I bowed my head in acknowledgment. "I couldn't have done it without Lei. She's an awesome mentor."

Ian's blue eyes gleamed with amusement and he squeezed my hand before releasing it. "You might be surprised at what you can accomplish without Lei. When you're ready to take that step, let me know."

I debated keeping my mouth shut for a minute, then I just went with it. "You blew it with her, you know. She loved you."

Ian's face hardened, but before he could reply, his gaze fixed on a point beyond my shoulder. When a steely arm hooked around my waist, I knew who'd drawn his attention.

"Jackson," Ian greeted him stiffly. "I hear congratulations are in order for you, as well."

Jax tucked me into his side. "I'm a lucky man who got a second chance."

I arched a brow at Ian, since Jax's words tied so neatly into what I'd just said. Ian's response was a tight smile.

Jax excused us and led me away, his hand cupped around my hipbone in a grip that sent heated thoughts through my mind. "I managed to get us the same room you were in the last time we were here together."

I remembered that trip well. It had been a turning point for us. The beginning of the end that kicked off a new beginning. "Are you being sentimental?" I teased, drawing to a halt and facing him.

"Still working on fixing past mistakes."

"Oh? What was the mistake?"

He ran the tip of his finger down the bridge of my nose and his dimple flashed. The one-two punch made me more than a little weak in the knees. "Leaving you naked and wanting. Gotta fix that, baby."

"I think you've left me hanging more than once. Maybe I should make a list."

Jax's grin widened. "Absolutely."

"It might be a long one," I warned, thinking about all the times he'd gotten me hot and bothered, then made me wait until I thought I'd lose my mind.

He reached for my hand and played with my ring. "Good thing we've got plenty of time."

A lifetime. Which might just be long enough.

ABOUT THE AUTHOR

SYLVIA DAY is the #1 *New York Times*, #1 *USA Today*, #1 *Sunday Times*, #1 *Globe and Mail*, #1 *Der Spiegel*, and #1 international bestselling author of over twenty award-winning novels sold in more than forty countries. She is a #1 bestselling author in twenty-eight countries, with tens of millions of copies of her books in print.

Visit the author at
www-SylviaDay.com